PENGUIN BOOKS
LOST IN TERROR

Nayeema Mahjoor is a leading journalist and fiction writer from Kashmir. She has previously worked as news editor (Urdu) at BBC World Service in London for two decades, and travelled from South Asia to the Middle East to Europe in search of the big issues facing people, particularly women.

Her unique style of short-story writing has earned her fame in literary circles and her work has been translated into other languages. Her novel *Dahshatzadi* was published in India and Pakistan in 2012.

ADVANCE PRAISE FOR THE BOOK

'This book gives deep insights into the universality of pain and how it transcends boundaries, forcing us to redirect our attention, to let go of the past and lean into the future that wants to emerge through us. Powerful real-life stories adorn the book, reminding us of the Palestinian, South African and South American freedom movements.'

KISHWAR NAHEED, PAKISTANI POET

'*Lost in Terror* probes into the painful wounds of Kashmir's past. It explores the struggle of one woman trapped between society and her own aspirations, as the heartbreaking realities of war and violent conflict shatter the idyllic beauty of this wondrous vale.'

PROF. GOPI CHAND NARANG, WRITER, LITERARY CRITIC AND SCHOLAR

LOST IN TERROR

NAYEEMA MAHJOOR

PENGUIN BOOKS

An imprint of Penguin Random House

PENGUIN BOOKS

USA | Canada | UK | Ireland | Australia
New Zealand | India | South Africa | China | Singapore

Penguin Books is part of the Penguin Random House group of companies
whose addresses can be found at global.penguinrandomhouse.com

Published by Penguin Random House India Pvt. Ltd
4th Floor, Capital Tower 1, MG Road,
Gurugram 122 002, Haryana, India

First published in Penguin Books by Penguin Random House India 2016

10 9 8 7 6 5 4 3 2

ISBN 9780143416531

For sale in the Indian Subcontinent and Singapore only

Typeset in Adobe Garamond Pro by Manipal Digital Systems, Manipal
Printed at Repro India Limited

www.penguin.co.in

MIX
Paper from
responsible sources
FSC® C047271

This is a legitimate digitally printed version of the book and therefore might not
have certain extra finishing on the cover.

My gratitude to those women of Kashmir who lost everything—
from their dignity to their relations—but never lost hope
for a better tomorrow.
My mother too among them.

PRELUDE

It was a perfect summer's day.

The blue sky overlooking the lush green valley was squinting at the remnants of the white snow at the peaks of the majestic mountains. At its foothills, the overgrown coniferous forests surrounded by wild flora and fauna had welcomed the new inhabitants, who wasted no time in erecting their makeshift shelters by the deep gorges of the river Jhelum. The summer heat had reduced the volume of Jhelum's waters, due to which its original inhabitants had moved further up, towards the source of the streams. New and unknown arrivals had started to fill the empty spaces without anybody noticing.

At the remote end of the tall mountain of Mahadev, there lived a septuagenarian, who had never seen the two-beaked bird with black patches on its tail. The migratory bird was perched on the poplar tree surrounding his old brick house. He was asking himself which country it had come from, and whether it had lived here before. He was eagerly waiting for his seven daughters to come home so that they would also get to see the unique two-beaked bird. The bird took flight towards the

Himalayas, where the sky had turned dark and the clouds had huddled together.

In the lawns of the entertainment and information centre, a lone gardener was tending the red-rose plants, which were getting eaten by the wild weeds with needles at the top. He was sucking his thumb, having been pricked by one such needle. It had caused a strong sensation within his body, and he was thinking about seeking expert advice from his master gardener so as to get rid of the weeds before they destroyed the lawn's well-tended bushes.

Inside the information centre, most of the rooms were filled with the sounds of loud laughter, music, arguments and the gossiping of staff, unaware of everything that was happening somewhere in the deep forests of the great Himalayas.

September 1988

The house of the Deputy Inspector General of Police was attacked by a gunman in Rajbagh. He was later killed by security guards during a scuffle. The eruption of the armed movement led to mass processions and demonstrations across the Kashmir Valley.

ERUPTION

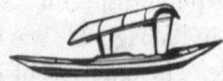

Tahira, my production assistant, was so irritated by my repeated glances at my watch that she stopped editing the interview of the young politician and said, 'Off you go, or I will run wild.' Without taking any notice of her agitated mood, I grabbed my purse, specs and book, and rushed towards the long, illuminated corridor of the radio station.

I was on my way to Baba's house. Somewhere in my mind I knew that Tahira would not only edit the interview but would also use it immaculately in the broadcast material. Glancing back through the oval mirror fixed in the middle of the heavy door of Studio Five, I could see that she had already started editing on her own. I felt great relief.

We had been having secret meetings since we all got married. My sisters lived and worked at different places and it had not always been easy to get together after our marriage. Additionally, our customs did not permit us to go frequently to our father's house without our husband's consent. We did visit Baba once or twice in a month with the permission of our in-laws. Of course, this was in addition to our daily secret lunch visits to his house. We sisters had, in fact, been implementing our secret pact to gather for lunch at Baba's house and share all the gossip we had about our in-laws, neighbours and colleagues.

One or two hours at my father's house were all I needed to recharge my energy, and I would return, refreshed, to do wonders with broadcasting.

Apart from Baba and my sisters, only Tahira knew that we all gathered this way for lunch at Baba's house. She had never disclosed it to anyone.

~

I could smell something in the air on my way from my office to the main street that joined with the lane to Baba's house, but I didn't know what it was. Maybe I had not slept well for the last few days due to the long hours at work. I had this feeling of restlessness.

Normally, it took me twenty minutes to reach Baba's house from my office. However, today, due to protests on the main road, my autorickshaw had to stop at various crowded places. So it took me twice as long to get to the house.

I felt a strong urge to eat something once I reached Baba's house; I was hungry and my legs had become jelly-like, perhaps due to the low sugar level in my body.

The moment I stepped inside the house, all fourteen pairs of eyes in the living room fixed their gaze on me. I greeted my father—known to all of us as 'Baba'—and uttered some excuse for being late. Baba seemed quite tense. He kept looking at me apprehensively as if something bad had happened to me.

My eldest sister, Sadia, hugged me, as if she had not seen me for ages.

'I'm receiving special treatment today! Is everything all right here, or have you had a bad dream about me?' I said to Sadia.

Sadia did not take her wide eyes off me.

'Please give me something to eat. I have no energy left,' I said, playfully shaking Sadia, who seemed to be playing the role of host today for us.

'Tell us about the incident that happened this morning in your area,' Hafiza, my second-eldest sister, asked impatiently.

'What incident are you talking about?' I was totally confused.

'How can you not know? I'm asking about the gunfight incident this morning near your house,' said Sadia in one breath.

'Are you really working in the media?' added Hafiza. 'A police officer's residence near your house was attacked by some gunmen in the morning. Didn't you hear the firing, you dumb girl? There are rumours that the mujahideen have come to free us.'

'Yes, the gunman was killed and people have come out on to the streets to protest against his killing. There are Azadi processions all over downtown,' chipped in Sadia.

'How come you know nothing about this incident in your neighbourhood? Baba was worried sick. We were concerned that you'd have to pass through the protestors on your way here. How are you so ignorant of all this? One thing is certain—you are not cut out to work in the media.'

My sisters were revealing so much information and pronouncing edicts at the same time that my head was all muddled up trying to recollect what I saw on my way. Why didn't I bother to find out about the unusual crowd on the road, or had I become that horribly absent-minded? I kept gazing at my sisters.

My sisters had given up their interest in gossip. They were suddenly keen to discuss and analyse all sorts of rumours about the beginning of an armed struggle in Kashmir against the central government.

Mehmooda, my youngest sister, who was ordinarily the most taciturn of us all, felt jubilant at the thought of freedom, or *azadi*. However, no one seemed to comprehend much about this idea of freedom. What it would bring to our lives, or what it really meant—we had never thought of any of it, except that it would be better to have our land with our authority over it. Among all of us, it was Mehmooda who was delirious at the prospect of achieving what we had lost during the partition of the Indian subcontinent. Everyone was brimming with enthusiasm about Azadi, as if it were the cure to our otherwise-mundane lives.

My father was present physically, but was mentally far, far away from us. He was thinking about the strange migratory birds that might come and perch on the peach tree. Baba seemed to have aged very fast in these few hours, perhaps anticipating the moments of uncertainty and turmoil that might become our fate in the future. I thought, maybe he was reminded again of the terror and torture he had gone through during the riots that followed the arrest of Kashmir's popular leader Sheikh Mohammed Abdullah in 1953.

Again, the question started to hover in my mind: Why was Sheikh Abdullah arrested in 1953 when he was the government's only supporter in Kashmir? Baba had never given us any satisfactory answer to this question, even though I had asked him dozens of times before. Instead, he would always praise Sheikh Abdullah's fight against the Maharaja of Kashmir. I was curious to know the reaction of his supporters when Sheikh Abdullah supported the accession theory, but he would never reply. Instead, it would make him furious and he would start pacing the floor in a frenzy. Sadia would place a steaming cup of tea in front of him and divert his attention by talking about her husband's business plans.

This was the first time after I got married that my father wanted us to leave quickly so that we could reach our homes as early as possible. He was worried about us having to travel through the protests. It could take an ugly turn as in the past.

Mehmooda and my two other sisters rushed towards the main street after taking Baba's leave.

'Stay together and board the bus quickly. Don't mingle in the crowd if you happen to pass through it,' Baba warned us.

Assuming that they would have crossed the street connecting the main road, I left my father's house with my sister Sadia. She would be boarding the bus at the same stop as me.

Sadia lived in Srinagar's interior town of Safa Kadal, which was famous for its wooden houses, close-knit neighbourhood and massive gardens of fresh green. In this old town, the people shared their sorrows, joys, secrets and vegetables. Sadia had become an admirer of her neighbourhood from the moment she first set foot in it.

Baba's neighbourhood, where we all grew up, was not very different from downtown Srinagar; it was also an old-city quarter congested with wooden houses of traditional architecture, with narrow lanes just big enough for two-wheelers to pass through, and without any underground drainage. Some houses were connected at the top floor by wooden footbridges. Due to the closure of the Nala-Mar canal that ran through the heart of Srinagar and the subsequent construction of a circular road, many wooden houses were demolished and only a few now remained in the interiors of the downtown area.

Baba's old brick house was sandwiched between the famous Dal Lake and lush green Takht-e-Suleiman hill. The hill, with its thick forest cover and bounty of wild fruits, gave us shade and comfort during the scorching heat of summer. Our front lawn touched the banks of the lake, which had become our personal swimming pool. Splashing water on each other, catching fish and growing floating gardens were an integral part of our childhood memories. We had enjoyed the majestic beauty of moonlit nights on the banks of the lake along with foreign visitors, who would stay awake through the night on their houseboats.

To live near the resplendent lake elevated my profile among my friends—because it was one of the posh areas in the valley and housed the private residences of ministers and top officials—even though our home was a small old brick-house with a shingled roof.

The lane from Baba's house to the main street was becoming longer and longer. At the first turning of the road, we saw some women from our neighbourhood huddled together. While walking past we could hear them talking in whispers. I felt their staring eyes.

Being the only educated family in our locality had alienated us in the eyes of our neighbours. They begrudged us our existence, and we always uttered prayers on leaving the house so as to ward off their evil eye. I did not know why this strange feeling crept into us that our neighbours would give us the evil eye. Maybe they did not like us . . . or perhaps we were just being paranoid.

Our father had advised us to silently recite the 'Ayat al-Kursi' (the Throne Verse) sura from the Quran to ward off their evil eye. Ever since childhood, we had made it a habit to start muttering the sura once we crossed the threshold of Baba's house. However, sometimes, I would forget to recite it when I had to leave the house in a hurry.

Our biggest sin, in their eyes, was going to school and getting educated. Among all his relatives and in the whole neighbourhood, it was only Baba who took the risk of sending his daughters to college in the early 1970s. It was something for which he had to pay a huge price. His relatives looked down on him throughout his life. In fact, my mother was his only real relation until her death.

When I got out from the snake-like curves of the streets on to the main road, I saw there was a huge crowd gathered near the bus stop. Everyone was rushing towards whatever bus, minibus or autorickshaw that happened to stop by for a few minutes before moving off again. People seemed to be in a panic to catch some form of transport to leave the area.

I approached a young boy standing close to a paan shop and asked him, 'What's happened here? Why are people in such a panic?'

The young boy beamed and replied proudly, 'Don't you know the freedom struggle has begun? There have been protests everywhere against the killing in Rajbagh. The first martyr of the armed struggle has laid down his life. We will soon get freedom, inshallah.' The boy ran away to catch a bus that had pulled up just near the bus stop.

A few metres away, two traffic police officers were trying to regulate the traffic and control the chaos on the road, but nobody seemed to be following their instructions. The officers' rage was rising for being thus ignored and disobeyed.

Sadia got on to the bus she was taking to her part of town. It was heaving with people, some on the roof and some clinging on to the metal ladder on the rear of the bus. She waved goodbye to me and the bus drove away.

In a fraction of a second, some paramilitary vehicles stopped near the bus stop and surrounded its entry gates.

'Don't move. Stay where you are,' one of the soldiers bellowed to the people waiting for the bus.

The situation was getting really tense. People scattered in different directions and boarded the buses in panic. I took my identity card out of my purse and showed it to the soldier who had demanded it. After a quick glance, he returned it. I walked quickly away from the bus stop.

I had not heard anything about the gunfight in my area. Ordinarily, if there was something, we would have heard something about it at the radio station where I worked.

Yet, when I left for work earlier that day, everything seemed normal. Maybe the incident happened while I was on my way to my father's house. News in Kashmir spreads like wildfire. The information about the Rajbagh incident had spread to my father's area near the Dal Lake much faster than I could physically get to his house from work.

On my way back home I felt a glimmer of hope, like some sort of anticipation. Inside me, I could sense a feeling of happiness and satisfaction. The idea of liberation had been buried in my heart, but something seemed to raise my hopes again. Even the mere mention of achieving independence made me happy, because my distaste had grown deeper and stronger ever since I had delved into the history of my subjugation. It was as if I had acquired a strong dislike by drinking my mother's milk. However, I never expressed this feeling openly. How could I? I would have lost my chance of working in the media that was controlled by the government.

If the news of the Rajbagh incident had reached my in-laws, I'm sure they would have started the celebrations at the mere mention of Azadi. They were so sentimental about achieving Azadi that its mention always brings tears to their eyes.

My husband, Asad, and his family had never supported Sheikh Abdullah or his policy of accession with India. Rather, they were loyalists of Mirwaiz Farooq, the leading Islamic cleric-cum-politician, and called themselves Bakras, meaning 'goats', and supported accession with Pakistan on the principle of the Two-Nation Theory. Kashmir had been divided into two factions soon after the popular leader Sheikh Mohammed Abdullah signed the Delhi Agreement with the government, thus making the state of Jammu and Kashmir a permanent part of India. Abdullah's supporters, called Shers, meaning 'lions', never dared to enter the downtown area as it was a Bakra stronghold, while certain areas in Srinagar's Civil Lines were barred for Bakras.

Visiting the bastions of the Shers and the Bakras was always dangerous for strangers. One of my neighbours was once caught in a real quagmire. He had gone downtown to buy spices for his daughter's wedding, when he was confronted by a group of people who asked him what leader he supported; when he replied with 'Sheikh Abdullah' he was grabbed, kicked and beaten by the group, who turned out to be supporters of Mirwaiz Farooq. Walking down the road he encountered yet another group of people and was asked the same question again. When he replied that he was a staunch supporter of Mirwaiz Farooq, the people became furious and left him half-dead on the road. It was by some miracle that the police found him and informed his family. He spent more than three months in the hospital recovering from his grievous injuries. Following the Partition, the constant feud between the Shers and the Bakras had torn asunder the Kashmiri society, often leading to violence even among family members. Like the rest of the Bakras, my in-laws had always supported the Two-Nation Theory and wanted Kashmir to join Pakistan.

After my marriage, Baba and my husband continued the political discourse, which sometimes took a nasty turn. Asad, representing the Bakra faction, and my father, the supporter of Sheikh Abdullah, would fight about petty political issues, making all of us laugh and weep at the same time. We were confused about whom to support.

At every mention of Azadi, Asad would become sentimental and remember his father's association with the cleric Moulvi Yusuf Shah, who fled the valley and took refuge in 'Azad Kashmir' (as Pakistani Kashmir was called) after the valley and its adjacent parts became conflicted territory between India and Pakistan.

Asad had repeated his words many times: 'After Abdullah deceived his people in 1947, my father was disappointed and joined the student's organization Al-Fatah (meaning "the victory"). He was unable to come to terms with what Sheikh Abdullah did in the end after a long struggle. On his deathbed, his last words were, "When Kashmir achieves independence, please come to my grave to tell me the great news. Only then will my soul be at rest."' Every time Asad spoke about his father's long-cherished dream, his eyes would become moist, and he would confine himself in his father's room for that whole day.

I often wondered: *If Asad was a supporter of Bakra politics, why did he support independence? Were independence and accession not two different ideologies—poles apart?* It created the same confusion in my mind as it had always created amongst our people. We were not taught the difference between Azadi and accession.

The Sher–Bakra fight lost some of its steam after Pakistan lost the war against India in 1971, a war that resulted in the creation of Bangladesh. People were disillusioned and disappointed with the idea of a separate homeland for Muslims. However, feelings of religious identity were rekindled when the Afghanistan jihad brought the Soviet Union to its knees, and Islamic revolution toppled the US-backed Reza Shah Pahlavi's rule in Iran. This began raising the consciousness of Kashmiris with regard to the humiliation they believed they were constantly suffering at the government's hands. The new armed struggle owed its inspiration to Islamic awakening throughout the Muslim world.

BOUNDARIES

My in-laws seemed to be traditional, but they were modern at the same time. The daughters of the family were not allowed to go to school or leave home without a chaperone, even though the family preferred to marry off their sons to educated, working girls. *Was it to give freedom to the daughters-in-law?* I would often ask myself.

I tried hard for one of the daughters of the family, Faiza, to be allowed to go to college for higher education. It proved to be a difficult challenge to convince her radical brothers to let her pursue her dream. However, she had already won her first war against her family when she made them surrender, long before I got married and came into this household—she was the first girl child of the traditional family who made history by entering the primary school in the locality.

The family felt pride in relating Faiza's stubborn attitude, but for a long time, my husband believed I was the one ruining the family's discipline and obedience to social norms. Working in the media was a taboo for most girls in our society. Fortunately, my in-laws had broken this taboo. They wholeheartedly accepted me and my job without ever mentioning it or complaining about it. I always wonder how they allowed it.

The family rules were rather vague about what amounted to 'shame' or 'dishonour'. There had always been a thick boundary line between the daughters and the daughters-in-law, as if it were a military line of control that nobody had a clear concept about. 'Honour' and 'shame' had somewhat different meanings when it came to the daughter-in-law.

Daughters were considered the repository of the family's honour. And they were expected to uphold that and the values of society. Male members zealously 'protected' them at every moment of their lives.

Like other conservative families, the girls in Asad's family had not been permitted to aspire for education, let alone higher education. Faiza was the only lucky one who got her way and broke with tradition. At the very least, the girls were required to avoid relationships or crushes that might bring the family into disrepute. Asad's sisters spoke bitterly about their family when they related the stories of their restricted childhood.

I had to make a lot of adjustments in Asad's house. It was too rigid for girls, mostly for the daughters, who had to take the elders' permission for any and every trivial matter.

For everything I had to ask for permission from someone. Can I go for a stroll in the morning? Can I buy my shoes in the market? Can I stay at Nina's house a bit longer? Each time, there was a nod from Asad. And if he was not present in the house, his brother would step up and place restrictions on me, even within the four walls of the house. Surprisingly, however, with the passage of time, they ceased objecting if I reached home late, left earlier, or travelled to distant places on work trips. I thought maybe they had developed a little confidence in me.

I had grown up in a somewhat open and free environment at my parent's house. It was a closed society, but there was still a little leeway for girls to develop. Baba's brothers and sisters were not much different from my traditional in-laws; it was only Baba who was a bit flexible and liberal with his daughters. Only when it came to marriage would Baba's decision prevail, irrespective of our choices, crushes or aspirations. We had to follow him blindly.

The Muslim society was deeply conservative on the whole. Only a few people were brave enough to try to push the boundaries of what was permissible. Even Baba's sisters bore malice towards him as they thought of him as liberal and open. His decision to send his daughters for higher education led to his becoming isolated and detached from his brothers and sisters. They did not invite us to marriage ceremonies or special occasions—as a form of punishment and boycott against our father—when all our neighbours and distant relatives were rejoicing at family gatherings.

Despite the government constantly boasting about having raised the literacy rate for women to 60 per cent, our society still looked at daughters and daughters-in-law as the personal property of men. Even if a girl hailed from a rich family and had several hectares of land to her name, she actually owned nothing in reality. She could not take any important decisions without the prior approval of her father, brother or husband. On the surface it might seem as if girls were given full freedom to fulfil their dreams of pursuing higher education, but they were, in actuality, ultimately always bound to follow the decision of the ruling menfolk.

Most of us had accepted this situation wholeheartedly and managed to live our restricted lives in good-enough spirits, as long as we got the chance to go to school or college to build ourselves up—thank heavens for these small mercies. My colleague Saira would often say with sarcasm, 'Enjoy your controlled freedom.' My sisters and me had enjoyed this chicken-coop freedom with pride and dignity.

I was more than happy to live under this blanket rule. However, the defiance of one's in-laws or keeping secrets from them amounted to not only rebellion but also the disrespect of family values, which could attract severe punishment. I always dreaded it.

Visiting Baba's house without the permission of my husband amounted to a breach of trust. Although I felt guilty going to my father's house frequently without my husband's permission, I could not give up this practice. On such occasions, I would often remember a teacher who had taught me: 'Do what makes you happy and make sure it doesn't hurt anybody. A little lie is forgiven.' Meeting my Baba and sisters made me feel happy and contented. I had never ever counted it as a sin.

All of us had vowed that we would never ever reveal anything about our luncheon meetings to anybody, let alone our husbands. We would never ruin the joy and comfort of Baba's presence, which we all missed so sorely after we got married.

My brother and his wife had to move to the winter capital of the state, Jammu, every year because all government offices were moved for the six months of the harsh winter. Baba was left all alone in his house. My sisters and I tried our best to make sure someone kept him company.

It was not just the lunch that I enjoyed with my Baba; I also looked forward to the intriguing stories he told of deceit, oppression and manipulation practised by our men, employers or foreign rulers in the ages gone by. Baba's knowledge had provided me with a lot of material for producing programmes on the radio, either on our glorious past or on our history of subjugation under the maharajas of Kashmir, and was much appreciated by the public. I never revealed my real source of information to my colleagues at work. It was a treasure to which only I had the keys at my disposal.

Baba's eyes remained fixed on the door from the moment the clock struck twelve. And my restlessness began the moment I left for work in the morning, like it was all just a facade to meet my father. All my sisters would come over and talk and laugh and make lots of noise to put life back into his house. Our presence made my Baba happy and jubilant. His cheeks would become red with laughter and stories.

Since the death of my mother, he had felt very lonely and isolated—though he had never expressed it. I had become a mind reader and could read his face and expressions in volumes together.

FORBIDDEN

Never in all the discussions that I had had with my father about the different careers I could consider had I ever expressed a wish of joining the media—and that too an organization that had a bad reputation and was forbidden for womenfolk. And neither did Baba mention this when I completed my graduation in science and started job-hunting.

It was only fate that placed me in the lap of radio work. No doubt, I was met with the ice-cold attitude of my colleagues initially, but there was something binding me to them permanently.

From the very first day that I stepped into the premises of the radio station, my work became my passion. I used to think I could only dream it but now my working was a reality. I hardly slept for almost one entire year, when I juggled around from one coaching centre to the other to broaden my skill set.

It was the era when women in Kashmir were confined to the house. Barely a handful of women had got the opportunity to attend school, forget working in the news and entertainment world.

The radio station was exclusively a man's empire—and a Hindu man's empire at that. A girl who had just left her carefree college life behind had dared to enter the entertainment world. It not only shook Baba's family like an earthquake, but I had to bear the malicious, hateful looks of male colleagues too.

Muslim employees were only a few, and worked either as peons or orderlies, watching the entry gates or sorting out the official post. One had to be brave enough to dare to enter the forbidden premises, and the entry was subject to passing the competitive examinations conducted by the government throughout the country—something that Kashmiri men and women had hardly ventured into in the past. I passed these barriers with a brave heart.

Later on, after joining the radio station, I found that the task assigned to me did not seem as difficult as it was rumoured to be.

When I produced my first radio programme on the political subjugation of Dogra rulers, believe me, I felt as scared as I might on the Judgement Day. The conference hall of the radio station was jam-packed, and every officer was hell-bent on shredding my programme into hundreds of pieces. I was shivering, sweating and shuddering.

'The facts were incorrect and the pronunciation was wrong.'

'Why didn't you interview the former Dogra heir apparent, Dr Karan Singh?'

'The research was below the standard.'

'The programme was lopsided.'

Looking upon their stern, mocking faces, I thought I would never ever enter the premises again. I had reached my breaking point.

While leaving the place with a heavy heart, I saw my old peon outside the gate talking loudly to other colleagues. 'Unless you have enemies in your life, you have no challenges. Your life becomes dull and you get bored with it. Without a challenge, you are a dead man.' He gave me a broad grin. There was something divine in him, and he seemed to me like Baba's dervish, whom I had painted in my mind since the day I heard about his miracles.

I decided to return to the studio and listen to my production again.

After only a few more productions, my colleagues were left with no choice but to recognize my professional excellence. It was only Sarla, the only female Hindu officer in the radio station, who did not come to terms with the idea that some Muslim woman had dared to stand beside her and broken her record of being the only female officer in the organization. We did not get along with each other for a long time, and she hardly spared a chance to undermine me. She had so much influence on the staff that she made me the laughing stock of the station.

It was my first documentary feature on Habba Khatoon, a sixteenth-century Kashmiri poetess, which marked my debut in the radio. Habba Khatoon was the beloved wife of the then king of Kashmir, Yusuf Shah Chak, who was deprived of his throne by Akbar, the great Mughal king of India. Due to simmering political unrest in the valley, Akbar called the king to Delhi for negotiations. Instead of talking about strategy to quell the unrest, Akbar incarcerated Yusuf Shah Chak for the rest of his life, thus making the valley a part of his empire. The king was never seen again by his subjects, or by his beloved.

It was from that time that the subjugation of Kashmir began—when the kingdom of Kashmir was lost due to the manipulation and treachery of the Mughal king. Habba Khatoon lost her lover and Kashmir its king at the same time. Habba Khatoon was devastated and expressed her pain and solitude in poetic verses. Some people declared her a lunatic and threw pebbles at her. She had become lost in the wilderness and kept roaming around in the forests and hills of the valley. Referred to as Zoon, meaning 'moon', she became the symbol for women's suffering. Her poetry was what every woman would remember by heart and sing on special occasions—or when facing the worst phases of life.

The documentary feature that I had produced raised a few serious questions about the proposed Bollywood film on the life of Habba Khatoon. It was believed that the sole purpose of the film was to make it a big commercial venture by exploiting and thus tarnishing the image of the poetess—something Kashmiri women would not have tolerated. My programme, on the other hand, was based on thorough research into historical facts, and was well-received by my colleagues and also won the hearts of the listeners. This made my resolve to stay in radio stronger and I started to dig deep into the history of Kashmir in order to present it in the right manner.

However, just when I was about to carve a niche for myself in the media market, it quickly started to wane and fall apart. The eruption of armed struggle not only halted my further productions but also left a very serious impact on every phase of my life.

FORTRESS

My office had turned into a fortress.

The radio station was under the complete control of the government. It had become a prime target for the mujahideen. The heavy deployment of armed forces throughout the premises of the station had made the working environment tense and full of suspicion. It was bizarre that regular employees and security personnel were allowed in the entertainment centre, while the artists, the lifeline of the station, were barred from entering.

Each employee seemed to be spying on every other person in the office and mentally noting their movements. Hindu employees avoided coming into contact with the few Muslims on the staff, as though the latter had, all of a sudden, become infected with some contagious disease and needed to be placed in quarantine.

In the morning meeting, where we deliberated on our daily programme content, the head of the station asked the staff to assemble in the conference hall and advised us to remain extra vigilant and avoid movement outside the office. 'In case of emergency, do not leave the office without security. If you feel protected at home, stay there and do not take any risks while coming to work. I will manage things here. And do not ever talk about militancy in the office premises.'

Pursuant to his orders, the Hindu and Muslim employees dispersed in two separate groups, whispering to each other. The wedge had grown bigger. However, the Hindu group was bigger than the Muslims because more than 80 per cent of the staff belonged to the Kashmiri Hindu community.

Those who, only yesterday, had praised my broadcast skills were now making every effort to avoid even the slightest eye contact with me, let alone talk to me. I found myself unable to trust my Hindu colleagues, while they felt intimidated living in a Muslim-majority region in the backdrop of an outbreak of armed movement. Mutual trust had become the first casualty in the rebellion. Kashmiri Pandits were seen as enemies of the freedom movement, just as Muslims were labelled anti-India, even though both communities shared the same space, spoke the same language and wore the same clothes. Hindus and Muslims had always pretended to live in a secular society. Yet, they despised each other's ideology and preferences in their allegiance to a nationality.

If one wanted to leave office during the working hours or take a lunch break, one had to obtain the station director's permission due to the concern behind the growing security risks to central government employees, who were being warned not to go to public places without a police escort. Rather than making us feel protected, the situation made us more suspicious in the eyes of the public. Working in government offices was treated as a betrayal to the freedom movement, thus we were a genuine target for public outrage.

My routine of sneaking out of the office and spending a few hours with my sisters at Baba's house had now become difficult to manage. Nobody was sure who was spying on whom, who would be declared an anti-national element and who would be included on the hit list of gunmen. The newspapers had started to publish death threats aimed at those working undercover for national intelligence agencies, as well as statements of those mainstream politicians who declared their non-allegiance to their political parties.

Everyone was besieged by fear and paranoia, which slowly started to rule our minds and souls.

1990: Jagmohan Malhotra is appointed as the governor of the state of Jammu and Kashmir. Chief Minister Farooq Abdullah resigns. Massive protest marches in support of Azadi continue unabated in Kashmir.

ENCROACHMENT

The fierce winds blowing through the hills and mountains of the Great Himalaya Range smelt of uncertainty and unseen danger. Grey mist covered the valley of paradise, the scene never seen before by Baba or anyone from his generation.

It felt as if we were caught up in vicious circumstances, over which we had no control. Baba would warn us of the danger ahead: 'Somebody somewhere at the far corner of the valley has taken the reins of our lives in his hands.' However, Baba never disclosed the identity of this 'somebody'.

Newspapers were inundated with the reports of sporadic gunfights that would be followed by a massive deployment of security forces across the valley. The national highway connecting the valley with India was stormed by the convoys of security force vehicles, due to which civilian traffic was suspended for many days. This raised the anger and anguish of the people. Security forces could be seen in enormous numbers at every crossroad, bridge, hotel, school and deserted building. People were surprised to find soldiers patrolling at every corner, shop and at their doorsteps. Most mosque-goers found it hard to walk freely when going for prayers early morning.

In our neighbourhood, a security bunker had been built overnight. The security forces were stopping people and inquiring about the size of their family and neighbours, and whether strangers had recently come into the locality. Unmindful of the impending dangers, we shrugged and sometimes giggled when they asked us about the presence of gunmen in the neighbourhood.

Once, when I went in the backyard to throw out the garbage in the dustbin, the sight of dozens of soldiers and the many shadows took life out of me. I froze and lost my speech for a few moments until my brother-in-law came and asked me to move back inside.

Asad's eldest brother had already warned us about the dangers ahead. I did not take it seriously. We knew about the gunmen taking shelter in our neighbourhood, but we never knew they had access to our house as well. 'We all need to be alert. They have some intelligence reports about us. Somebody has given the wrong information to security agencies that the mujahideen regularly take shelter in our house. Every time you leave the house, make sure you do not leave the gate open.' Asad put his head down when his brother was revealing this information, and left the room in silence.

Despite the warnings of the security risks, the huge deployment of security forces, and the anticipation of worse times ahead, my family was hopeful that we would achieve our azadi, independence, very soon. Our mujahideen had raised our hopes so high that liberation seemed only a short distance away. It made us laugh and dream about our new destiny every moment we got together at Baba's house. We even changed the time on our clocks.

However, a small section would ridicule the mujahideen and their armed struggle. One of my firebrand Muslim colleagues at work would speak openly against the armed struggle: 'If the gunmen think they can fight the government, they live in a fool's paradise. A few charity guns cannot defeat the army.'

'Have you lost your mind? It is not a matter of rented or charity guns, but a mass uprising against bloody democracy that has impressed, so far, only you!' another Muslim employee lambasted him.

'If it is a mass uprising, it doesn't need guns from Pakistan, it needs leadership to nudge it in the right direction. The gun has never resolved any conflict! It has only brought death and destruction to the people. If Pakistan is sincere in resolving the issue, it should not place weapons in teenagers' hands. It should allow Kashmiri leadership to talk to the government and not incite them against each other!'

'I think you are writing your own death warrant by talking against the movement. If you wish to die a martyr for the government, be my guest. But I will suggest that you keep your opinion to yourself and don't ever talk against the freedom movement.'

'Don't tell me what to talk, I have a grandson your age! Have some respect for my grey hair. This is all a result of the gun, that brings lawlessness and indiscipline into society.' He banged the door and hurried past him with a stern look on his face.

I was worried about my older colleague's anti-Pakistan outburst. He was really brave to raise his voice against the mujahideen at a time when the whole population had become euphoric about Azadi. Tahira told me that he was on the payroll of national intelligence agencies. 'Stay away from him,' she warned me. Every time I would happen to run into him on my way, I would change my path.

I came to know a week later that he had disappeared while returning from the mosque in the evening. His wife had come to the head of the station to ask him to help her find him. The station head soon lost interest when the police refused to file a First Information Report for the missing employee. The wife performed his last rites by placing a stone on a mound of earth, symbolizing his grave, and declared herself a half-widow.

CRUMBLE

Realizing that the situation was getting out of control, and that the initial few erratic incidents of violence were now giving way to a mass movement for freedom, the state government, headed by the Jammu & Kashmir National Conference, resigned. Kashmir was now under the direct rule of New Delhi, and a new governor, who was considered to be a Hindu nationalist, had already been dispatched. He carried out a reshuffle of the state administration. Officials were brought in from outside Kashmir to handle key posts, while local officers were transferred to other departments of lesser significance— perhaps as punishment for being considered supporters of the anti-government movement.

Local employees called for a strike throughout the valley, which resulted in the total collapse of the state administration. I could not decide whether I should observe the hartal being an employee of the central government, or whether I should go to work. A small number of Muslim employees working in central government offices were more euphoric about Azadi than their counterparts in the state administration. Yet, some sort of suspicion persisted among the population against central government employees.

The valley was in an utter mess. We hardly knew who controlled our state. The administration was invisible and everything collapsed. We were either at the mercy of the gunmen or the security forces. Baba said the government could not afford to lose the Kashmir Valley and that it had deployed hundreds of thousands of personnel in a bid to re-establish control. On the other hand, Asad boasted that the state had come under the direct control of the mujahideen backed by the Pakistan Army. I did not know whom to believe and who would eventually succeed in gaining control of the situation. However, the majority of the population would follow the separatists' call for a complete strike, and public participation in the protest marches grew bigger and bigger throughout the valley.

CRACKDOWN

I rushed to Baba's house to share every bit of news that I had gathered in the office. At one o'clock, I slipped out of the main gate of the office compound and chose the shortest pedestrian path amongst all, which were usually patrolled by security forces, keeping a close vigil on every passer-by. I avoided their gaze and walked briskly to reach Baba's home. I did not let Tahira know about my mission and left her wondering in the studio. Rebellion had embedded itself in my soul.

Overnight, the valley had become a garrison, as we had been pushed in between a war: on the one hand, there were the soldiers who were everywhere, and, on the other, there was an invisible enemy, as claimed by the government. On my way down the road, I thought about the latter. Around me I saw only frightened and angry people, walking in silence. There was no trace of the gunmen who used to avoid fighting soldiers during daylight.

The roads and streets were studded with bunkers put up by the soldiers. Everywhere, one could see security vehicles driving furiously, and soldiers patrolling the streets, staring at people suspiciously. We had become strangers in our own street.

The national media broadcast statements of officials warning Pakistan of dire consequences for training and sending militants into the valley.

In the main road of my neighbourhood, there was a big manhole right in the middle of the road. I had witnessed many accidents happening here. Once, a child fell into it and it took five hours to pull him out. Another time, a dog was stuck in the manhole for at least one week and the whole area was on the verge of a cholera outbreak. Even after so many incidents, the municipal corporation did not bother to have the manhole covered. It fell to the soldiers in the nearby bunker to fill it with sand and cover it with a metal lid. I was moved by their gesture, even though their intention was simply to deny militants any hiding places to store improvised explosive devices (IEDs). Incidents of landmines being used to blow up security vehicles had become a routine part of news bulletins. Listeners were only curious to know how many security personnel had been killed.

At the entrance to the street leading to Baba's house, dozens of armed soldiers were disembarking from their vehicles and entering a newly built but empty hotel, taking with them their weapons, kitchenware and bedding. Many children had gathered around them, giggling and shouting, 'We want freedom!' Some of them started pelting stones at the soldiers, whose anger was rising with every pebble hurled at them.

Anticipating the confrontation between the soldiers and the children, the women and elderly men nearby rushed out of their houses. They grabbed the children and scolded them. But the children were struggling and trying to break free from the elders' grip; they wanted to exhibit their courage by pelting stones and shouting 'We Want Freedom' slogans.

I saw one soldier land a hard slap on the face of a young boy, who could hardly have been nine or ten years old. Other children rushed forward in a flash, grabbed the soldier and started beating him.

Everyone was raising slogans for Azadi. The voices of the elders and women rose above the children's. They kept protesting and pelting stones at the soldiers. Among their shouts the firing shots were heard. Everyone froze. And then again continued further shots into the air. The children's smiling faces transformed into looks of horror. The soldiers who came rushing out of the hotel building immediately took their positions, their fingers ready on the triggers. The sound of firing was coming from the adjacent street and slowly grew more and more intense. For a second or two, there was silence. All eyes were fixed far away on the horizon, where thick black smoke was billowing up. *Whose firing is this? The gunmen or the soldiers?* We were all making assumptions in our mind, but our eyes remained fixed on the soldiers who were waiting for orders—commanding them, perhaps, to fire on us. Time seemed to have stopped.

I was struggling to breathe. The strange smell of smoke and the noise from the gunshots was spreading all around us, making us cough and anxious. In the fraction of a second, the soldiers were ordered by their officer to encircle us. They were separating the men from the women. The little boys were clinging to their mothers, but the soldiers were dragging them towards the men's line. I was desperately looking for a way out from here. The possibility of fleeing was out of the question.

The soldiers took control of everything—the people, children, the streets and houses. I was scared to death, more scared of the fact that my in-laws would come to know about my being caught up in a crackdown, when I happened to be on my way to Baba's house without their permission. My secret would be found out, and I knew my husband would react to this out of proportion, as he always did.

This was the first crackdown that I had encountered. 'Crackdown' was the local term for a cordon and search operation that the security forces would launch when they suspected there were militants in a particular area. They would place a cordon around a locality, ask all the people to come out of their houses, separate the men from the women and then search the houses for 'militants'. The crackdown could continue from a few hours to a few days. No matter the weather or the situation—be it day or night, winter or summer, or whether one was old or sick— every single person had to behave like a meek lamb and obey orders of stripping naked or face harsh beating.

The soldiers dragged some children towards the hotel building, threatening severe punishment if they repeated what they had done a short while ago. We were now in the midst of a siege. The soldiers were inquiring about the presence of gunmen, their hideouts and an arms dump in the neighbourhood. We ignored them, their inquisition and their threats of demolishing our houses in case any 'militant' had taken refuge in our houses. After about two hours, the soldiers ordered us to disperse without arresting anyone.

The elderly were now laughing and making jokes about the situation they were just in, as if letting go of the humiliation, but the children were silently watching the soldiers boarding the vehicles.

Making my way to the secret gathering was out since I had lost my ability to go to Baba's house for lunch. I was anticipating another crackdown at home, when I would have to face my husband, Asad, in case he had come to know about my clandestine visit to Baba during lunch and caught me in the throes of the crackdown. The situation that was waiting for me at home was more petrifying to me than what I had seen on the road.

BRUTAL

The days had become dry, hot and dusty. The nights were humid, suffocating and airless. The paradise on earth that Kashmir could once claim to be had now turned into a desert due to a heat wave. And the presence of the unknown faces at every turn made us think again: *Is this the same place we have been living in?*

When we were children, Baba would take us to the alpine resort of Gulmarg to get away from the hot weather of the plains, though it was not as hot then as it is now.

Between the snow peaks of Gulmarg and Khilanmarg, the small valley running deep down the gorge was the abode of the nomads of Kashmir, whom we call the Gujjar. We used to spend a few days in the summer in their mud house, and would watch the sky get suddenly shrouded by a thick mist, which would be followed by torrential rain. At times, it was only one's eyes or shadows that could be seen in the flicker of the candlelight inside the house; the rest would get absorbed in the mass of mist, clouds and forest. It was here that I learnt the skill of climbing mountains without bruises or broken bones. The head Gujjar of the clan would warn us of the wild bears that would often come down the stream in search of food. 'He is not a man-eater, but he eats the wild fruit that grows around the streams. Do not disturb him,' he would caution us repeatedly.

After years of the chasing and counter-chasing of militants by security forces, the wild bear had reached further down the village and dozens of the inhabitants there had become his prey now.

Kashmir used to be called 'the Switzerland of Asia' by European travellers for its majestic beauty and lush green forests. The Mughal kings had referred to it as 'paradise on earth' and had made it their place of rest and refuge from the scorching summer heat in the Indian plains. The valley was losing everything from its peace to its beauty in the turmoil. The soldiers had covered every mountain range in the valley and established checkpoints at mountain passes to stem the infiltration of militants; the environmental damage, deforestation and pollution of streams, carried out by smugglers were a threat to everything: forests, streams, beauty and tourism. One of Asad's relatives from his village said that the security forces ruled almost all the mountains and villages and that the local population had moved out in droves.

In the plains, nobody dared open a window or ventilator to let fresh air in—they were fearful of the unknown gunmen roaming around, who were known to force their entry into any house they felt was safe from the soldiers. We encountered many unknown faces those days, once we opened our windows. We would either see the security forces patrolling the streets, or see strangers shrouded in pheran—the Kashmiri traditional dress stitched like a long, loose shirt, with an opening at the top—running about in panic. Sometimes it seemed as though the security forces and strangers were playing cat and mouse with each other. If, by chance, the strangers took refuge in our house, we would have to face the wrath and terror of the security forces the following day. We preferred to roast in the scorching heat, behind the shut windows and doors, rather than risk unknown guests in our homes.

Every night, Asad would make sure at least twice that all the doors, windows and ventilators in the house had been shut. All the curtains remained drawn in the evening time and the lights were kept switched off even in the darkness. All this was just to give the impression that we were asleep. We could hardly sleep in this atmosphere of terror. The most we were able to do was pretend to be asleep.

After closing all the windows and ventilators, Asad came into the room, beaming. This was unusual because he had lost his ability to smile after the Rajbagh incident, and had since become serious and withdrawn and remained lost in his thoughts.

When I asked him what was making him smile that day, he related to me the fight between our two hostile neighbours, who had each been supporters of different ideological groups. One had been a staunch supporter of independence, while the other was supporting accession with Pakistan. At least they were clear about their thoughts on the solution for Kashmir. Asad had enjoyed the fight, the argument and the tension between them.

In the recent days, the pro-Pakistan lobby had become much stronger. It secured more support from Pakistan—material and financial—even though it was the independence movement that enjoyed mass appeal. I was sure the fight would leave its impact on our close-knit neighbourhood. But I could not understand why Asad was deriving pleasure out of the fight. His attitude was rather mysterious. Looking at his grinning face again, I made him understand the sensitivity of the situation we were in. He brushed my fear aside, saying, 'You are looking too deeply into it. The gun will finish all apprehensions created by the agencies by floating too many possible solutions through its spies.'

I was surprised and also worried about his ignorance of the reality. He was living in a fantasy world, where the gun was the cure for all our problems. 'How can you live in the neighbourhood if it is torn apart by the differing loyalties of two different factions?'

'There are no different factions. We all cherish Azadi. If this is not acceptable to some factions, they will have to face the consequences.' His face went red and the anger was rising in his eyes. I tried to avoid the argument and went to bed to get some sleep.

Regardless of whether it was due to exhaustion or fear, I started yawning and covered myself in a quilt to go to sleep early. Asad came towards the bed, put his arms around me and started rubbing his body against mine. This felt very irritating to me. I could see mischief in his eyes when he stroked my hair. My yawns became too frequent. I turned to the far side of the bed. He was looking at me in surprise. And I was surprised to see his mood change so quickly: from anger a short while ago to this interest in lovemaking. His face was changing expressions every moment I glanced at him.

The more I shifted to the edge of the bed, the closer he came to me. He was muttering to himself that he had to wait so long for a child and how I couldn't bear him a son to carry forward his clan. 'My friends make fun of me for not having a child. They challenge my . . . How can I tell them that you have let me down? You have dashed all my hopes.'

He seemed to get more and more irritated while continuing to look at me.

And then, in a flash, he became so furious that he dragged me by my hair towards him, took his quilt off and tore his clothes off in a hurry. While undressing himself, he kept quoting verses from the Quran, which, if I understood correctly, threw light on the duties and loyalty of a good wife—qualities that I lacked, according to his rants. He grabbed me from behind and grinned at me, placing his face very close to mine. I felt his breath that was full of smoke and fear.

Initially, I had thought he was just mocking me. I pleaded to him politely to let me go, saying I needed to rest for my early day the following morning. He seemed completely unbothered at my helplessness, though he did not take his eyes off me. I could not wrap my head around what was going through his mind. What I came to know later was that he had found my resistant attitude insulting and a challenge to his manliness. And so he had become outraged—his eyes were bloodshot, and he started abusing me physically and mentally. I was gasping for air; my breathlessness nearly killed me.

However, Asad's passion and lust lasted for only a few minutes. He turned to the far side of the bed and went immediately into a deep slumber, unremorseful, and oblivious to what he had put me through by imposing himself on me.

I went numb and silent. Everything in the room disgusted me. I wanted to vomit all over the wooden floor, on the blanket, his clothes and on the book on 'successful marriage' that had been a part of my trousseau. All these things seemed meaningless now.

I did not dare to look at my face in the mirror opposite my bed. I was terrified that I would catch a glimpse of my own cowardliness, which had not let me stop Asad from having his way. Everything turned acidic in my stomach. I felt nauseous and went to the bathroom to vomit it all out.

Throughout the long and dark night, I was raving and reeling inside. I could see no reason for Asad's inhuman behaviour. *What could have changed him into a demon?* I kept asking myself. The horrible incident kept replaying in my mind constantly. The more I recalled it, the more I feared him.

Baba would always say, 'Marriage is a sacred relationship based on mutual love and trust.' I found neither trust nor love in my marriage in that moment.

I did not know how and when 'force' entered my relationship. When I finally realized it, I had lost everything: my honour, my dignity and my self-respect.

I could not afford to mention this to anyone. People would ridicule me. In our society, the husband was the sole proprietor of the woman he was married to—just like how the government treated Kashmir as her property. My motherland and me, we were both enslaved by our oppressors, though each of us never realized it.

I thought about the things that had never crossed my mind before. My eyes hurt when I turned my face towards him. My heart threatened to stand still, but the next moment it was about to explode. The whole issue of marriage grew inside me like an embryo grows inside the womb. Every moment my torment increased and I started to concentrate my anguish upon the huddled mosquitoes on the ceiling. My sense of isolation filled up my brain and prevented any other thoughts from seeping in.

The sound of a huge blast somewhere in the neighbourhood shook our house. All the mosquitoes huddled on the ceiling fell down to the floor, with some going straight into my mouth. I started vomiting again and spat on the mirror. My image in the mirror was more terrifying—my guilt overpowering my timidity had made me undignified in my own eyes. I could not endure the feeling and started crying silently.

~

Feeling numb and depressed, I stayed home all day. My garments were scattered all over the place—some left on shelves in messy piles, some dangling out of the closet. My collection of books, that I got no chance to read, was scattered around the bed, under the table and inside the cupboard. To divert my attention from the nightmare, I engaged myself in tidying up the room.

There was little space left for more garments to fit in the cupboard. I chose a few dresses for daily wear, while the rest I placed in a suitcase to give to Asad's sister in-law, his brother's wife. She would take all my clothes to the village and distribute them among her servants. The light-blue dress that Asad had bought me after a few months of marriage was lying at the top of the suitcase. The colour of the dress had faded.

Now the room looked different. Everything seemed to have been immaculately placed at the right place. The room had a new and clean look. Except for me—the ugly, unclean feeling did not go even after many showers.

In the evening, Asad was ironing his 'Khan dress' in a corner of the bedroom. The Khan dress comprised a loose, long shirt and trousers; it had been made the national dress of Pakistan by the military dictator Gen Zia-ul-Haq, and was mostly worn by the Afghan mujahideen during their fight with the Soviets. During the Kashmir movement, the dress became a symbol of support for Pakistan; by this dress code, people would be able to recognize the mujahideen, who would keep their guns hidden under the loose shirts of the Khan dress.

Asad acted normal, though immersed in his own world. His skill for ironing was unique, as if he had worked all his life in a dry-cleaning shop. Men in my family only liked ironing among other household jobs; I'm sure they sometimes secretly ironed their wives' dresses too.

Suddenly, we heard a series of big thuds on our main gate. I peeked through my bedroom window to see who had come. I could only see shadows in the street, as if somebody was pacing back and forth, waiting eagerly to enter our house.

Asad hurried past me, pushed me away from the window towards the wall and descended the flight of stairs quickly to reach the main gate. I heard some people talk to Asad in a whisper near the living room adjacent to the kitchen. For a long time I could hear voices coming from downstairs, sometimes whispering, sometimes loud voices; in between, I could also hear thuds, as if something heavy was being dropped on the floor. I knew there was something amiss.

I waited for Asad to come upstairs and tell me what was going on. Yet, he took a long time. My tossing and turning in the bed was causing the wooden floor to creak. I was afraid. What if there were patrolling soldiers outside? Even a squeak, in those days, was enough to provoke them to enter a house solely on the suspicion that there were 'militants' hiding inside.

After a few hours of restlessness, I heard Asad climbing the stairs. He was again smiling callously, showing his teeth that had recently turned yellow. I lost my temper over the fact that he was boasting about some mujahideen taking shelter in our house. He wanted me to cook food for them.

'About a dozen of them are going to stay here tonight. They are hungry, cook some food quickly.'

'What, are you out of your mind?! You want me to cook food for them in the middle of night? Don't you know the patrolling soldiers would know immediately if I switch on the lights in the kitchen?'

'You do not have to raise an alarm by illuminating the whole house. You can cook in candlelight. My mother used to cook *wazwan* by candlelight. Why do you make such a fuss of everything?'

'How can I cook food for twelve people by candlelight? I am not your mother. It is out of the question.'

'You know what your problem is? You have become too big for your boots, and it is entirely my fault that I let you open your big mouth. I will deal with you, but not now. Go and cook food quickly.'

He closed the bedroom door so that the men downstairs would not listen to our conversation. We could hear a lot of whispering, as if they were eavesdropping. Then there was silence. I tried again to make him understand the consequences of keeping the mujahideen in our house. He ignored my apprehensions.

'Do you realize they are fighting for our freedom, laying their life down for our future? They have left their families and dear ones for our Azadi. Do you want me to throw them out of my house? You have no right to talk to me in that high tone. You can at least show some respect for what they have been going through day and night. If you do not know, let me tell you, they are chasing death whilst you are sleeping in a cosy bed!'

After a long lecture on morality and freedom, Asad gave me a contemptuous look, as if he were about to spit on me.

'Come down into the kitchen quickly, cook food for them, or they will eat you.'

'Why are you treating me like this? Don't you have any regard for me? I had never thought that you could stoop so low.'

'Because when you ask for it, you get it. If your father had taught you how to treat your husband properly, you wouldn't dare to talk to me so disrespectfully.'

'Has your father taught you how to behave with your wife, or have you only inherited the trait of imposing your will upon a woman?' I retorted.

'How dare you talk to me like that? Had you been married to my brother he would have kicked you out a long time ago. You're talking like you have given me dozens of sons. You have not been able to bear me a single child, and you know you are barren. You have ruined my life and my sense of dignity in the family.'

'Before you blame me, you better get yourself checked by the doctor,' I said. He raised his hand to slap me, but before he could do anything, someone called him from downstairs. His scornful look took the breath out of me. He left me wondering what to cook for our visitors. It was very hard to recognize him any more. He had totally lost control and it seemed there was only hatred left in him for me. Was he really Asad, or had he turned into some monster?

Outside, the sound of heavy boots made me petrified. I peeped through the window to see if soldiers had come to our gate. I could only see shadows on the walls of the fence.

There was a butterfly trapped in the small crack of the windowsill, struggling to free itself. Its feather was stuck in the crevice and so it seemed to be in a lot of pain.

My legs were heavy as I made my way to the kitchen. Trying not to make a sound on the wooden stairs, I looked for the candle that I kept on the shelf in the middle of the staircase. The flicker of light was like a flicker of hope. I thought about Azadi and drew a big circle in my mind. I kept revolving around the circle in a way that the butterfly dances around the candlelight until it strikes the light so hard that its life ends there. The circle was growing bigger and bigger and I was losing count of the orbit. *What does 'liberation' mean exactly?* I asked myself. The idea of liberation is great, but it depends on the definition of the word. Liberation can mean life, it can mean death, or it could mean the end of marriage.

Sounds of shouting came from downstairs. In between all the noise, Asad's voice was prominent, requesting the others to calm down. Then somebody tried to leave the house and was stopped from opening the door. Asad told him, 'The moment you step out of that door, the security forces will shoot you.'

The door closed again and the men went inside and continued shouting at each other.

I thought the end was near because the security forces, in the past, had razed many houses to the ground because they had information that 'militants' were hiding inside.

I brushed my fear aside and started to cook in the middle of night, but we had no stock of meat, chicken or vegetables left—there were only a few packets of lentils in the cupboard.

Even if we all have to die, I will not let them die on an empty stomach, I vowed to myself.

~

I could not sleep. I only pretended to sleep and waited for dawn to break. I wished I could leave before the mujahideen left.

Surprisingly, I saw no sight of them when I went into the kitchen just before light broke. All I saw were used cups, saucers, plates and cigarette butts littered on the floor, as if we had been burgled during the night. It took me a few hours to clean the kitchen with cold water; still, I could not clean the lentil stains on the carpet. The blankets, duvets and bed sheets were piled on top of the table. The men needed hot water for a wash. I kept the tea and bread ready for breakfast and then got ready for work.

Asad was snoring in the adjacent room. The clatter of dishes being washed woke him up and he came to help me tidy up the kitchen. This was very unusual of him because kitchen and household work never suited him. Our men considered it below their dignity. His brothers and sisters would ridicule him if they saw him cleaning dishes in the kitchen. It was difficult to understand what he wanted to prove with his grand gesture. However, he was silent like a graveyard. There was no remorse or guilt on his face.

Did I have a nightmare, or had some gunmen really come to stay at our house for the night? I felt unsure of everything that had happened.

Without saying a word, I went upstairs and grabbed my purse. I was just about to leave the house when Asad came up from behind me, wrapped me in his arms and started kissing me passionately on my cheeks. It was a bit of a surprise, but more terrifying than anything else. A devilish grin had appeared on his face.

He whispered in my ear, 'Don't tell anybody about the mujahideen. The slightest hint of it would put our whole family in danger. Try to forget what I said earlier. Remember, we are all in this together. If we cherish Azadi, we have to make some sacrifices. At least, you will be able to proclaim in the future that you once cooked food for our visitors.' He kissed me again and pressed my hands tightly.

Regardless of whether it was a warning or the manifestation of his love for me, his face still wore a blank expression, which made me very uncomfortable.

However, his kissing and cuddling had started to make me feel guilty at the same time. I felt that maybe I was being too harsh on him and my heart started to melt. I wanted to reassure him and tell him not to worry about it, but as I turned to look back at him, I saw he had closed the door behind him with a big thud and left. My legs felt heavy, like lead, with every step I took towards the road, but I made sure I kept my mouth shut, eyes closed and ears blocked.

The more I thought about the situation, the more it hurt me. It felt like I was walking on fragile eggshells all the way to office.

UNCERTAIN

The office rooms were more or less empty.

Those who had managed to show up for work were the least interested in producing programmes for the listeners. Those who had stayed home were dreaming about joining office after Azadi.

I was neither mentally present in office, nor was I thinking about home. I was somewhere else. The employees present had to seek the permission of the station director in case they wanted to leave the premises during office hours, and in the event they did get permitted to leave office, they had to take police escort. So nobody bothered to leave the premises. It was unsettling for me.

My yearning to see Baba and my sisters was making me restless. I could not wait to tell my sisters the nightmare I had gone through. I could not keep everything in my chest bottled up, and it was too heavy to carry on with. My Baba had a right to know what I was going through when the mujahideen were sleeping in my house. What if our house got blown up by soldiers, with the hiding 'militants' inside? Baba would never forgive me for keeping that a secret.

Should I go to Baba's house or stay quiet at work? I was indecisive as usual.

I kept looking at the white walls in my room that had lost their original colour the way my relationship with Asad had lost its character. The constant altercations with him were becoming too much to bear.

I had not shared this with anyone, let alone Baba. Whether it was good or bad, I had been coping with it in my own way, alone. I never wanted my father to repent his decision of having me married off to Asad. He would feel guilt that would eat him from within. It was after a lot of persuasion that I had agreed to marry Asad. The moment I saw him I became restless. I shared my anguish with my sisters, but they couldn't influence Baba.

Soon after the marriage, however, my sisters changed their opinion about Asad. They considered him a kind, sincere and caring person—which he was initially, I suppose. It was only a few months after our wedding that something changed him and he became harsh and imposing. I thought he would come around and that it was probably a temporary phase, so I never attempted to show my resistance to his behaviour and waited for him to realize it himself. Mentally, he went far away from me, and I had to bear the pain silently.

The intrusion into my house, Asad's proximity to the gunmen and his abusive language and tone with me—all this became too much to endure at the same time.

I thought, once I saw Baba, I would tell him about the mujahideen taking shelter in my house, even as security forces were patrolling the streets. I would warn my sisters that it was likely that Asad's every move was being monitored by the security agencies and that they were never to allow him to bring any guest into their homes.

Should I also tell them how Asad had been tormenting me with his callous attitude? I was unsure about that.

My timidity always engulfed me. I could not muster up the courage to walk on the road that led to Baba's house. Instead, I started walking on the road going back towards Asad's house. It was not fair to frighten Baba unnecessarily, because he knew the consequences of being close to the mujahideen—the security forces never stormed houses where the mujahideen were hiding; they simply destroyed them by shelling them.

I felt an ache inside me.

~

Near the bus stop, I spotted Sadia running after a bus. I ran towards her. Before she jumped on the bus, I grabbed her arm. She turned her head and looked at me in astonishment. Without any smile or greeting in response, she continued quickly towards the bus and rode away on it.

That was unbelievable! How could she ignore me?

She seemed indifferent towards me, as if I was not her sister but some stranger. Why was she doing this? I could not wrap my head around it. Something was wrong with her, and she tried to hide it from me.

Why was she acting so terrified? Does she know that the mujahideen are taking refuge in my house? Is that what made her keep away from me? Does she fear that some sort of catastrophe would fall upon her family if she were to come close to me? Or had something happened to her as well, that she was trying to keep a secret from me? My thoughts were all over the place. I could tell from her eyes and behaviour that something very strange was going on. The bus sped away. I could not get myself on any bus.

Instead, I wandered around the bus stop for many hours. It seemed I had lost sense of time and space. I had even forgotten the way to my house.

FEAST

The summer of 1990 was lost indoors. Those days were long gone when we used to sit outside, on the threshold of our houses, to catch up with the neighbours. Our evenings were the most precious of our lives, when we would all go outside and form different groups, of young girls, boys, men and the old.

All of us would be talking, gossiping and laughing, and sharing our joys and sorrows. But autumn had spread its dark wings everywhere. Our poplar trees had started to get stripped off their leaves and greenery. The barren mountains had become like skeletons, and the streams running through their heart had become grey and muddy.

We had lost communication and connection with each other. There had been no lunch gathering at Baba's house for the last few months. I wondered how my sisters were enduring the volatile situation around them, how Baba was coping all alone in the house and why Sadia had ignored me that day at the bus stop. I pondered over all of it all the time. We were separated even from our close neighbours. We had no telephones and no means of communication. The curfew imposed by the government, or the strikes called by the Azadi leaders, had confined us to our homes.

I was dying to see Baba and, even more, dying for the delicious food that was always served at his house. It was hardly a grand feast—the turmeric-rich potatoes with fresh mint, saag pickle, onions washed in vinegar and potatoes cooked with green chillies had always been a speciality at Baba's house. Due to a recent shortage of green vegetables in Srinagar, people had become used to eating potatoes, which were more easily available, and were coming up with innovative ways of cooking them. Aloo gosht, a meat curry of potatoes cooked with meat, was another sumptuous dish we had enjoyed since childhood.

While enjoying the potato dish, Baba would remind us, 'After Partition, Sheikh Abdullah insisted that people grow and eat their own potatoes to become self-sufficient, rather than go begging to others for help. Abdullah's time has returned, though this time the people are enjoying eating potatoes, rather than feeling resentful at being forced to eat them.'

I wanted to ask Baba why Abdullah had encouraged people to become self-sufficient when he had actually acceded Kashmir to India. Baba's reaction was worrying at times, and I could feel his pain when he cursed Abdullah. Perhaps he was repenting his association with him. Because of all this talk of potatoes, probably, he got reminded of Abdullah's time, while I was reminded of the big feasts my mother used to cook for us. My mother's favourite dish was spicy lotus stem cooked with fresh lamb chops and a special Kashmiri rice called *mushkibudhaj*. On top of that, we were each served a big tumbler of buttermilk. The potatoes cooked with green chillies would turn the meal into a grand feast; I tried to replicate it dozens of times, but always failed.

At every celebration of Eid or on big family occasions, my mother would become sentimental while serving us her special delicacies. She would boast about the past, when her grandfather used to invite all the powerful and influential people to his house for grand feasts. My mother's grandfather was a wealthy landowner who left hundreds of acres of land for her father. Unfortunately, Abdullah snatched away the family fortune when he implemented communist-style reforms under the 'land to the tiller' principle of law, whereby all the land was redistributed to the cultivators. My mother would curse Sheikh Abdullah, the great polarizer of opinion, while looking deep into the eyes of my Baba, who was a supporter of his. We could see a big grin on his face.

It was worth having to wait for hours to be called into a room adjacent to the kitchen. Mama would call us one by one, and our eldest sister, Sadia, would make us sit around the *dastarkhan*, meaning the sheet of cloth upon which the food was served. Baba's place was fixed in the middle, close to the window where Mama had kept a big pillow for him. We were not allowed to touch the food until Baba finished reciting the Quranic verse. We would all silently watch his lips move and then he would finally finish by saying *ameen*. Mehmooda's burp on ameen would make us laugh throughout dinner.

All of us, except Mehmooda, wept for weeks when our mother died. She was asking everybody during the mourning period, 'Who will cook potato for us?' When my *bhabhi*, my brother's wife, joined our household, she took charge of all the cooking, but she could not match the taste of my mother's cooking. However, her own potato recipes outmatched my mother's.

My brother had made Jammu his permanent abode instead of subjecting himself to the risk of travelling on the dangerous national highway that had claimed hundreds of lives in avalanches and accidents. Baba did not agree to leave his nest in Srinagar and preferred to stay behind, all alone.

We did not want to see Baba left on his own. My sisters had made a plan to spend one or two days in a week in rotation at Baba's house. It had not affected our married life. Our in-laws had displayed magnanimity by not complaining about this arrangement, even if it had sometimes caused some unease in the family. For the first time since I was married, Baba was left alone.

1990–1992: An estimate by a local human rights organization revealed that more than 5000 Kashmiri youth had crossed over into Pakistan for the purposes of training and procurement of arms.

MISSING

Like the rest of our neighbours, my family too was getting frustrated over the frequent search operations and crackdowns being carried out by the security forces. Sometimes, different groups of soldiers would come to search our house from the top floor right to the basement. We had to leave everything untouched and had to give them the freedom to carry out the search as they wished. However, they never went to the attic, which was full of junk. Asad never let us throw the junk away and kept the attic locked most of the time.

Whenever a search operation took place, all the men would be ordered to gather in an open field. They would have to walk before a vehicle, from inside which a masked informant inspected them in order to identify people's identities: whether they were militants or their helpers. Some of those who earlier took up the gun to fight the security forces had surrendered during their time in custody and now worked for the government to re-establish its writ in the valley. Most of the youth identified during such raids or search operations were innocent. The mujahideen usually managed to escape an area before a search operation started. They had a stronger intelligence network than the government's intelligence organizations.

Due to the numerous calls for strikes given by the armed groups and the public's support of the continuing search operations, all offices and educational institutions remained mostly closed. My family fully supported the strike call. The growing violence had made parents reluctant to send their children to school, which had remained closed for almost a year now. The shops closed before dark. All the streets became deserted after six o'clock and only uniformed personnel could be seen on the roads in the evenings. The general impression among the public was that the fighting between the mujahideen and the security forces was bound to take place.

Despite the fear of cross-firing or crackdowns, people tried to lead normal lives and go out to see one another. It seemed a bit relaxed on the road even though there was a huge presence of security forces around. As I began to feel an eerie sense of calm, I decided to visit Baba. I took the shortest route to reach there.

Only the corner shop at the far end of the street was half-open, but was without customers. A couple of dogs were rubbing their bodies against an electric pole. Popular Hindi-film music was playing in the precincts of the school, where the soldiers were busy cleaning their guns with chemicals.

Before crossing the threshold of Baba's house, I peeped through the kitchen window to see who else had come to visit my father. Luckily, all my sisters had come, but they looked sad and gloomy. Instead of ascending the stairs at a normal pace, I climbed them two at a time.

My eldest sister, Sadia, was holding Baba's hands. She was crying and did not look at me. And I did not take my eyes off her. I hugged Baba, who I felt had become frailer. Sadia's wailing became more intense and uncontrollable the moment I greeted her. Baba wrapped her in his arms. He was trying to comfort her by giving reassurances about something. 'Do not lose heart, my daughter. God will help us.'

'Will anyone tell me what has happened to Sadia?' I looked straight into her tearful eyes.

'What can I tell you? I am ruined—my home, my future and my life—everything is destroyed.'

'What has happened, can you please tell me?'

'How can I tell you what disaster has struck my family? Please promise me not to tell anyone, not even your husband, as I have no courage left to keep answering people,' Sadia said, punctuating her words with sobs.

I exchanged looks with my sisters. We nodded our heads in unison, as if agreeing to make a promise that we would not share her secret with anybody. I wondered if Sadia's sadness had anything to do with Hassan, her husband, or Aziz, her son.

'You all know that Aziz had gone to Bangalore to study information technology last year. He was doing fine, passed the first semester with top grades. Since October, he has not been seen around the campus. We got a call from the college principal about his sudden disappearance. His friends and the staff looked for him, but he was not found. We tried everybody we knew, he was not in contact even with his close friends. Hassan went to Bangalore to find him, but he returned disappointed. Now Aziz's friend Ali has recently discovered that Aziz has gone across the border for arms training and has joined some militant organization,' said Sadia, crying and beating her chest.

'Across the border?' we all exclaimed in unison. Going across the border meant we would never ever see Aziz again as long as we were alive. Many divided families had perished without even a glimpse of their loved ones after the partition of India and Pakistan in 1947.

The border demarcating the Line of Control had remained closed for almost sixty years now. There was a time when both countries had agreed to permit their citizens to visit their relatives across the border. But this was not allowed for those who lived across the Line of Control because the issue of dividing Kashmir was an unresolved dispute between the two countries; thus, this movement across the border was barred for Kashmiris on either side. It had been a distant dream for every Kashmiri family to visit their relatives across the border, which had been put into place at a time when both India and Pakistan achieved independence from the British.

'Is there any way to get him back? Can we send him a message?' I asked Sadia, knowing in my heart that she would have already exhausted, in vain, all options of trying to reach him by now.

'Nobody can help. Hassan blames me for everything: for sending him to Bangalore and for not keeping track of his activities.' Her sobs became loud wails now.

'And what was Hassan doing all that time—playing cards with his friends? He should not blame you. He is the one who never took any interest in his children, their education or their activities. His business adventures and dream of becoming a millionaire overnight is all he cares about. He should be held responsible for everything.' I kept accusing Sadia's husband of neglecting his family, although I knew that he was the most caring father among all my brothers-in-law. My rants did not ease her pain and agony.

She was crying her heart out. Baba felt helpless, looking at her grief-stricken face. My thoughts were running wild. I was visualizing the worst scenario all around me.

With an AK-47 rifle hanging from his shoulder, Aziz was firing at soldiers indiscriminately. Some of them were falling to the ground after being hit by him, while others were running to overpower him. Aziz was running and firing simultaneously. Furious soldiers were chasing him from all directions. He was in a panic and kept running wildly. One of the soldiers came close to him from behind and kicked him down. Another hit him at close range. In an instant, the AK-47 fell down and so did he. Blood was gushing out of his head like a stream. He was screaming and abusing the soldiers. He was fading away. His breathing stopped. He opened and closed his eyes. We were all crying around him, pulling our hair. Sadia was running wild here and there. Baba was taking him in his arms and crying silently.

'No! No! It cannot be true!' The loud, shrill cry burst out from my chest and I started to run around wildly in the room. The blood seemed to have frozen in my veins, my heart was pounding like a drum and it appeared that my brain was not aligned to any of my actions.

Mehmooda landed a slap on my face to stop me from running and crying.

'Am I dreaming this, or has his death become imminent?' I stuttered.

We were reeling with shock. All of us were contemplating the worst that was yet to come and how we were to prepare Sadia for what lay ahead of her.

I woke up from a nightmare and found Sadia wailing and weeping.

Baba took her in his arms and tried to console her. He raised her blind hope of finding him: 'Have faith, he will come back, inshallah.'

My sisters were crying within. Yet, they were trying to hide the pain with a facade and displaying a brave face to each other. However, the water in their eyes was ready to flood over and dissolve the charade that was being played out.

After so many months of separation, our lunch gathering had made us numb and cold. We sat silently, staring at the walls, listening to Sadia's crying and Baba's long sighs. The house was haunting us and we all wanted to flee from it, perhaps never to return—but nobody could move from their places.

1990–1992: Most Hindus, including the entire Kashmiri Pandit community, flee the valley after the killing of two prominent Pandit judges.

DASH

A storm, in the dead of the night, had bruised and scarred the face of the valley. Fossilized, old chinar lay uprooted everywhere, houses ripped down and damaged, walls razed to the ground, electric poles broken flat across lanes and litter strewn all over the streets. Stray dogs were sniffing through the piles of garbage and playing with the fluttering polythene bags.

However, all this had no impact on the patrolling soldiers, who had moved their fingers on the triggers of their guns and had their eyes fixed on our windows. Those soldiers, who had been peeping through the small window of a nearby bunker, had been enjoying watching the fighting among the dogs over the flying empty plastic bags. At least, they had found something to entertain themselves with in our tense neighbourhood.

There was no sign of people on the roads; it was as if the whole valley had gone into hibernation. The sight was eerie.

Home seemed the safest place on earth in such circumstances, provided there were no crackdowns or raids at 'militant' hideouts by security forces. For the last few days, we were spared the search operations. It appeared that the gunmen had left our neighbourhood for other hideouts. Still, people preferred to stay indoors.

I had not seen Kashi Nath or his daughter, Nina, since the previous Sunday. But I was not sure if I would be able to visit their house to overcome my boredom because Asad had not been going out like he used to. I visited Nina only when Asad would slip out of the house.

In our backyard, towards the left corner, was the house of Kashi Nath, who had been living there for almost fifty-five years. He had been a teacher throughout his life and there was hardly anybody left in the neighbourhood who had not been his student.

When I assumed my new identity of daughter-in-law, I became familiar with Kashi Nath through his daughter, Nina, in the neighbourhood. She became my friend and close confidante only after we shared a brief encounter at a wedding ceremony in the area. Nina proved to be good company and an 'informer' about everything that happened in our vicinity. She even knew all the oddities and pleasures of my family life. I relied on her to keep my secrets.

The only problem with her was that she never disclosed to me her own secrets, which often made me wonder whether she had any of her own? Or did Pandit girls have none?

I often went to visit her on Sundays and we discussed everything from politics to her plans of joining the media. Her huge personal library always made me envy her. I wished I could read all those rare books that her father had collected throughout his life, during visits to remote corners of the valley. Being a daughter-in-law, I was not supposed to be seen reading books, even if I had finished all my household chores. It came across as rude to my traditional family if I started reading a book in the presence of my in-laws. They considered it an attempt to belittle the daughters of the family, who were mostly illiterate or uneducated. Still, I kept a book in my bag to read at work during my free time. Only Faiza would sneak into my room, in Asad's absence, to discuss her favourite subject: Kashmiri Sufi philosophy. We always made sure the door was securely shut.

Nina would often challenge me by asking about my choices: 'Why did you marry Asad? He does not seem normal to me.' 'How can you tolerate him?' 'Did you meet him before the wedding?' 'Were you forced to marry him?'

To avoid the subject of the state of my marriage, I would change the subject and talk about her plans of joining the media.

Nina knew about my strained relationship with Asad, yet I never encouraged her to give me her opinion. I dreaded the fact that she would advise me to leave him—and that was something that was not permissible as per our social norms. Moreover, I personally had no plans of abandoning him.

Asad and I would fight over the frequency of Nina's visits every time she would come to see me. He insisted that I tell her not to barge unannounced into every room since we now had more regular visits by gunmen in our house. But I could not do it. Nina was the one who had encouraged me to read books, and evade my sense of isolation, within and outside.

But she had a very strange habit. The moment she entered my house, she would go to every room and open every closet, which often made me angry. Yet, I knew her actions were benign and she didn't mean to snoop for clues about our personal matters. Despite the family pressure, I never stopped Nina from visiting me; though I made every effort to stop her from going towards the attic that Asad had kept locked.

Asad considered Nina an 'informer' for the intelligence agencies. I did not. We argued about it every evening. In the past, it was Asad who had been very close to her father, who used to be our special guest on Eid or other family occasions, yet he despised Nina. Perhaps he was not happy with me, as a consequence of which he despised everybody who was close to me. I believe, in fact, that he hated my guts.

I had heard a rumour that a Muslim girl in my neighbourhood had eloped with a Hindu soldier, and they had been caught by the local police near the town of Banihal, on the national highway. The father of the girl had had a heart attack and was in hospital. I wanted to share this information with Nina and was longing to hear the real story from her.

After about two hours of cleaning and dusting in the kitchen, I looked around for Asad, who had already left. I rushed to Nina's house. I was curious to find out if she had made any decision about taking up a job at the radio station. She had already received an offer for the post of scriptwriter, which was considered very prestigious. I used my influence to make sure she got this job, partly because I would have her as company on my way to the office and back. It was ironic that Nina received a job offer at a time when most Hindu employees in my office were leaving the valley.

I sneaked out from the backyard door without telling Asad's sister-in-law about my secret rendezvous.

The street was silent and deserted. A few yards away, I heard some whispers, from behind Nina's house, that became insistent when I came closer to the fence. The old traditional wooden gate of her house had a big padlock hanging on it, and there seemed to be no trace of anyone inside the house.

Why is her house locked, where have they gone? I wondered.

It was very unusual to see Nina's house locked when it was usually the only house in the neighbourhood whose door always remained open. We kept our doors shut to keep the gunmen out, but Nina's house had the advantage of having a security bunker close to its fence. My neighbour would say, 'The security forces know whose fence they are guarding. There is an internal bond between Hindus and the security forces.' Therefore, the mujahideen would not dare enter a Hindu house.

Drawing closer towards the locked gate, I became nervous, being the only one walking on the street. Two soldiers came out of the bunker facing the fence, looking a bit suspicious. I was looking around for any clue as to where the family might have gone. The windows were closed and the curtains fully drawn. The family would often travel to other Indian states, but somebody would always be around to guard the house, mostly Muslim servants or Nepali immigrants.

Finding me lost in my thoughts, the soldier leapt towards me—perhaps trying to figure out my intentions.

'Stop there, or I will shoot you!' the stout soldier shouted at me.

I was scared to death, staring at the raised gun pointing towards me.

'What are you looking for? What do you want to steal?' barked another soldier close to the fence at the back.

Angered, I thought: *Steal? How dare he? I wish I could smash his head.* But I couldn't. Instead, I pointed towards my own house, trying to make them understand that I lived there and that I had come to see my friend.

They failed to understand me and my gestures, or they didn't believe me.

This was painful. I had been visiting this house for the last five years without seeking anybody's permission. Nobody had stopped me from meeting Nina—even Asad gave up in the end and his family caved in. What had changed overnight that the soldiers were now objecting to me being in my own street? Can't I walk freely in my own locality, live in my own house or see my only friend? I was frustrated and losing the ground beneath my feet.

'Nobody lives in this house any more. The family moved to Jammu last night. They were threatened by militants to leave the valley. We are here to guard the house.'

You better guard it properly because my memories with Nina are written all over the house. I have spent the best time of my life within those walls. I wanted to tell them that, but my courage had died inside me.

'Leave this place quickly, just run, or . . .' the soldier shouted again.

They were watching my every move and that of the surroundings.

Something dreadful must have happened to Nina that had forced her to leave her house, neighbourhood and relationship behind in the darkness of night, so suddenly, without even saying goodbye. The soldiers' constant gaze scared me about being alone on the street. I wanted to run, but I felt stuck in the spot I was standing in. I could not move.

Had we lost everything between us, our friendship, our relations, our secrets? Has everything gone down the drain? Who has robbed us of everything? Soldiers, gunmen, or some other force was scheming against us. The suspicion against each other, among two communities, had deep roots, even though they had been living together for centuries and boasted about the tradition of their secular culture. It never occurred to me that the situation would get so bad that Pandits would have to leave in the middle of the night.

The soldiers did not take their eyes off me, trying to gauge me.

'Run . . . you . . .'

Without looking at them, I ran back towards my house. Expecting a shot from behind, I visualized my fall to the ground. I heard loud laughter instead. I closed the gate behind me with such force that, startled, my neighbours peeped out through their windows.

One more chapter of my life had been erased.

~

Asad descended the stairs two at a time, hurrying towards me, and landed a slap on my right cheek so hard that I nearly fell off the steps.

'Why were you talking to soldiers?! Do you not realize they have come to destroy our nation, our respect, our honour? Don't you have any respect? Do you want to shame me in the eyes of my family and neighbours? What were they asking you? And what did you tell them?' He was shaking and fuming with rage and fear.

I could not reply, my right ear was hurting so much that I felt like it would burst open if I moved my hand away from my face or opened my mouth.

Asad's fragility and cowardliness was written all over his face. When his brawling accompanied physical abuse, I did not feel frightened. Such moments were worth enjoying, not worth worrying about. He was the most cowardly person in of all humankind. I could see he was under tremendous stress and worried about something I had no clue about. He never told me his secrets.

There was nothing to discuss. We were beyond that stage now. For a few seconds, my eyes remained fixed on him, and he kept avoiding me. We were both scanning each other to read the other's thoughts.

'Was there anything to tell them?' I said, managing to speak at last.

He gave me a look that was piercing and humiliating. His glances were trapping me.

'Did you tell them anything about the mujahideen? Were they asking any questions about me?' He was shaking me back and forth, making me dizzy. I was losing my balance and about to fall on the staircase. His anger, fear and terror were showing more and more on his face. 'Has Nina taught you spying? She was a bitch. If anything happens to my family or me, I will hold you responsible. Your whole family will have to bear the consequences.' He was threatening me. I could hardly believe it. My husband was threatening me with dire consequences. I wanted to laugh at him.

Asad was looking at me because of my association with Nina.

The soldiers were looking at me because of my being the wife of a suspected militant.

And Baba was looking at me because I reminded him of the past, of the day of my birth, when he was arrested by the Bakshi government.

They all had trapped my mind and soul. Their constant staring was tearing me apart and making me mentally weak. Wherever I went, they would chase me and abuse me.

I did not know what they expected from me. Did they want me to live in terror or die in terror?—or rot in terror?

Leaving Asad would have meant rebellion against society. Baba would not have been able to bear the thought of it. But living with Asad had become my worst nightmare. I was left in despair.

The fight against the orthodox and irrational social norms was harder than the fight against government rule. The realization dawned upon me like a slap on my face.

ACTOR

I had barely seen Asad in over a week. The Azadi movement had turned him into a shadow for me. And I dreaded his shadow at times. Nothing was left between us: love, affection, sympathy or any sense of a relationship—everything just vanished into thin air. We were poles apart. We hardly knew anything about each other any more, and I especially had no clue about his inner or outer circle of friends. Why he left so early in the mornings, or where he went, I was not in the slightest bothered any more.

He knew nothing about me, whom I worked with, or what I was going through. He did not give a damn about any of it. A few weeks earlier, when our neighbour came to tell us that the soldiers were inquiring about Asad and his acquaintances again, I asked my husband about his connections with the gunmen. He was so infuriated that he left the house and didn't return for a few days. His eldest brother blamed me for that. After that day, I hardly asked him any questions or spoke to him.

It was ironic that the armed movement had helped in the development of close relationships among strangers in the valley. On the contrary, for me, it created a wide gap between my husband and me. We were living under the same roof, but our worlds had become different and unknown to the other.

The Azadi struggle had made the majority of the population vulnerable, as we suffered humiliation every day at the hands of the security forces; but at the same time, it made some people strong, cruel and arrogant. These people were not gunmen or the mujahideen, but their henchmen, who exploited the Azadi movement to make their own fortunes and empires. Asad did not become a gunman, but he was close. He did not make a fortune, but displayed his power and influence to such an extent that he turned into a berserk elephant, trampling everybody who came in his way. Consequently, he jeopardized his own relationships, home and future. He had no idea of it though.

Asad's younger sister, Faiza, felt his arrogance and warned him to behave like a decent human being. He ignored her and refused to talk to her until she begged for his forgiveness. Faiza would often come to my room to comfort me. She would beg me not to lose heart and have patience with her brother: 'I am sure he will come to his senses. Please have faith in him. He has come under bad influence; it will not last long, I promise you.'

Faiza told me Asad, of late, had become too sentimental about Azadi, just like his father, who left his family in the early 1970s to cross the border to start a campaign against the government. She said, 'It was a Gujjar shepherd who saved him from a near-death experience and brought him back while he was crossing the rugged mountains at the Line of Control.' Asad cherished his father's dream of Azadi and hoped that one day it would come true.

But how his arrogance and rudeness would help us achieve Azadi, I was unable to understand.

In the presence of our extended family, we were like professional actors, we behaved like the ideal couple. Except

Faiza, nobody knew nor felt any tension or strain between us. Asad's brother and sister-in-law would sit close to each other and share their food to show their love and respect for each other. Asad would come close to me and place mutton chops on my plate. From the corner of my eyes, I could see his changing expression. He was cursing me in the core of his heart. My blood would boil with inner turmoil, but I would keep a smile on my face to conceal my inner self. We always played the happy family in the company of others.

After the feast, we would go to our room and sleep with our backs facing each other.

MURDER CENTRE

O ur house swelled each day.
　　The increasing number of guests was neither noticed nor mentioned by anyone. Everybody was welcomed with open arms. I could not question the unknown visitors or relatives that my neighbourhood had become used to receiving. These guests, who would come from distant villages to stay with us, would keep changing their hideouts from one house to another, every night. Apart from them, we had additional guests from Asad's ancestral village.

Every time some relative entered the gate, Asad would make sure they were looked after and fed properly. He never cared about the fact that the increasing number of people meant more cooking and housework and general stress for me. He had no patience if there were any delays in offering food or hot drinks for the guests.

Moreover, it was my salary, only, that kept our kitchen running. Asad's business of exporting Kashmiri handicrafts was in a shambles, as he never thought about it or took care of it. Azadi had made him generous when he had no income.

The day the security forces were deployed in Nina's house, all the boys and the mujahideen arrested during crackdowns were brought and put under interrogation there. Their mothers, fathers and relatives had to wait for hours outside the gate to get information about their arrested relatives. Some even fell asleep under the shade of the chinar in our garden until dusk. I could feel their pain, but could do nothing to comfort them.

The nights were dreadful. We could hear the boys screaming and shouting during interrogation, which kept us awake all night. The whole neighbourhood did not sleep. We wanted to listen to the screams only to find out if any scream sounded familiar to us, so we could pass on that information to the relatives.

Nina's house had become a big interrogation centre in Kashmir. Most people called it the 'Murder Centre' of the valley.

I could hardly bear to listen to the screams coming from the house that used to treasure not only the memories of my laughter with Nina but also the books her father had collected throughout his life. I had to nail shut the window on the side of Nina's house.

ARREST

It had now been almost over a week that Asad had been coming home and going straight to his room.

I peeped through the door and saw him enjoying a routine siesta. Perhaps he had not slept the night before, when there was firing in the neighbourhood.

Where he was spending his nights, no one in the family knew, nor did they bother to ask him, even if his sister-in-law saw him in the lobby. He hardly spoke to anybody and silently went to sleep.

Without disturbing him, I sat near the cupboard and made a list of the tasks that had to be finished by the following day. I kept forgetting about even the most routine domestic chores now . . . There was a sense of decay that was seeping into me.

Asad's younger brother, Tahir, barged into the room without knocking, even though it was a practice to knock before entering anybody's bedroom. The turmoil had begun to turn us into a 'lawless society'. Intentionally or unintentionally, we had crossed all moral barriers. Tahir did not even bother to cough before he entered our room. I was terrified by the ghastly look on his face.

'Asad, we are in serious trouble, get up quickly!' Tahir kicked Asad in the back and tore the quilt off him.

'What trouble?' Asad was startled to see his brother in our bedroom, as this was unprecedented under normal circumstances.

'Ali has been arrested and taken to the Papa 2 interrogation centre.'

'Papa 2! When? Who else was with him?'

'Momin Khan [declared a dreaded terrorist by the government]. It was early morning only when the security forces cordoned off his house. Both were arrested during the search operation.'

'Shit! I knew Ali was a weak soul, he can't handle it. I should not have left them . . .'

'What? So you know he was with Momin Khan?'

'So what, you think he would ever listen to me?'

'You should have stopped him.'

'I tried to warn him, he wouldn't listen. Momin Khan hired him to write his statements and articles in support of the freedom movement. He did it openly and repeatedly offered him shelter at a time when the security forces were searching for Momin Khan in the neighbourhood. This had to happen at some point. Still, I feel proud of my brother. At least he showed courage and resolve.'

'What are we going to do to get him back from the clutches of the Army?'

'Tahir, he is not a criminal.'

'That's true, but still, we cannot leave him to languish in a prison. We have to do something to get him released. Our bhabhi and the children are terrified.'

'What can I do? He should have been more careful while sheltering Momin Khan. We all knew we were under surveillance. Only yesterday, I warned him that the security agencies know everything about him and that they are waiting for the right moment to pounce on him. Instead, he offered the gunmen food, money and support. Can you believe his act of stupidity?'

I was listening to their conversation silently. Asad was trying to talk in whispers and avoiding my gaze on him. He seemed to have forgotten that he had made me cook for dozens of gunmen only a few weeks ago.

'Hypocrite!'

I spat the word out loudly, unintentionally. Nevertheless, they did not hear it.

'Asad, please get changed quickly and think about how we can get him back, that is all that matters now,' Tahir said, distress dripping from his voice.

Asad, with his head in his hands, muttered, 'Who will help in his release when they find out about his connection to Momin Khan?' He was punching himself with his fists.

Tahir went closer to the window and shouted, 'Asad, can we first go to the police station to lodge an FIR! Otherwise he will disappear from the face of the earth like the others.' He left in a frenzy.

Asad looked on in despair.

I took an ironed pair of trousers and a shirt out of the cupboard and handed it to him. For a long time, he stayed in bed, thinking hard about how to get his brother back from the clutches of the security forces. Back then, all captured dissidents or militants were mostly killed while in custody.

But before I knew it, in a flash, Asad had stood up and was coming towards me. He was beaming, a broad grin on his face. Pulling me towards him, he started kissing me passionately.

I was looking at him in shock, wondering how and why his brother's arrest had evoked this animal passion in him. It was not hard to understand that he was happy about his brother being arrested for the cause of Azadi. Was it freedom—or me—that evoked this passion in him? His gesture made me sentimental too and I came close to him and leaned my head on his shoulder. I looked deep into my heart to find out what had made me melt so quickly. Was it his emotional surge, my own timidity or the thought of liberation?

I lost control over myself. Tears rolled down my cheeks. I could not bear to look into his eyes that were beaming with a devilish glint.

SURRENDER

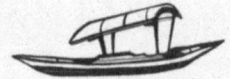

Asad spoke to dozens of government and police officials on the phone, but there was no hope for Ali's release. At least he was able to get some information that his brother had been placed in the notorious Papa 2 interrogation centre. Most arrested boys end up either as custodial deaths or remain unidentified for a long time.

The electronic media led its news bulletins with the capture of Momin Khan, branding it a big success for the security agencies. For the forces, he was a big catch, and they distributed sweets among themselves to celebrate his dramatic capture. The local population was sad and mourning. It was a big blow to the liberation movement.

Asad put the phone down and put a woollen jumper, towel, soap and bathroom slippers into his rucksack for his arrested brother.

Tahir was impatiently waiting for him in the kitchen, muttering abuses at Ali the whole time.

Asad came into the kitchen aghast and agitated. I gave him a cup of tea. After taking a few sips, he looked deep into my eyes, as if recalling something. His expressions were constantly changing. He looked like he was busy working out some mathematical calculations in his head.

All of a sudden, he asked me about the home secretary, Haleem, and whether I had seen him lately. Haleem had been my classmate at university and I did see him often at meetings, when I had to visit the civil secretariat.

'Why are you asking?' I asked, sounding quizzical.

'He could be helpful in securing Ali's release,' Asad replied, his voice full of hope.

'I am not so close to him.'

'You do not need to be close to him to get Ali released.'

Tahir had left the kitchen. I could sense his presence outside the kitchen door, eavesdropping. He gave me a stern look, but remained silent until I came out of the kitchen to offer him a cup of tea. Perhaps I had startled him; he looked apologetic.

'Can you please help? I know it would be a bit embarrassing for you, but we are family and we need to help each other in times of need. Ali is our brother and we all have to make an effort to get him released as soon as possible. Otherwise, we will not be able to get him back alive. Look at his family now,' pleaded Tahir, as though I would magically be able to get his brother out of prison.

Without a word of assurance, I put the kettle on the table and left the kitchen, so that I would not get involved in any other argument. Asad followed me towards the door.

He blocked my way and came very close to whisper in my ear: 'Do what Tahir just said. We are family and it is everybody's responsibility to try their best to get Ali released as soon as possible. If you live in this house, learn to behave like a responsible member of this family. You should learn some manners and not ignore your family, and hear and help them when they are in need. Don't you feel any of the pain we are going through?' Asad burst out.

'How did Ali shelter a Momin Khan when he had a family to look after? It is only a miracle that he has escaped death and the wrath of the security forces on his family. Why didn't he think about us then, or does one inherit this trait of ignoring one's family? How embarrassing it would be for me to barge into Haleem's office out of nowhere and beg him to release Ali.' The words came out of my mouth like bullets.

Then I saw the anger rising in his eyes and his face turn red— my uncompromising attitude in the presence of his brother was boiling his blood. He would have strangled me had his brother not been present in the room. He raised his hand, like he was about to slap me, but stopped in mid-air as his brother came close to him.

'What is wrong with you two? Is this the time to settle old scores or help our brother?' said Tahir, tapping his shoulder.

Asad did not hear him. He stepped towards me, infuriated, and whispered in my ear, 'You will go to the secretariat and talk to Haleem. You will only come back when you have Ali's release order in your hand. That is the end of the story. Ali's release is more important than your embarrassment. Do what you are told and don't ask questions, ever. We do not have this custom of women asking questions when their men give them orders. They just obey.'

'Oh, and is it custom to send your women to officers for help too?' My words were a bullet that pierced his heart. He had sweat all over his forehead. His pride was wounded and he could hardly swallow the lump in his throat.

Ali grabbed him from behind. Asad grabbed his rucksack. They both walked past me with contempt in their eyes.

The tea in the untouched cup on the table was left cold and colourless. I was restless.

~

It was after a lot of cajoling and persuasion from my own self that I decided to seek Haleem's help.

But to enter his office, I had to cross many hurdles and pass through long concrete barriers. The building of the civil secretariat was weaved into security bunkers with huge stone slabs surrounding the main gate. I managed to access his office, which was like a fortress, but to convince his peon at the door was yet another hurdle. The peon was more powerful than his boss. He was probably in his late fifties. The hair at the top of his ears had turned almost grey. If he had not been wearing the khaki uniform, nobody would have noticed his significance: he was the only local gatekeeper of the only functional office in the valley. He was dozing and seemed the least bothered about knowing who went in and out of the VIP room. But when I approached him, he stood up quickly, like a flash of lightning, and gestured me to go into the adjacent room, where the security personnel were watching, with piercing eagle eyes, every soul that entered the premises of the home secretary.

After making them believe my connection with their officer, the security personnel sent me to another room, where policewomen were all set to search every part of my body and every corner of my bag.

Looking at the special entry pass issued and stamped by the policewomen, the middle-aged gatekeeper ushered me into the office. The cumbersome and humiliating process took about half an hour. I was pissed off, and my heart was cursing Asad's family.

Walking in, I thought, this had to be the only building in the valley with functioning light bulbs, painted walls, fresh flowers on the corner tables and piles of files all around.

The maps of the valley—with bold red boundary markings at certain places on the Line of Control—were hanging on the wall behind his seat. Why were there red marks on the Line of Control? Maybe these were thought to be the 'infiltration points'. I was trying to resolve the riddle like some detective.

Haleem was on the phone, telling some police official to send re-enforcements to the area; he was suggesting the use of force to quell the protests, in case of an emergency—because the government did not want to see the insurgency turn into a mass movement at any cost. 'If it seems like the situation is getting out of hand, use force, but don't let the mob take over in any way. I can arrange for further deployment,' he said.

I could not believe this conversation: he was ordering the tight security measures to somebody over the phone in order to curb the movement.

I thought about how much he had changed in these last few years—it was beyond my imagination. What he said made me look at his Kashmiri roots with suspicion. *How could he order a shoot-on-sight on his own people?* I wondered. There were hardly any Kashmiri officers who would dare to act like him. He knew the real situation: the people had genuine political demands, but they were being silenced by bullets.

His physique was the same though, and his general aura and personality had not changed much. He had the same big protruding eyes, weak chin and red cheeks. The only difference was that his hair seemed thinner now and his complexion had become darker—this could be because his job had become too stressful due to the Azadi movement. But mentally he had moved too far away from his people.

I had not taken any prior appointment to meet him, as was expected from any visitor, but he did not seem to mind my unexpected visit. He looked a bit surprised initially, but gestured to me to take a seat. He motioned to his old peon, who was watching my every move, to bring some tea. His office was too brightly lit, due to which the map behind him was reflected on the glass tabletop. Perhaps it was left deliberately in such a position so that he didn't have to turn around to view it.

Haleem was not married, or was he? I had no idea; his face did not look like that of a worried man concerned with leaving work early to buy groceries for the house or change the nappies of his child.

He had a successful career, no doubt about it. In just a few years' time, he had reached the top of the bureaucratic ladder, whereas I had been stuck at the same place since I passed the civil service examination—no thanks to the central government for its stagnation practice. Haleem had never been a gifted student, but he was undoubtedly born under a lucky star. He was possibly the only Kashmiri Muslim who had been retained during the major reshuffle in the administration recently. The armed struggle had brought luck and fortune to some. Haleem was at the top of the list, and he seemed to be enjoying it.

In the early years of the freedom movement, Haleem had become a household name in the valley for being an intelligent and shrewd officer. It was rather his strategy of counter-insurgency that had worked well for the government, and he was rewarded for it.

Was he indeed a successful man? It was very difficult to ascertain this because the changing expressions on his face were uncomfortable for me. I was trying to solve the puzzle of his life, from job to family, fame and fortune, in my mind's eye. My analysis remained inconclusive. What he had achieved in the last four years was incomparable to what I had lost at the same time. I was still struggling to find a niche for myself in the media, while at home I was declared the worst wife.

After a long conversation on the phone, he replaced the receiver in its cradle and gave me a broad smile, as if to show that he was pleased to see me.

'What have I done to deserve the pleasure of your visit, my dearest friend?'

Was he being sarcastic and making fun of me? I did not care.

'I just wanted to know how far you have gone in life.' I tried hard not to sound sarcastic, as he was not in the mood for sarcasm, but I did notice a little bit of it in my tone. It obviously bothered him, it was written on his face.

He was looking deep into my eyes, 'Tell me if something is bothering you. I am ready to help.'

I felt knots forming inside my stomach, my eyes became watery.

He kept looking at me. I was suddenly reminded of our university days. I went back to our last day on the university campus, when we were at the end of our educational journeys. Our campus was on the bank of the Dal Lake, surrounded by enormous, old fossilized chinar trees. It was the replica of heaven on earth. Sitting by the bank of the Lake, I was very upset over leaving the university. It was the end of our carefree life and our first step into the real, practical, problematic world. Haleem covered my eyes, coming up behind me, and said, 'What is bothering you? Why don't you open up your heart? I have a solution for all your problems. Tell me about your worries.'

'You are making fun of everything. I feel really bad about leaving university. Who knows which direction we will all take? We might not even see each other any more.'

'If you really want me to go with you in one direction, give me your hand for ever, let me become your shadow. I promise, I will bury all your sorrows in the Dal Lake, or I might bury myself in the lake like Nagrai did for Heemal.'

I burst into loud laughter at his words and he joined me.

'I have nothing to do from tomorrow: no job, no studies, no friends, and no you,' I said.

'You will have a career, a life, a home and children. Who says you will be unemployed? There is so much to do now.'

'I do not think there will be any offers so soon.'

'I offer you my hand; make me the happiest man in Kashmir!'

He promised me, that on the convocation day, he would meet Baba to ask him for my hand and promise to spend his life with me. I forced Baba to wait for him three times and shared my secret wish of marrying him with my sisters. He did not come to see Baba, so he never fulfilled his promise. It was a long wait marked by anguish and humiliation.

I saw him again, when I went to university after the convocation. He remained silent and never explained why he broke his promise to me. I never asked him either and left him to suffer in silence as I had. These days, we happened to cross each other's paths more often at meetings and government functions.

Even after I got married, I would sometimes cry, thinking of the pain and humiliation he had put me through. How easily he had forgotten that day, his promise—and the moment he had waited outside my house for three days when I was unwell, just to catch a glimpse of me.

'Hello! Are you with me, or are you lost somewhere again in the Dal Lake?' He was the same, light-hearted in his conversation. I wanted to come close to him and feel his breath, his warmth, and assure myself that he was not pretending to be so carefree and was also feeling the pain of our separation.

I put a leash on my emotions, some heavy weight over my chest made my breathing difficult. I wanted to tell him quickly why I was in his office, but it was hard to get it out of my chest, which became compressed with every breath.

'I have a personal request; my brother-in-law was arrested yesterday . . .'

While taking notes on the paper, he was shocked, like he was struck by lightning, when I told him Ali's home address. The pen fell from his fingers.

'Is this the same address from where Momin Khan was captured?'

I became mute with worry.

He started to draw lines on the paper, browsed through his letter pad, read something and asked, 'Is your husband's name Asad?'

I did not look at his inquisitive expression.

'Do you really know your husband?' Haleem asked with fear in his eyes.

'I was destined to become close to people I never knew.' I felt pain in my chest and wished I hadn't come.

I was overwhelmed by the turmoil around me. My thoughts were wandering around the Dal Lake, where he had dreamt to make his own nest with dozens of children. 'My father had taught me to swim in the Dal Lake when I was a child. I wish my children would swim like me. You know, we will have dozens of children. We will break my grandfather's record; he had twelve children and twenty-seven grandchildren. My only concern is about this majestic lake: will it survive until we have had our children and grandchildren?' He used to talk a lot about the dreams he had for his home, children and the Dal Lake.

Whilst writing in the letter pad, he became serious and tried to divert his attention towards the files lying on the corner of the table. He seemed very disturbed and tried hard to keep control over himself. Had I unravelled his memories of the university? Or was he troubled by the request I made?

We were silent for a long time, both lost in our own worlds. Then I stood up to take his leave. He hurried past me and walked towards the entranceway to open the door for me.

Outside his office complex, he regained his official composure. Yet, asked in an easy-going tone, 'Is your husband taking good care of you, or do I need to send him to the interrogation centre?'

I laughed, tears rolled down from the corner of my eyes. I tried to hide my face.

He touched my hand and pressed it. We were both laughing like small children who found a treasure in the woods.

The laughter filled him with life, emotions and vigour. He was the same person I had lost on convocation day.

My internal turmoil made me cry on his shoulder and I was just going to ask him why he had not fulfilled his promise and had humiliated me instead. I failed to find the words. He took a few steps away from me and walked towards a car that had just pulled up near the gate.

A little girl in a pink dress, along with a woman, came out of the car. The girl walked fast towards him.

'Papa!'

'My darling!'

I was frozen in my spot. A woman in a crimson dress walked elegantly out of the car and smiled at him. I could not believe my eyes; it was Rahat, my friend from university, who used to make fun of my involvement with Haleem. When I had told her about Haleem's promise to meet my Baba on convocation day, she became hysterical, ridiculed me and told everybody in the university that I had started daydreaming. Initially, it was she who had pushed me towards him. When I got emotionally involved with him, she started to despise me and him, both.

Unbelievable, I thought.

Haleem hardly looked behind him; I had become just another barricade surrounding and securing his office from all sides.

The khaki-uniformed peon was scratching his head, waiting for me to walk out of the gate.

He started coughing loudly.

The daughter of the Home Minister of India is kidnapped by armed men in broad daylight.

RESTRICTION

My office bore the heavy brunt of the escalating bloodshed, which was exceeding anybody's wildest imagination. All the rooms and studios were empty because the employees had either left the valley, or had not bothered to show up.

The vernacular press was full of stories about the fleeing Kashmiri Pandits, who had left the valley without a trace or intimation to their bewildered neighbours.

A majority of the Muslims viewed their fleeing as a betrayal and some were suspicious too. Media reports had revealed that the security forces had helped them pack up their belongings and made arrangement for vehicles to take them away from the valley in the darkness of night. There was anger, surprise and distrust against them.

Low attendance was recorded in the case of Kashmiri Pandits, who otherwise constituted more than 80 per cent of the workforce, and mostly held key positions. Most of them had left for so-called 'safe havens' after some instances of the gruesome killing of Pandits thought to be working for central intelligence agencies.

The office rooms that were empty, the cupboards left open, the chairs facing the wall and the piles of files scattered on the table were reminiscent of a burglary scene ransacked by bandits.

The controversial newsroom, the only source of information to the valley, was in total disarray, as though it had been consciously wrecked. Muslim employees would hardly enter this room under normal circumstances. The Pandit officers usually dominated the newsroom, except for a few Muslim newsreaders, who had no role in editorial policies.

The Muslim employees were rejoicing on seeing the place empty and dilapidated. It was a general belief among the Muslim staff that if the government still had control over Kashmir, it was because of this newsroom and, besides, more recently, due to the deployment of hundreds of thousands of security personnel across the valley. Considered the mouthpiece of government propaganda and the secret hideout of intelligence agencies, the newsroom had been shifted to Delhi along with the Hindu staff. However, the perception was that the overall control over the state/people would be nevertheless tighter by employing the use of satellite technology in the transmission of propaganda programmes.

Security was tight around the office, and no participant in any of the programmes was permitted to enter the premises without the prior approval of the head of the station. Only the few of us who had special permission passes were allowed to enter the office, albeit after being thoroughly searched and frisked by the paramilitary forces.

Lunch boxes, face creams, painkillers and soft drinks were not permitted inside the premises. I was strictly prohibited from carrying even Crocin tablets in my handbag.

Once, a policewoman, while frisking me, asked, 'I want to buy a Kashmiri shawl for my mother. Could you tell me where to find the best one?' I could only stare at her, because I did not know where she would have been able to buy the embroidered Kashmiri shawl in those trying days. I never thought of suggesting Asad, who had left bundles of embroidered shawls untouched in the balcony. He would not be interested in his business, it seemed, until he achieved Azadi.

Tahira was happy to stay at home on the pretext of security. She would always pray to God for the curfew to continue for days, whereas I would always pray to God for it to be lifted. But I strongly believed God listened to only her prayers.

I felt uncomfortable spending my days in my house with some unknown people—who were roaming around with so much familiarity, as if they had been living there for ages— although, they never spoke to me, and I also never gave them any chance to talk to me. They never touched me, but I never felt safe in their presence. All they did was sit silently in our living room and spend hours staring at the walls.

Earlier I spoke to Asad about their whereabouts; he would say they were from his ancestral village. I had been to his village so many times in the past, but I had never seen any of these people.

MURDER

It was announced on the radio that the curfew would be lifted for two days so that the people could get a chance to acquire some essential commodities. It was for the last ten days that Srinagar had been under a curfew, after huge processions demanding Azadi had stormed the streets. Many processions had turned violent. The clashes between the protesters and security forces had left dozens dead and injured. When the situation went out of control, shoot-on-sight orders were issued on loudspeakers throughout the valley.

At about noon, the curfew was lifted at last. I reached the office without wasting any time waiting for the official transport to pick me up. A long walk on the banks of the Jhelum river was all that I needed to stretch my legs, and it was quicker than waiting for the vehicle.

I did not care about the volatile faces on my way and reached office on time—punctuality being the only trait I had inherited from my Baba. It was hardly surprising that I was the only female present in the office. Nobody had cared to report for duty, let alone be on time. Only after an hour did Tahira surprise me by her presence.

The lifting of the curfew seemed to make no difference to people, as most of them had preferred to stay indoors. Only a few vehicles were on the road. When I reached the State Bank of India building on Residency Road, I could see a few people walking past the security vehicles, trying to enter the bank building. Perhaps people had run out of money. Or maybe the rumour was true, that Kashmiri account holders were closing their accounts in SBI and other central banks and transferring money to the local Jammu and Kashmir Bank, which was believed to be a safer bet, in case of Azadi being achieved.

~

In another few hours, all the cast of the play reached the office for the recording that was scheduled for broadcast on all channels of All India Radio in the evening. Shiasta, one of the performers, had still not arrived though.

We wanted to get done with the recording quickly, so that we could all get home before it got dark. There was always a risk of the reimposition of curfew in case the protestors re-emerged on the streets in the downtown area. This had often happened in the past.

We waited for Shiasta for a few more hours, which felt like an eternity. She had to perform the lead character in the play. Without her, we couldn't record it. She did not turn up. Ultimately, the recording had to be cancelled.

I had been talking to the artists to fix another date for the recording and was about to leave, when Tahira came rushing into the studio and gestured to me to stay back. She was breathless, sweating and about to burst into tears.

'Shiasta was shot dead!' she shrieked.

'Dead?'

'How?'

'Why?'

We were all over her with our questions.

'Her body has been found near the gutter in Watal Kadal. Shiasta's mother was informed in the morning by her neighbour.'

Tahira was revealing the gruesome details as though she were recording the tragic scene in a play.

'Who killed her?'

'She was kidnapped by some gunmen two weeks ago, when she was leaving the radio station after the rehearsals for the play. Her mother says she had been ordered to take some AK-47s to Anantnag, which she had refused to do. And after Friday, she did not come back home.'

How can that be true? Somebody has concocted the story. She was probably somewhere with a friend or relative, I reassured myself.

'She was tortured to death and then her body was thrown into the gutter. Her mother has identified her body, which was found with a letter warning others of the same fate if they are found spying for the security forces.' Tahira's chilling information made goosebumps spring up all over my body.

We all stood motionless—staring at each other— dumbfounded and shocked. Nobody dared leave the studio nor did they move from where they were standing.

I saw frightened and shocked faces around me. There was pin-drop silence in the studio. I could find no consoling words. My fragility was sending shivers down my spine. Why was the curfew lifted? Why did I come to the office? I wanted the earth beneath me to crack open and swallow us whole. The situation was becoming unbearable.

Shiasta's fellow artists started wailing and beating their chests. I did not. I had to put on a brave face, even though I felt the most vulnerable at the time.

My emptiness was filling me with fears and I had no place to run to feel safe.

How ironical it was that all these people were hardly wailing over the loss of Shiasta's life; they were wailing over the justification given for her killing. It was more dreadful to imagine that the same story would be circulated in public.

Tahira was crying, saying, 'The killers had labelled her an informer'.

That meant she would be declared a traitor not only in life, but after her death too. They had insulted her mother, ostracized her family and ridiculed her sisters. How could her mother bear the shame? How could her sisters walk on the road with their heads held high? How would they bury her? Who would talk to them, console them and be a balm for their wounds? The neighbours would not let the family bury her because she had shamed them too. How ruthless the world was.

Could this movement be so cruel that it was now claiming innocent lives? I dreaded the Azadi movement, but felt an ache at the thought of it.

Shiasta had hardly been twenty-five years old. She had no father, brother or male relative to look after her family of six women, including her old mother and four unmarried sisters. Being the eldest one among the girls, Shiasta had to work day in and day out to earn enough to feed and look after her family. She preferred hard work to begging and did not ask anyone for help. At times, when the whole valley would sleep in the comfort and warmth of their cosy homes, Shiasta would lay awake, working on her different roles in drama. The artists were talking, crying and cursing, as if they were performing on stage.

She would juggle around from radio to television to acting on the stage, all to feed six stomachs at a time. Nobody knew the cruel truth of her life. Because she was always smiling, people around her thought she was a successful artist of the radio. Instead of encouraging this young girl to remain firm on the ground, she was humiliated and tortured to death.

'If freedom requires truth, justice and humanity to be wiped away from society, let us prefer slavery instead. The people who had dreamt of Azadi would not want us to die a death of shame and disgrace. We did not object to the gun when it was forced into our society, but we never believed that it would be used against us,' Tahira burst out, crying and wailing.

'How could they be so cruel? To torture her by ironing her private parts? Who says they are liberators? They are criminals and barbarians, more dreadful than soldiers!'

I wanted to prevent them from making inciteful statements, but I couldn't. The least I could do was close the heavy door to the studio to prevent anyone from eavesdropping.

Tahira and another young female artist were embracing and crying loudly. 'Shiasta was a brother to her sisters, a husband to her mother and a lover to herself. She made people laugh though she was weeping inside all the time.'

The screaming grew louder and louder, it sounded like we were recording the death scene of a Greek tragedy.

'What a waste of a talented life.'

'An unfortunate family robbed of their sole breadwinner.'

'Her family lost their only hope.'

'And she lost her life, dignity and honour.'

The liberation movement had become a very deadly weapon. And we had a feeling that we were falling into an abyss of shame and disgrace.

Most of the print media would write what Shiasta's assassins want them to write. And most people would believe every word of it. The people would spit on Shiasta's mother, ridicule her sisters and would not let her mother bury her daughter in their ancestral graveyard.

Only a few days ago I read a report in the newspaper about a girl who was abducted by gunmen on the suspicion of spying for the security forces. The story related how the mother was not allowed to bury her daughter in the ancestral graveyard and was forced to leave her home, neighbourhood and life behind.

Surprisingly, I did not feel any pain at the time of reading the report.

MARTYR

To reach home safely was a miracle, and to find every family member safe at home was a bigger miracle. It was very rare if we didn't have to pass through crackdowns, cross-firing or search operations on our way to work and back.

At the first turning of the road, where the street stretched to the long row of old, unplanned wooden houses, people had gathered in groups, raising slogans for Azadi.

A lot of crying and wailing was coming from inside the five-storey brick house, but nobody seemed to care. Perhaps somebody had died a natural death. A natural death was a rare phenomenon at the moment though.

Walking past the red-brick house, I took a left turn at the crossroad. After only a few hundred yards, I could see there was a huge crowd in front of me. Men, old and young, were marching ahead in many rows towards the open field at the end of the road. The soldiers had surrounded them from all sides. Women were chasing after the soldiers, shouting freedom slogans, beating their chests and arguing with them to let their men and boys go. The soldiers were mocking them in return.

Suddenly, I saw that another group of soldiers had surrounded the bunch of boys. I went blank and froze on the spot.

The soldiers were using many tactics to apprehend the mujahideen. They were dragging the teenage boys by their hair; some had been bundled up into white vans, while some had their faces covered in black cloth.

Presumably, the mothers were begging the soldiers to release their sons, touching their faces and shoes and crying their hearts out to have mercy on them.

'My boy is not a militant! He is too young to be a militant. He just came from his tutor. Please leave him, I beg you.' One of the mothers was touching the heavy shoes of a soldier, who kicked her in her face. She fell down on to a mound of sand nearby. Aghast, she was folding her hands repeatedly, begging them not to arrest her son, who, she said, was an asthma patient.

Her cries fell on deaf ears though. There was no sign of mercy and no let-up in the terror. The soldiers threw the boy into a white Gypsy.

At a little distance, a group of soldiers took the clothes off a youth. He looked around for help, but nobody dared to come forward. The boy was paraded naked in front of the crowd. The flock of men were watching in shock and awe. Further down the road, women huddled together were beating their chests.

A tall woman wearing a black pheran and scarf jumped on to the Gypsy and tried to pull her son out of it. A plump soldier pushed her out of the vehicle, kicking her in the back. Blood was oozing from her nose, but she came rushing back towards her son, begging them to have pity. The boy could not bear the pain of humiliation his mother was being subjected to; like a flash of lightning he went to the soldier and slapped him so hard that his gun went flying and fell on the ground. The other soldiers close to the Gypsy immediately grabbed the boy and placed the nozzle of a gun in his mouth. They kicked him on every part of his body.

The mother lost her voice and could not even make gestures any more. She became numb, staring at the mob in utter helplessness.

The boy fell down on to the concrete slab and laid unconscious there. Not a single soul came close to him as the soldiers were watching every movement of the people. The mother's eyes remained open. She fell down beside her son. The crowd did not blink, nor did they let their tears flow. They did not want the soldiers to derive pleasure out of their misery and helplessness. They remained silent, like lava in the heart of the mountain.

It was not until the security forces had left that the people around finally came close to the mother and son. They were found motionless. The Imam Sahib of the nearby mosque declared them dead, and both were buried together in the mosque graveyard, which had been named 'Martyr's Graveyard'.

I could hardly walk. My legs were numb. I begged my neighbours to take me home. They did not hear me as they had gone away for the quick burial.

On my way back, I saw countless eagles perched on the rooftops of almost all the houses in the neighbourhood. During my childhood, my mother used to throw pebbles at them to scare them away. She thought they were evil and would cast a spell on us. There were so many vultures hovering over our rooftops now, but nobody dared to scare them away. They were scavenging for food because, for the last few days, hardly anyone in the neighbourhood had cooked. People had lost their appetites waiting in anguish for the painful crackdowns and search operations.

~

I lost count of the incidents of murder, rape, kidnapping and crackdowns that occurred all around us. Not a single day passed without a violent incident.

With the passage of time, such incidents became routine. If I saw anybody being killed or being arrested in front of me, I just hurried past.

The 'new being' inside me helped me swallow my conscience and pride. I was not the person I used to be. My personality had changed altogether.

I did read a lot about the violence in the newspapers. Earlier, when there was a natural death in the family or neighbourhood, I would cry for days. My sisters and relatives used to ridicule me for being so mentally weak. I wished I could tell them I had become strong now.

The violence on the roads would be reported in the newspapers the following day. We relived and remembered every incident in our hearts and minds. We would discuss it every day. There was a report in most newspapers that some survey had been done by a non-local NGO, which stated that over 50 per cent of the women in Kashmir were suffering from severe mental ailments, mainly depression.

Unfortunately, the agency did not mention those women who had become statues, those who had turned into a stone from the inside. These women never laughed or wept, sighed or whispered.

To become a stone had helped them in a way, for they hardly felt pain any more, despite the relentless killings.

I thought quite a lot about why our male population was not surveyed by the non-governmental agencies. Asad's sister-in-law said the survey meant to create a wedge between the male and the female population. She was talking as if she were a professional detective. 'Our men are killed, humiliated, arrested and maimed. That is the reason for depression amongst women.

How can men not be depressed when going through this hell?' I thought she had a point.

Fortunately or unfortunately, the violence developed some resilience in me. I kept waiting for another crackdown, another beating, more humiliation and another dead body. I hardly reacted over the situation. If soldiers ridiculed my demanding Azadi, I laughed at them and did not take it seriously. My family shouted slogans upon seeing soldiers—it was only to vent our emotions. The soldiers felt more and more comfortable with our resilience.

Everyone I knew, my family, neighbourhood and relatives, they were all waiting with a lot of patience for the day to come when we could achieve freedom. I was one among them.

STRANGER

Despite the growing size of our household, I felt lonely and isolated.

It was not just me, all the daughters and daughters-in-law faced the same dilemma. We had to suffer through our pain and anxiety silently. Our society had a strange belief about daughters-in-law, who were considered naive and timid before their marriage. Overnight, she would be deemed strong enough to bear the pain and agony silently, once she achieves the new identity of daughter-in-law. Women were normally expected to endure more than the men do, but daughters-in-law were expected to maintain calm and act unruffled.

I did behave like a motionless creature sometimes, but there came a few moments when it got very bad. It was hard to believe that unknown people had become the masters in my house. I was about to lose the last bit of control over my household. Somebody else was deciding my destiny according to his likes and dislikes. They decided, they chose and they talked freely. I was reduced to a non-entity, and my task was to make sure everyone was looked after properly and received every comfort in the house. I tried hard to perform a good job, even if nobody at home cared or bothered about me. Asad did not even look at me, let alone praise me.

When I was a young girl, I would ask Baba for only one favour, 'Baba, please let me stay in my room.' My passion for reading had made me crazy and I would read anything I could get my hands on. Baba only bought books for me. I would get absorbed in my reading in a way that I forgot to eat dinner at times. My sisters had to keep shouting at me to join them for dinner.

But time had changed me like my surroundings. My marriage snatched my book away from my hand. If I stayed alone in my room now, the volatile situation snatched my solitude away and scared me to death. I kept wandering around the house because I had nobody to talk to, not even those who lived in our house—that was not permitted in our family, especially for daughters-in-law. Asad did not like it. And he had no time to listen to my fears. I was left to suffer in silence.

I would come out into the open to inhale some fresh air, and the soldiers near the bunker would become alert and start staring at me. More recently, they asked me weird questions about Asad, who was forced to take refuge in Moulvi Sahib's house to evade possible arrest on many occasions. His connection with the mujahideen had come to the knowledge of the security agencies and he was thus under their surveillance all the time.

My heart felt heavy like lead. Everywhere I turned my head, there was terror and humiliation. I wanted to lean on Asad's shoulder and cry. But he was miles away from me. He did not want to share my grief and ensure my safety. Instead, sometimes, he seemed more terrifying than the soldiers themselves.

Asad avoided even talking to me, let alone spending time with me. If I forced him to talk, our arguments became fights, the differences turned into abuses—and the tension ended in violence. His pushing and punching was a new phenomenon in our relationship. Many romantic relationships may sour, and many couples may fight or separate, but, still, a marriage never usually reaches the point where it is as dreadful as mine had become. Asad was not in the right frame of mind. He had fallen into an abyss—and he was taking it all out on me.

When I saw him sad, I felt guilty and cursed myself.

After I got married to Asad, my friends would feel jealous of me and say, 'You are lucky to have Asad. He is a handsome, honest and caring person.'

A few months after our marriage, Baba had invited Asad and me home for lunch. Due to some indigestion, I started vomiting and felt very sick. Asad was so worried that he rushed away barefoot to bring a doctor quickly, as if I were on the brink of death. Baba felt bad at my condition, but he was very happy, at the same time, to see Asad caring so much for me. It was a bit embarrassing to find Asad not leaving my bed even for a second. That was a very unusual, odd gesture in our culture.

I believed that Asad's love and respect for me would last at least another seven lifetimes, but unfortunately it all ran out and did not last even seven months.

What changed Asad so much as person, I did not know. What I did know about was his association with those who used to hide guns inside their pherans, chase security forces and take shelter in our neighbourhood. They preferred our house, due to its backyard full of shrubs and huge trees, where one could hide without anybody noticing. Asad was under their spell and sacrificed everything for them.

I wondered sometimes, if Asad were given a gun, how dangerous would he be? He had already become so rude and arrogant on account of his closeness to the gunmen.

Perhaps it was an overall phenomenon. The day the gun entered our society, something strange happened all around us. The opinions of some people changed for the worse. I wanted to ask Baba: 'Who had cast this evil spell on my fate? Where is your dervish and his miracles? Why is he not saving my home and my future, and saving me from falling into this abyss?'

I had lapsed into silence and stayed indoors most of the time, staring at the ceiling. My room was cold, dank and dark. I hardly slept. And when I did, I had horrible dreams.

Outside, the crying was growing stronger. The constant barking of the dogs near the security bunker was most annoying. The sight of Shiasta's mutilated body was suffocating me. I had lost control over myself and everything I had.

'Please don't kill me, please let me live for goodness' sake. I do not want to die. Baba, please come to save me. I cannot live this life any more. Somebody is killing me silently.'

How long was I crying or talking? I saw Asad's sister-in-law sitting beside me, wiping the sweat off my forehead.

HERO

Shiasta's murder had become a headline in almost all the newspapers in the valley. The papers sold like hot bread in the market.

Like others, my in-laws were eagerly waiting for the paper, so they too could get a glimpse of Shiasta's tortured body and read the story behind the murder.

We were all huddled together in the living room talking about her. It was only the living room where we could afford to keep warm in the winter. Due to the first heavy snowfall in the mountains, the valley was under the grip of intense cold. Chillier, though, was Asad's stare, when he kept turning the pages of the newspaper that had published every possible angle linked to the murder.

The fallout of the gruesome murder was that the media had emerged the big winner. Most of the papers had published a photo of Shiasta's mutilated body on a full page, not considering it a crime.

In such a charged and sensitive atmosphere, if anybody was labelled 'anti-movement', it was taken for granted that even God would not be able to save that person.

'The war for liberation was sacred, so it had the sanction of God to kill anybody it declared guilty of anti-movement activities,' read a line in one of the leading newspapers, under Shiasta's photo. Madness and criminal intent was declared a sacred act. It was all done in the name of Azadi.

Asad was whispering to a villager and showing him Shiasta's photograph: 'Who knew such an innocent girl would turn out to be so dangerous?'

I pretended not to hear him.

I despised the photographer who had made money out of all this misery; I loathed the editor who published the letter found tied with the body and, more than anything else, I hated Asad, for sounding like such a callous person and laughing at the heinous crime that had given a bad name to our liberation movement.

The freedom movement was doomed on the day an innocent girl was tortured to death. It was buried on the day the gunmen blew up into pieces a clueless passer-by labelled a spy, after they had wrapped him in bombs. The cause perished on the day it got shrouded under a religious cloak. Tahira's shouting was reverberating in my mind.

I dreaded Azadi.

I was scared of the person whom we called 'mujahid'. Baba told us about his courage and strength, of how, after a daring attack on security forces, he had escaped unhurt by throwing himself from a five-storey building. He was our hero and superman, and we all dreamt of seeing him. We created his image, and in his praise we sang songs that we sang on special occasions. At every festival and special event, we remembered his deeds. They had made us proud of being so strong and courageous. After Shiasta's murder, he seemed to be the bad man. Instead of fighting for Azadi, he seemed to be depriving us of our honour, dignity and freedom.

Our hero had stunned us by his actions and turned us into mute spectators of death and destruction.

I started to despise him.

And I despised myself for believing in him.

I kept myself shut in my room. I felt rotten inside and wanted my external self to rot too.

There was not a single soul to listen to my silent cries. I cried and cried to my heart's content, without making a sound.

There was a knock on the door. I was terrified. It was very unusual those days for somebody to knock before barging into the room. The permission to enter into one's bedroom was not asked any more, no matter the state or position we were in.

There was one more knock.

Perhaps it is some civilized person, or maybe Asad has come to his senses and learnt his lesson, I wondered.

I believed the people who called us a lawless society. We had crossed every moral and social barrier there was.

Why was somebody knocking at the door, why can't they just come inside?

'Who is there?' I shouted in anger; my sobs became prominent.

'It is me! Baba!'

'Baba!'

I jumped down from my bed and ran towards the door, quickly opened it and saw my Baba standing at the doorstep, a forced smile spread over his bearded face.

I ran towards him and embraced him. His warmth was like the soothing monsoon rain after a period of scorching heat. I was crying like a child.

'My child, I have come to see you. I wanted to find out if you were behaving as a responsible woman.'

Baba took me into his arms. I wanted him to hold me forever. I stayed wrapped in his arms until my heart felt light and empty.

In the evening, I left with Baba to stay with him for a few days.

GLIMMER

What a pleasant surprise it was to see the golden calligraphic invitation card from Fareeda. Thank God, Moulvi Sahib had finally succeeded in finding a good match for his daughter. After a long spell of death and destruction, the message filled me with a new hope for life. It was an indication that we were not stuck in the wilderness but were somehow moving forward.

It was ironic that Moulvi Sahib, who resolved the most complicated problems in the neighbourhood, could not find a suitable match for his daughter until she had completed thirty laps of her youth.

It turned out that only a few weeks ago Fareeda had got engaged to a boy whom she had known since her childhood, though, both had never known that they would come together in their united destiny.

So what if Fareeda was not married yet, she was still full of youth, charm and integrity. She was the queen of her house and the beauty queen of our neighbourhood. However, her beauty had sometimes become a curse for her, and a source of embarrassment for Moulvi Sahib, who had to be on his guard at all times, since the security forces occupied an empty house in the vicinity.

The soldiers did not only look for gunmen in the area, they also kept an eye on everybody who entered Moulvi's house, so that they could get a glimpse of Fareeda when she saw the guests off at the gate. The soldier with the pockmarked face always coughed when he saw Fareeda at her doorstep, though she would keep her face covered with a scarf.

It was common gossip amongst the young girls in our neighbourhood that most of the young boys prayed just to create a good impression on Moulvi Sahib. That might give them a chance to get close to Fareeda. Some boys would go to the mosque just to get a glimpse of her in the window, which was parallel to one in the mosque. The recent deployment of forces in the vicinity had worried Moulvi Sahib because a few soldiers were always seen at his doorstep.

Fareeda was the youngest of her three brothers. Being the only sister among her siblings, she was the most loved in the family and the apple of Moulvi Sahib's eye.

Except Sajid, all her brothers were married and lived separately in different parts of the valley. Sajid disappeared three years ago without saying a word to anybody. The family bore the pain silently and came to terms with his absence to keep the issue under the carpet, without even mentioning his name or revelling in his memory. Moulvi looked serene and calm, as if he had never lost anything precious in his life. He kept himself busy with the complicated relationships, property disputes and neighbourhood issues of the people.

I often wondered how he had given up on finding his disappeared son—or perhaps he knew something that he did not want to share with anybody. His mysterious ways of dealing with the tragedy made me concerned about his state of mind. Due to our callousness, we would even cite his example to Sadia, when she cried her heart out, 'Look how Moulvi Sahib was bearing his pain with pride and silence.'

But I knew there was a volcano forming inside him.

Fareeda had spent thirty years of her life under strict family restrictions. She silently compromised on everything— education, relationship and, now, perhaps marriage too.

Her fiancé was, in fact, a distant relation living in the remote village of Kupwara, who often came to stay with them. He happened to be the sole heir to a huge family fortune. It was the only bargain Fareeda had preferred in this relationship, which would at least elevate her profile in society and certainly cement her status in her own family.

~

For the wedding, Moulvi's three-storey brick house was glowing with colourful lights, paper decorations and newly green painted walls. The street had been closed on both sides and the space had been used to accommodate the innumerable guests in a fashionable colourful tent. Whatever the circumstances, there had been no compromise on the decorations and feasts, which were certainly grand. Without the pomp and show, the ceremony would have looked colourless and lifeless and the neighbours would have looked down upon the family for the rest of their lives. And because she was the only daughter of Moulvi Sahib, he had made sure to make the event impressive, one that would be remembered by the neighbourhood for a long time to come.

Moulvi's long-time friend, the grand imam of Jamia Mosque, had been specially invited to perform the nikah ceremony and was busy giving a sermon on the significance of marriage and family values. All the male guests were sitting encircling the Imam Sahib and listening to him intently, as if they had no idea of the duties and responsibilities of husband and wife, or the significance of the procreation. The women were not allowed to sit in on the nikah, due to which, some elderly women sat on the stairs outside the hall to listen to the sermon, which might bring blessings to their unmarried daughters at home.

Outside on the lawn, the guests were laughing, singing and merrymaking. The Bollywood music on the stereo was blaring at a high volume, and young boys and girls were talking and joking with each other, having a good time. The women were holding one another in a chain, singing traditional wedding songs, mostly those that had been written in honour of the mujahideen. A group of traditional chefs, *wazas*, were making the final preparations for the grand feast which would be served in the dastarkhan, for which everyone was eagerly waiting.

The soldier with the pockmarked face looked sad, but had kept an eye on the people going in and out of Moulvi's house. Most of the soldiers seemed to be enjoying the wedding.

Moulvi was emotionally fragile today; his tearful eyes were fixed on his daughter, who was a resplendent bride in her white dress studded with pearls and fake diamonds. So great was her bridal beauty that I felt compelled to put a black dot on her face in order to protect her from the evil eye. Women were singing around her in circles, the girls were dancing and the boys were rejoicing behind them.

Half of Fareeda's face from the top was covered in a pashmina shawl, because the heavy dupatta did not sit properly on her hair.

The moment the women spotted Moulvi Sahib entering the tent, they covered their faces with their scarves and stopped singing out of respect.

Fareeda looked pure and elegant. The tears were rolling down her cheeks at the sight of her tired, emotional father, when she was peeping through the cutwork embroidery of a dupatta.

'Mubarak! Mubarak!' Celebratory voices were coming from the hall where the Imam had just completed the *nikah-khani*. Fareeda was now a married woman. After embracing and shaking hands with the groom's father, Imam Sahib was emphasizing the blessings of and secrets to a successful marriage.

'Your sorrow and happiness depends upon your trust in each other. The husband has to fulfil the responsibility of protecting his wife, who has a duty to comfort her husband at every moment.' It reminded me of my own wedding vows.

Imam Sahib had no idea what he was talking about. He was raising the hopes of some ideal world, which would never be possible in today's age.

Like Fareeda, I also had dreams. I also thought I was the most fortunate girl in my family to have been married to a smart and elegant person, who had pledged to protect and love me for the rest of our lives.

But who protected and who comforted whom in today's world? I was yet to find out.

But why was Imam Sahib lying again?

I felt a pang of anger and disgust inside me. He was lying through his teeth in the presence of hundreds of guests. I wanted to tell him off and tell Fareeda that the real world was opposite to what the imam was saying. It is only you who will have to protect everybody. And it is only you who will have to guard your own honour and respect. Nobody else will do it for you. 'Husband' was only a word, and a 'nikah-khani', at the end of the day, translated to only a piece of paper, which had no meaning in the real world.

Whether your husband was a rogue, an alcoholic or an offender, his actions in most situations would never be considered shameful. Society mandated that norms, customs and restrictions be followed only by the wife, not the husband.

We were living in a society that was against womankind. There was a false sense of justice as far as women were concerned.

I looked at Fareeda, who was being hugged by a few elderly women. Imam Sahib came into the makeshift tent, where he was offered kahwa, a traditional Kashmiri hot green-tea drink blended with spices.

After he greeted Fareeda and gave her his blessing, he began a speech on the current political turmoil. He cited many cases of the atrocities of security forces and advised the guests to fight back with commitment and demonstrate strong resolve.

I could not take any more of this.

I left the wedding ceremony before Fareeda was bid farewell.

MISERY

Shiasta had cast a spell on me. I could not wipe away her memories. Regardless of whether I was at home, a wedding or in the wild backyard of my house, I was always thinking about her and the tragic end she had met. Did her death serve any purpose at all for the Azadi movement? The question hung over my head like a cloud.

It was early morning when I saw Asad creeping inside slowly from the backdoor of the garden, quiet, as if hiding from somebody. He took quick steps towards the attic and closed the door behind him.

Asad is in real danger. I had a horrible thought that the security forces were waiting for the appropriate moment to apprehend him. And then he would disappear off the face of this earth and I would never see him again.

Without taking any notice of Asad's sister, who was staring at me, I left the house and closed the main gate behind me.

Just outside our gate, there were a few strangers talking to the soldiers in whispers. As they saw me, their whispering stopped and they looked at me suspiciously. I walked at a normal pace and showed no fear.

I rushed to the hospital to see Shiasta's mother, who had been admitted to the psychiatric ward a few days earlier.

Shiasta's mother was lying on a hospital bed. Her face was pale, grim and expressionless. She seemed to be staring around at everybody in the ward, as if lost somewhere. The doctor said she was still in a state of shock since seeing her daughter's lynched, mutilated body that had been found in the gutter.

She had neither spoken nor eaten after the incident.

The doctor was making every effort to try and revive her and make her say something, or even cry or eat. But she seemed to have lost her words, her appetite and herself.

Dr Muzaffer said to me, 'If she doesn't talk, she will go into a coma without anybody even noticing. She will turn into a vegetable.'

Shiasta's youngest sister was sitting beside her on the edge of the bed. She was holding her mother's hand and looking at her grim face. She listened to what Dr Muzaffer said to me. She urged the doctor to give her some medicine that would help release her tension.

'Please, doctor, do something to save our mother! We have nobody left except her. We are destroyed and ruined,' she said hysterically. She started shouting Shiasta's name, described the state she was found in and abused those who had killed her. She made every effort to evoke her mother's emotions, but Shiasta's mother did not respond and showed no emotions. She did not even blink.

Not a single relative or neighbour had dared to offer their condolences, share the bereaved family's misery or cry with them. Nobody could afford to face the wrath of the cold-blooded killers.

Shiasta's family was suffering the pain, disgrace and humiliation all alone.

It was not only Shiasta though; she was just one name in a long list, silently bearing the punishment for a crime she had not committed.

Dr Muzaffer and his team came into the ward again, discussing perhaps the worst case of depression in Kashmir. The doctor whispered in my ear, 'Somebody needs to talk to her constantly; make her cry, scream, do something to break her silence. I do not have any medicines to give her, she needs to wake up if she wants to live.'

I looked at Shiasta's mother's expressionless face. She just stared back at me. I spoke to her. She did not.

I cried, shouted, slapped and shook her. My screaming scared the other patients. The hospital ward came to a standstill.

She was motionless. I pushed her from the bed in frustration, she fell to the floor like a corpse. I tried to open and close her eyes. She did not even move her eyelids. I slapped her repeatedly. She was static. She was constantly staring at the cobwebs in the windows in the corner. The spider hanging in the middle of cobweb was about to fall on her.

All the patients in the ward were looking at me in horror. The attendants did not dare to come close to me and stop me from becoming hysterical. I was shouting at everybody. I ran wildly out of the ward and sat on the main road, crying and wailing. People moved away from me, thinking of me as a crazy person who might harm them. The security forces patrolling the entrance gate of the hospital came close to me and one of the soldiers offered his hand to lift me up from the ground. I just stared at him.

~

This was the police's version of Shiasta's murder, published in one of the reputed national papers the following day.

Shiasta had been very close to her cousin Ahsan, who had faced a lot of difficulty in finding a government job after completing his post-graduation in physics. It was after a lot of hassle that he was successful in finding a job, but it did not suit him as he had to shuttle between Delhi and Srinagar once a month. He had nobody to look after his old mother, who refused to move to Delhi. He could not cope with the pressures and became disappointed with his job and life.

The local politician, who had become a staunch supporter of the armed struggle, capitalized on Ahsan's vulnerability and got him in touch with one of the militant organizations. Ahsan did not pick up the gun to fight, but opted to do some upper-ground job, which was everything from information gathering about the security forces' movement to the carrying of ammunition—everything except actual murder. In doing all these chores, he involved Shiasta to help him sometimes. Being emotionally close to Ahsan, she did not refuse and, later on, became actively involved with the gunmen.

One day, Ahsan was waiting at the village of Tahab for Shiasta, who had been ordered to pass on a gun to him, so he could carry it further to the other gunmen as well. Carrying the gun underneath her burka, Shiasta realized that the area she was passing through was under the control of the army and that she would get caught by the security forces. She threw the gun away somewhere in the rice fields and fled to a nearby house for shelter. Luckily, she did not get arrested and left the area to continue her journey further, but without the gun. When the gunmen did not receive the gun on time, they ordered Ahsan to kidnap Shiasta and hand her over to them. He had no choice but to obey them.

'The police were looking for Ahsan and his accomplices and had put a huge bounty on their heads,' the report added.

The story made me think of Shiasta's mother who was still in hospital. I placed the paper on the table and went upstairs to get ready to go to the hospital.

Asad was not in his room. He had left the place in a mess: all the closets were open, papers scattered all over the floor and towels dangling from the shelves. While I tidied up the room, I found a photograph of a group of unknown boys with guns placed against their shoulders. In the left corner was Asad, standing with them. It made me uncomfortable, but I continued cleaning up. I looked at the photograph again to try and identify the boys in it. I could not recognize any of them.

What should I do with the photograph? If I destroy it, Asad will be angry. If I keep it, the security forces might find it during a search operation. I decided to hide it beneath the carpet. I left the house without informing anybody.

~

At the entrance to the outpatient department were many vehicles carrying the injured and the dead; they had been caught in the cross-firing between the security forces and the gunmen near the crowded market of Kukar Bazaar and had been brought to the hospital in shreds. Some bodies were wrapped in white bloodstained cloth, perhaps having been declared dead, while the wounded were waiting for the medical staff to attend to them.

There was mayhem everywhere. The soldiers and civilians, both, were bleeding and crying for help. The doctors seemed to be under tremendous pressure, unable to decide whom to treat first. They were overwhelmed by the situation, and were calling all the technicians, nurses and orderlies for additional help.

One of the soldiers was holding his almost-severed left leg, which had only a ligament connecting it to the upper part of his body. He was in excruciating pain. The bearded technician was finding it hard to hold his foot down underneath. Next to the soldier, a baby was suckling on the breasts of his mother, who lay unmoving, motionless.

I walked past the dead bodies and injured to take the right exit to enter the psychiatry ward. I did not shed even a single tear. I only felt the knot inside my stomach getting tighter.

Inside the psychiatry ward, most of the patients were just staring at each other: silent, dumb and lost.

There was no trace of Shiasta's mother or her sisters. Her bed was empty and so was the bed next to it. The attendants kept looking at me, expressionless. I asked them about Shiasta's mother; they knew nothing. I asked the doctors, who ignored me and rushed to the other wards. I knocked on the nurses' door, they did not open it. I even tried the other patients, but they remained tight-lipped.

Somebody had silenced them; it was written on their faces.

I waited in the corridor for some time, hoping that, out of pity, somebody might give me some information about Shiasta's family. In the end, I had to leave disappointed.

Since that day, nobody knew where Shiasta's mother and sisters went.

Where Shiasta was buried remained a secret.

Where Ahsan had disappeared to, we never knew.

When and where did Ahsan's old mother die, nobody ever spoke about it.

CROWD

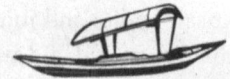

Our house had turned into a shelter. Most of the relatives from Asad's ancestral village were now permanently staying with us. Some had fled because of the intimidation of the security forces, some had left to avoid the frequent visits of the gunmen, while some had left their villages and homes for the safety of their womenfolk.

Every room in our house was crowded with people, every toilet had become filthy and every utensil lay dirty on the floor.

It was difficult to keep count of the people coming in and going out of our house. Most of them, I did not know. And it was not in my jurisdiction to inquire about them either. The security forces not only knew how many people there were, but they had all other information on the tips of their fingers too.

A village girl called Pasha was living with my brother-in-law's family and had come to see a doctor in the hospital for some stomach ailment. She was not willing to go back to her village, which, according to her, had become 'unsafe'.

'I will go only when Bhai and Bhabhi go back to the village. I would rather die than live alone in that house.'

Asad made her help in keeping the house clean and running the kitchen. She took control of the housework in such a systematic way, it seemed she had some inherent talent for housekeeping. She could understand and fulfil everybody's needs without anyone needing to voice them. Most of all, she managed to keep a smile on her face, regardless of how tense the situation was around us.

The situation got out of hand when Asad's uncle's family came to stay with us. There was no room left, no spare bedding, not even a corner to accommodate five more members.

Having failed to convince his relatives to return to their village, Asad quickly found a way out. He wanted me to give up my only personal space—my room.

'No, I will not leave my room or allow anyone to sleep in the same room as me,' I refused outright.

This was rather unexpected for Asad. He came up with another suggestion, that I go to Baba's house for a few days till he could encourage the relatives to return to their village. I would have loved to spend a few days with Baba, but leaving the house in such circumstances did not feel right.

I argued with Asad for being so naive and easy-going with his relatives. When he did not budge from his stand, I became suspicious that Asad maybe wanted to get rid of me. And I had no choice but to accept his plan. I put forward one condition: that he would accompany me to Baba's house and ensure that this arrangement was only for one week's time.

Asad agreed without even listening to what I was saying. He had promptly left the room in a tearing hurry to tell his uncle to make himself comfortable in my room—before I could even manage to grab my clothes to take with me to Baba's house.

Asad was one of those people who had not learnt to say no to his relatives, no matter how demanding or imposing they were. However, he never hesitated to turn on me, even if I suggested the most sensible thing to him. He had accommodated most of his relatives at my expense and had gone so far now that I was being forced to leave my home in order to make room for his uncle's family. How I felt did not really matter to Asad at all.

I prepared myself silently to leave for Baba's house. I knew he would be more than happy to see me. Yet, it didn't seem right to leave my home for people I hardly knew.

HUMILIATION

Since the day Sadia's son disappeared, she had not stayed indoors, nor did she rest. She went to every house in the village, spoke to every family and asked every shopkeeper if they had any information about her son Aziz.

Leaving the house at dawn had become her daily routine, and to find Aziz had become her sole purpose in life.

If we sometimes suggested she rest for even awhile, she would become agitated and hysterical. She looked exhausted and worn out, yet she was not willing to give up her fight.

Baba was uncertain whether her son would come back. He tried to prepare her for the worst, but she had stopped listening to anyone's advice.

When she was at home she turned into a ghost and stared into space. She would keep listening silently to everything people said, looking for clues that would help track down her son. Then she would start talking incoherently.

The shopkeeper at the street corner came to our house early one morning. He said that he had seen Sadia's son in Bandipora district along with some gunmen, after there had been a deadly attack on the military camp there. The reports were that the attack had left dozens of soldiers dead and maimed, but the militants had succeeded in their escape.

Sadia instantly decided to leave for Bandipora along with the shopkeeper. Baba tried to make her understand the difficulties she would face on her way: 'There will be so much security-checking, and the military convoy and barriers created at certain places on the road make the three-hour journey into one that takes seven or eight hours. It would be useless to leave today. Let us leave early tomorrow instead, so that we reach there while there is still daylight.'

Sadia did not heed what Baba said. Instead, she was ready to embark on yet another futile search. Meanwhile, we heard an announcement from the minaret, directing all the men and boys to gather at the cricket ground. Our mohalla had again been put under crackdown, with all the roads closed to our area.

Looking from the corner of the window, I could see all the neighbours—the old, young and the sick—walking on the street towards the cricket ground, like herds of cattle. Countless soldiers followed them. The women were huddled outside their houses, shouting, preparing themselves for another disaster.

Baba came rushing to look for his shoes that were behind the dining-room door, when a soldier kicked the door open with such force that Baba crumpled to the floor. The soldier pointed his gun at him, told him to put his hands behind his back and run.

'Officer, let me wear shoes; I will do what you want me to do.' Fear had spread all over Baba's face.

'Just run you old man. How many terrorists have you produced? Do you also want Azadi?' The soldier placed the muzzle of his gun against Baba's chest.

Baba's courage died. He wanted to run, but he could not. His eyes were fixed on the nozzle. His face had become pale, and beads of sweat appeared on the bridge of his nose.

Should I run or stay? Baba was juggling with the idea in his mind.

'Officer, do you want me to leave or . . .' Baba's words trailed off.

The soldier shouted, 'I will tell you what to do! First, tell me who gives shelter to terrorists here?'

'I honestly don't know! There is no mujahid here.'

'Mujahid, you old dog, say *terrorists*.'

'I don't know, I am sorry.'

'Tell me how many persons live in your house?' barked another soldier, with a writing pad in one hand and gun in the other.

'I am the only one here at the moment. My daughters often come to visit me. My son and his family live in Jammu because of his posting there,' Baba said in one breath.

'We have reports that your grandson is a terrorist—he is a Pakistan-trained bastard, why didn't you mention him?' the soldier pointing the gun at Baba asked ferociously.

Sadia turned white and tears came rushing out of her eyes.

Was Sadia crying at Baba's humiliation or at the mention of her son? I looked at her, aghast.

'No, no! I don't know. He is studying in Bangalore.' Baba's voice was breaking. Pearls came down his cheeks. He lifted his right arm, which was aching with pain, while I was aching with humiliation.

Sadia and I were both watching our Baba, who looked crippled.

Baba, a symbol of courage and strength, was begging the soldiers to spare us from further indignity.

Another group of soldiers searched our house, right from the bathrooms to all the bedrooms, the kitchen to the attic. They were looking underneath the beds, inside containers of rice, behind the cupboards and around the thick shrubs with the metal detectors. After about twenty minutes of an intense search, they left open containers, cupboards and rice and clothes scattered on the floor.

The search operation was over, but the ache inside me had become so severe that I did not raise my hand from my chest. The soldiers left in a row, talking to one another in a language alien to us.

Baba had covered his face in his arms and wept like our mother used to when she was ridiculed by her relatives on giving birth to a girl every time. Sadia took Baba in her arms and they both cried until the darkness turned them into shadows.

CHANGE

I read this one page of the newspaper over a dozen times.

The paper carried all the claims and counterclaims made regarding the fighting, information about the number of crackdowns, about the infighting among the different militant groups and the statements that Kashmir was about to achieve its most cherished objective.

During the turmoil, every aspect of life had almost fully collapsed except for the newspaper industry, which had thrived at the expense of the growing bloodshed. Schools were closed, commercial activity was defunct, offices were shut and life came to a standstill.

I bought a newspaper to find out how many violent incidents had happened and where, how many were killed, and who had crossed the Line of Control—who could not have had any country-issued sympathy statement for us. The general perception among people was that the national papers published reports that were filtered by the intelligence agencies. However, due to the constant calls of strike and the curfews in force, the national papers hardly reached the valley.

The local papers comprised only one or two pages, and were all flooded with the news of militant action and counter-insurgency operations. There was not a single news item about social and economic life.

I did not know much about the outside world that seemed to have forgotten Kashmir. The international community was perhaps wrapped up in its own issues and hardly knew what we were going through.

The government-controlled electronic media was tight-lipped on the issue of crackdowns, disappearances, water shortage, basically, the dead administration. Instead, every violent incident was classified as a 'law and order' issue. Even protests against water shortage were labelled a terrorist plot. Nobody dared to question or demand answers about it.

However, the turmoil was changing us in many ways. Our way of life, our habits, our neighbours and our traditions were all undergoing tremendous change. I was keenly observing every moment.

Like others, to buy a newspaper and read it word by word had become my sole obsession. I could remain hungry for days, but I could not live without reading the newspaper, despite knowing the fact that the news published was far from the truth. Most of the content was manufactured on the advice of the intelligence agencies or the militant outfits. Still, I would read it voraciously because it was my only connection to the valley. In the earlier days, only one person would buy the paper and then read it out to his entire neighbourhood. The paper would pass through dozens of hands. The tradition had changed, only in the sense that most people, despite the security risk, would now leave home early to buy a newspaper.

During the curfew hours, my family would sit together to discuss the changing political landscape, the UN's role in the Kashmir conflict, Pakistan's deliberate silence, India's rhetoric of 'integral part' and the militants gloating over their daring attacks. In case the discussion turned into a heated exchange coupled with blows, I would perform the role of an umpire.

But it was always Mehmooda, my youngest sister, who had been born with the gift of disciplining people if they got out of control. Most of the time, my family would disagree on the possible solution to the Kashmir conflict. Mehmooda would promptly ban them from further discussion and impose her own solution on Kashmir: 'Let both countries leave us. We do not need anybody's crutches to walk, and we do not need guns to fight for freedom.'

My family would laugh at her speech and sometimes ridicule her.

The continuation of the curfew imposed by the government for almost a week now was just too much to bear. We were all running out of patience. We were tired, and feeling crippled and jittery. Most of all, we had run out of topics to discuss.

In my neighbourhood, when all the patience had completely run out, the people came out of their houses in a procession. Some young boys took the lead in getting people out of their houses and directed the nearby shopkeepers to open their stalls.

The soldiers camped in the school were silently watching. But they did not dare stop the crowd. The shopkeepers raised the shop shutters in a frenzy, one glance at the soldiers and another at the crowd. People thronged the shops with demands for milk, roti and other eatables. The shops were cleaned out within the hour.

There were some old, shredded newspapers in one of the shops. Some people were so frustrated with the curfew that they took them home to read, considering them the trophies of the day.

After a while, there was an eerie silence on the streets; the people had shut their doors and windows.

IRRITATION

Moulvi Sahib, standing at the threshold of his gate, was lost in his thoughts. I could tell that he might have been missing Fareeda. He would be remembering the thirty years of her life from birth to marriage, tantrums to modesty. How quickly time had passed. I suppose he must have felt that it was only yesterday that she was a little baby, crying in his arms, looking for her mother, who had died soon after giving birth to her. Now she had become the daughter-in-law of another family, which would never consider her naive, simple and innocent, like he had.

My Baba was Moulvi Sahib's only friend, with whom he shared his treasure of memories. However, he never shared the secret behind his disappeared son. He remained tight-lipped throughout his life. It was not only Moulvi Sahib who concealed the disappearance of his son, but many more did the same. The slightest whiff of a disappearance was enough to invite the wrath of the security forces and result in the inquisition and potential arrests of the family members of the disappeared persons. The best these families could do was to find them through underground connections to gunmen who had either come back from Pakistan or were planning to cross the border soon.

Due to the curfew, Moulvi Sahib could not visit us, nor could Baba pay him a visit after the wedding ceremony of his daughter. The curfew was so strict that the soldiers shouted at me even when I was about to open only a window by the roadside.

It was on the day Moulvi Sahib married his daughter off that the curfew was imposed. Many relatives remained stranded in his house. Moulvi Sahib could afford to feed his relatives for months, considering he was the richest person in our neighbourhood, but he was more worried about the tradition he may not be able to maintain.

According to the custom, Fareeda was supposed to return home after an initial seven-day stay with her husband, but this did not happen. Fareeda had been gone for two weeks now and still nobody had any clue about when the curfew would be lifted.

The proud father did not want to give the impression to Fareeda's in-laws that he had not tried to manage her return on time, although they were also witness to the current turmoil. Still, they had every right to think anything was possible, being on the bridegroom's side. They would always enjoy the upper edge. These trivial things mattered a lot in our society.

In order to avoid the gaze of the soldiers, Moulvi Sahib walked slowly towards the fence and used the back door to enter my house.

Nobody knew who was master and who was subject in these uncertain circumstances. We were at the mercy of the soldiers, and it was they who decided who would live and who would die. They decided how many breaths we could take.

While sitting beside Baba, Moulvi Sahib asked me, 'Can you find out from your office if there is any possibility of the curfew being lifted?'

I tried to contact the duty officer at the office, but he was not picking up the phone. Perhaps the last stronghold of government control had slipped away, or maybe we had been left alone after all this bloodshed. I kept trying other phone numbers at the radio station, but there was no dial tone, let alone any reply.

Should I try Haleem's phone? I thought for a while.

'No, not at all!' I loathed myself over the idea. Moulvi looked at me from the corner of his eyes.

I reassured Moulvi Sahib that I would keep trying.

'Moulvi Sahib, the situation is not in our control. Do not be upset, the curfew will be lifted. Fareeda's in-laws live in the valley. They know the situation. You just prepare for her return, everything will be fine.'

My reassurances did not bring any relief to Moulvi, but at least Baba was proud that I had learnt to talk sensibly.

'Yes, my child, it is beyond our control. May God take care of us. Every moment is a nightmare.'

I dialled again, still no contact.

Moulvi Sahib became restless. He kept moving from one corner to the other and did not want to sit beside Baba to listen to his comforting suggestions. Whatever Baba advised him, he quickly rejected. He kept speaking to him in a loud tone. Baba just looked at him in astonishment.

I tried again, but still no luck.

Baba stared at me and sometimes at Moulvi Sahib. Perhaps he was wondering who was more disturbed, Moulvi Sahib or me?

'We are treated like dogs. They control our life, our land and our future. Why don't they bomb us all? Why torment us endlessly like this?'

Moulvi Sahib kept muttering to himself and, without saying goodbye to Baba, left hurriedly from the back door. Baba wanted to see him off, as he always did, but Moulvi Sahib did not give him a chance to get up. He was gone in a flash.

PROJECT

The crowd of people in my house had become intolerable.

There was no place to sit or sleep, every bit had been taken over by our relatives. I had to wait my turn to go to the toilet or use the bathroom for a shower. Our relatives had no intention of returning to their villages or towns, they were all just happy to stay together for as long as it took the situation to get back to normal, which seemed a distant dream.

They enjoyed each other's company while I became more and more isolated.

What did 'normal life' mean? I did not remember. I repented returning from Baba's house. At least, there was enough space to live there. How marriage changes the life and attitude of a girl, it dawned upon me for the first time. Baba's home was the safest and cosiest place on the earth for me. After my marriage, however, it changed its meaning and character altogether. I found it hard to stay there beyond a few hours. The mould for a girl is so unique that it keeps changing with every change in her life.

At present, we had three kinds of relatives in our house: those who were from the village but did not want to return to their houses because they dreaded the intimidation of the security forces; those from the city who wanted to go home, but had been stranded due to no relaxation in the curfew; and, finally, those who had no name: who came, stayed and left early in the morning for another hideout. We hardly had a chance to see or recognize the third category of people.

Sometimes, our house would turn into a battleground, as the many different relatives believing in different ideologies had to live under the same roof. They argued over the daring attacks on security forces and praised their ideological outfits.

A relative related this story: 'Let me tell you the story of the Hizb-ul-Mujahideen area commander's daring attack on the army convoy. Early in the morning, the army was taking its supplies to the camp headquartered in the school behind our house. Five mujahideen were watching from the small windows on the top floor of the empty building near the school. Once the army vehicles reached outside the camp, they were stormed by the mujahideen with rocket-propelled grenades, followed by intense firing. The vehicles along with the troops inside it were burnt to a crisp. The gunmen fled the area, breaking the security barriers. The soldiers, in retaliation, took their wrath and anger out on us by beating and torturing the young boys. We were stunned by the courage and the swiftness these young mujahideen had displayed during the action because they came back the same evening to see what the security forces had done to us.'

Even the subject of the rural–urban divide came into play during the heated discussions, which usually ended in a fight over the issue of the role played by rural–urban groups. Urban relatives would gloat over the fact that the armed struggle was solely their brainchild, whereas our rural relatives would boast over the number and strength of the gunmen, mostly belonging to rural Kashmir. The arguing would become as heated as the situation at the Line of Control, where Indian and Pakistani forces were set to begin an all-out war against each other.

All the impassioned arguing was entertaining at times, but it created new groups among the family members. One could say that the war of 1965 was fought in my living room.

Asad rather enjoyed all this a little too much. He would incite them and engage them in a heated debate and then leave when it reached its climax. I was sick of sitting quiet all day, listening to their tall claims of gunfights and gloating about Azadi. They were still dreaming of achieving freedom.

To avoid the heated discussions, I looked for different chores to do. All my efforts went in keeping myself occupied with anything I could find—else, I would go crazy.

Kitchen cleaning, bathroom washing, furniture dusting, I started doing it all, repeatedly. I was caught up in some sort of frenetic state of mind. Strangely enough, I was reluctant to read a book, which was once my passion in life. After my marriage, I hardly got any time to read, but I still kept buying books that kept getting piled up in my bedroom. I didn't dare to read them at home. It seemed rude to read in the presence of my in-laws. Apart from reading, I was free to do any damn thing, as long as it didn't hurt anybody's pride.

When I looked at the backyard of my house, I was surprised to find such a wasteland, overgrown with weeds, shrubs and thorny grass. If somebody would have told me to remove the mountain from its place, I would have never hesitated and would be more than willing to do the task out of sheer boredom.

I accepted a big challenge. I resolved to turn this wasteland into a blossoming garden. *Yes, I would make this into a kitchen garden. So what if I could not create stories, I can create something more real here.* And it was time-consuming job.

I began to cut the grass and shrubs and even involved my family and relatives in this gigantic task. It took me three weeks to turn this wasteland into something useful. Asad got so agitated at the cutting of the shrubs and bushes that he got a villager to replant them. It was thanks to his eldest brother who came to my rescue and supported me. Asad was forced to give in.

My hard work and labouring from dawn to dusk changed the landscape of our backyard and turned it into a beautiful kitchen garden. The fragrance of the flowers from the different plants and saplings spread in the air all around. It was only after a few weeks of toiling that we had fresh tomatoes, aubergines, chillies, gourds and spinach to eat. Our relatives—from the village as well as from around here—started involving themselves in the gardening rather than spending their time arguing on matters of politics. The neighbours visited us more often to collect fresh vegetables.

Suddenly, I could feel a tremendous change in Asad's behaviour too. The sight of and smells from the garden changed his attitude in a way that I could find him smiling at me. I did not know why my urge to come close to him and share my joy of gardening grew stronger every time I saw him looking at me from the corner of his eyes. He would get up early in the morning to join me in watering and tending the plants. He did seem to enjoy it more than anybody and decided to expand on it further.

Gardening had had a positive effect on everybody in the house. The surplus vegetables we grew were being wasted, so Asad taught me how to dry vegetables for the winter season. I made garlands of gourds, aubergines, tomatoes and chillies.

'Add garlic paste and salt on to the garlands. They will remain fresh and keep insects away from the vegetables,' instructed Asad, when we were making dozens of vegetable garlands and leaving them to hang in the attic.

I was feeling at home. Moreover, I had won over Asad once more, and he was around me when I needed him. Faiza would give me a devilish smile and say, 'See, I told you he would come around. He is a gentleman.'

I kept looking at the beautiful flowers. My faith became stronger with every second I spent looking at the colourful blossoms sprouting out of the soil. Somebody, somewhere in the sky, was making our universe beautiful and worth living in, even if we were hell-bent on destroying it. After all, it was man alone who was making life hell.

MIRACLE

I was unable to go to the office, even after the curfew was lifted, due to a severe pain in my abdomen. I had been feeling extremely weak and had been constantly vomiting and sweating profusely. The severe cramps in my lower abdomen were making it much worse. Strong painkillers did not bring any relief and left me cringing with pain during the many sleepless nights. I thought I was suffering from some dreadful disease.

During these turbulent times, many diseases, previously unknown in the valley, were being diagnosed. My family believed that the security forces were the hosts and carriers of these unknown diseases. They had polluted our water: our streams and rivers. The security forces had set up their base camps everywhere on the banks of the Jhelum, which was lifeline for the whole valley's population. Our water was so polluted that we feared the outbreak of an intestinal-disorder epidemic.

Due to an increase in the numbers of ailing people and the unabated violence, some parents had managed to send their sons to study outside the valley in order to prevent them from taking up the gun like other youths. Most of the boys got their medical degrees from countries in Central Asia and came back to practise it on every lane and street, where the sick and the depressed could be found in pain. And so it had happened that a new breed of doctors had emerged simultaneously, at the time when some professionals were leaving the valley for good.

Private health clinics mushroomed and were crowded with patients, who often blamed the doctors for unnecessarily advising them to get X-rays and MRI scans, just so they could earn their commissions. There were no checks and the health sector was the lowest priority for the government.

The next morning, when the pain in my stomach became acute and unbearable, I sent a message to Baba. Asad had not returned home since the previous day. Nobody knew where he was. There was not a single male member at home to take me to the doctor. Baba managed to send Mehmooda, my youngest sister, who accompanied me to the doctor's clinic, where there was a long queue of patients waiting for their turn.

I was in terrible pain, but had to wait for my turn to see the doctor. The clinic had been set up in a four-room flat. There were doctors in each room, examining patients and spending between five and ten minutes with each.

After an hour of waiting in pain, I was asked by the receptionist to go inside the doctor's room. Without even looking at me, the doctor examined my abdomen for about a minute. He pressed hard at certain places, where I felt the pain. Instantly, he advised me to get a urine test done along with some other checks. In order to relieve me from my dry vomits, he offered me a tablet with a glass of water.

I was so weak that Mehmooda had to practically pull me to the nearby laboratory for a urine examination. I saw sad and gloomy faces all around me. Many had come from far-flung areas, where proper healthcare was still a dream. Again, there was a long queue, but upon seeing me in a bad condition, the patients agreed to let me enter the laboratory first, out of turn. Meanwhile, the pain in the abdomen had subsided and I had to wait for the test results for almost another hour more.

Eventually, my test results came in, but I could not understand them. I rushed back to the doctor's clinic.

The doctor looked deep into my eyes and asked casually, 'How long have you been married?'

'Seven years. Why, what am I suffering from?'

'Is this your first child?'

'What??'

What Dr Lateef was saying was beyond my wildest imagination.

'You are pregnant.'

'What? Are you sure?' Mehmooda asked the doctor repeatedly.

'Quite sure, according to the test results.'

I was in a state of joyful bewilderment. A miracle had happened. I *was* capable of conceiving. I was carrying life in my womb. Oh my God, I had been worried that I was carrying some dreadful disease. My mind raced through my seven years of marriage spent waiting and hearing the sarcasm from relatives for not being able to bear a child. Moreover, Asad's changing and many unpredictable moods—his indifferent attitude in the beginning, his help in nurturing the garden and, now, back again to his losing interest in me—had left me without any hope.

At last, the moment had arrived in my life, when I could say with pride and dignity that I had the ability of nurturing another life within me. I was over the moon with joy; the world seemed to have become meaningful. It gave me a purpose to live. God had not let me down. He had bestowed the most precious gift upon me. I was overwhelmed with happiness.

Somebody, somewhere, in the universe was weaving the beautiful web of my life.

I looked at the doctor for reassurance that I would be able to carry on with this pregnancy without any complications.

'There is no reason to worry. What makes you so apprehensive? You are in good health. Is there anything else I should know about?'

'No, no, I am just overwhelmed by the news.'

Had I not become so physically weak and fragile, I would have run to Baba's house and announced to my sisters that I was carrying a baby in my womb and that I was not, in fact, barren.

Mehmooda took me back to my house, where everybody was waiting desperately to see if I was all right.

'She is pregnant!' Mehmooda announced before stepping into the room.

In a flash, my family was rejoicing and making the most of this moment.

Baba and my sisters came to visit me and made every arrangement for the preceding months.

Baba had a lamb slaughtered and sent turmeric rice cooked with meat to Dargah Sharief as a thanksgiving offering to God.

As a precaution, the doctor advised me to take complete rest for the first few months of the pregnancy. He emphatically said, 'The initial period of pregnancy is very crucial and critical for the baby. So take no risk, please.' So I was careful not to carry anything heavy or do any hard chores that might endanger my baby.

In the early months, my pregnancy virtually incapacitated me and I had to ask for help from almost all the members in the house, even for everyday things.

'Could you please scratch my back?'

'Could you hold my hand to lift me up?'

'Can you bring me some moisturizer to soften my itchy skin?'

My demands grew each day. But the people around me remained patient and put up with my mood swings and emotional outbursts.

However, I became just a liability for Asad, who initially took good care of me, but soon became withdrawn and stayed away. It had only been a few months of euphoria. He soon lost interest in our unborn child and me. And again something had happened to him.

Earlier, when he had stayed glued to me, watching my every movement, I had asked him, 'Are you taking care of me, or are you making sure your child is safe?'

He had burst into laughter, looked deep into my eyes and said, 'You cannot avoid my watching you—you are carrying my child!'

It was after a long time that he had laughed. He spoke the way he used to earlier, caring and loving, just like when we were first married. But unfortunately this was just a brief moment.

Soon, he wasn't bothering to come home for days together, and when he did come over, he preferred to remain confined to his room and stare at the walls. He never talked about the arrangements we needed to make for the birth of our child, or its upbringing.

I soon realized that, in the core of his heart, he despised me. He was only waiting for his child to be born. I felt a knot in my stomach and my body ached with pain.

'Try to stay relaxed and happy.' I remembered my doctor's advice and kept thinking of the good times spent with Asad.

Since the baby had started kicking inside me, the itching on my skin had got worse—it was now intolerable. My emotional outbursts were making me abusive and violent at times. Nobody reacted to my actions or said anything. They were watching my swelling belly with an air of mysteriousness. Asad's eldest sister would often warn me, 'I think you are carrying twins.'

Due to my fright and anxiety, I requested the doctor to conduct a scan on me. He advised my family to support me and be patient with me: 'She is under lot of stress and is anguished. It is very hard to cope with the present circumstances. The least you can do is not frighten her.'

It was mostly Faiza who was an angel with me. She did not leave me alone even for a moment and bore all my tantrums. Yet, my mind would get full of dreadful ideas about her silence and constant staring.

The thought of losing my baby got on my nerves. I kept tossing and turning on the bed.

What if my labour pains start during a crackdown or when we are under curfew and I lose my baby?

Who would take me to the hospital? Would I survive to see my baby alive?

My skin crawled at the horrible thoughts. I was sweating profusely. The closer we got to the delivery date, the more nervous I got. The hormones and overwhelming feelings of motherhood were making me emotionally fragile and vulnerable.

I prayed to the Almighty to give me strength and courage: 'Please let me live to see my baby in my arms!'

CARNAGE

I had moved to Baba's house for my delivery.

With the exception of Sadia, all my sisters were looking forward to helping me get through this critical period. Sadia had drowned in an ocean of despair. She did not care who lived or died. Her world had been destroyed the day her son disappeared.

The baby was due in about ten days and I still had a final check-up left.

My sisters had planned to stay with me, turn by turn, so that I would not be left alone at this critical time or only at Baba's mercy.

Baba had made all the possible arrangements, right from the booking of the taxi to the issuance of curfew passes in case the curfew was imposed again. An electricity generator was brought in to avoid any inconvenience due to the frequent power cuts, and the water tank at the top floor of the house had been kept full. Baba did not want to take any risks in such circumstances, when there was no help expected. Despite the worsening situation on the roads, my sisters would come and see me every day to make sure I was okay.

The last two days were painful. I was restless and I found it difficult to breathe as well. My body ached and I could hardly sit due to my swollen, overweight body.

The doctor had announced that the baby was due anytime. Neither Asad nor his family came to see me after I had moved to Baba's house for the delivery. A pregnant woman or a woman in bad health was always considered her parents' responsibility. But when healthy she had to do chores at her in-laws' house. So Asad was not technically at fault if he did not come to reassure me that everything would be all right.

The sounds of slogans being shouted, coming from the backyard of our house, grew more and more intense every moment. The noise made me tense and frightened. Something dreadful must have happened in the neighbourhood, as people were running in panic and all I could hear was crying and wailing.

Baba rushed into my room and sat down on the edge of the bed beside me. He held my hand and read some verses from the Quran to ease my tension. It soothed me a bit, but the shouting was coming closer to our backyard. The shouts and cries grew intense. Moulvi Sahib and Fareeda's crying became prominent and conspicuous among the voices.

I crawled close to the window and peeped outside. People were running in a frenzy towards the park for the identification parade. The soldiers surrounding them from all sides were shouting abuses on Azadi, militants and Pakistan.

Moulvi's newly-wed daughter, Fareeda, was crying and begging the soldiers not to take her husband, who was being dragged away by the soldiers towards an army vehicle.

'He is not a militant, he is my husband. And we married only a few months ago—ask my neighbours, ask the people, they will tell you. Please don't take him, leave him!' Fareeda was desperately trying to persuade the soldier, who was pushing and punching her husband into the vehicle. Her husband was looking around in desperation, but realized that he had to bear it all alone.

Moulvi started running barefoot after his son-in-law, pleading his innocence, but no one was listening to him or to Fareeda's wailing. He sat near the vehicle, begging for mercy, but the soldiers laughed at him. One of the soldiers came close, kicked Moulvi in the face and dragged him by his long, white beard; the other soldier punched his abdomen. Moulvi fell backwards on the grass. Fareeda came quickly to help him up from the ground. Instantly, the soldier carried her husband further down the road to throw him into the vehicle. Fareeda left her father and ran towards the bigger vehicle. The soldier, dragging her husband, went close to the vehicle and ordered him to jump into it.

Fareeda, feeling helpless, begged again for her husband's life. She even touched the soldiers' shoes. She kept running between her father and husband. The security personnel were making fun of her, as if watching a Bollywood movie at double speed. All the neighbours were watching the horror on their street, behind their curtain-drawn windows. Most of the women in the nearby houses were crying behind the doors, feeling useless, helpless—waiting for their turn to come.

Baba caught my hand to take me away from the window, but I was morbidly watching the scene, glued to it.

When Fareeda's cries were ignored, all of a sudden, she pounced on the soldier dragging her husband, grabbed his gun and pointed it towards him.

'Leave him or I will shoot you to a hundred pieces!' The mixed emotions of courage, anger and pride were written all over her terrified face. Her husband went pale.

The soldier took his hands off her husband and looked at his companion, who was behind Fareeda, making a mental note of how to overpower her.

Fareeda came close to her husband and told him to get up. He had no strength left to get up. Fareeda tried to lift him with her left hand. He stood up with a lot of effort. Fear and sweat were dripping from his face; perhaps he knew that this game was going to end very soon.

Within a fraction of a second, the soldier behind Fareeda caught hold of her, took the gun and kicked her hard in the head. She fell flat on the ground. Her husband was once again surrounded by soldiers; one of them came behind him to tie his hands.

Fareeda remained unconscious for a few minutes; blood was oozing from her mouth. She regained consciousness, stood up and again ran towards her husband, who was being dragged away.

She was pale, shivering and coughing. She knew she had lost the battle, yet she kept her gaze on the soldier, who was now beating her husband ruthlessly.

Like a tigress, she pounced again on the soldier and slapped him on the face so hard that his gun went flying in the air. The soldier guarding the vehicle fired a shot, first in the air and then at Fareeda's husband. The bullet pierced his chest. He fell to the ground like the leaf of an autumn tree, blood gushing out in a stream all over the green grass.

Fareeda ran to hold him, lifted his head and placed it in her lap. She tried to put pressure on his wound with her chador. The flow of blood did not relent.

Her husband was fading. His body was becoming motionless. His eyes were fixed on Fareeda, perhaps, struggling to tell her to run far away from the soldiers, who were taking pleasure in watching Moulvi's beautiful daughter covered in mud, blood and agony.

The beauty queen of our mohalla was begging the soldiers to do something to save her husband. Instead of looking at the people, she was looking up at the sky. She shouted, 'How can you destroy me and watch silently? What have I done to deserve this fate? Why this punishment?'

Soldiers had ordered the people in crackdown to disperse and return to their homes. They assembled near the vehicles, ready to leave after finishing their job.

Moulvi was glued to the ground, speechless. He dared not look at his newly-wed daughter, who had just become a widow after only a few months of marriage.

Fareeda was crying, talking to her dead husband as if he was listening to her. She was laughing, screaming and shouting, 'We want freedom! We want Azadi!'

Her voice was deafening, and ripped apart my heart and soul. My crippled body was not moving. I called the neighbours to help her up and console her.

I had no idea if I wept or wailed, but what I do remember is that I felt like vomiting out everything inside me. My mind went blank and I could hear nothing for a few moments.

When I woke up I saw that the soldiers had left the neighbourhood bruised and humiliated. Our street was crowded with people giving vent to their anger and helplessness.

Women were still screaming, beating their chests and accusing the government of savagery.

Fareeda had placed her dead husband's head in her lap. She was not letting people come near her. The body was wrapped in her chador. She was stroking his hair, kissing him on his forehead and whispering in his ears. 'How can you get freedom without me? You come back or take me with you. You cannot leave me here alone.'

'Baba,' I said.

'Baba, I can't breathe.' I felt suffocated. I could not move my heavy body an inch. I felt a dampness in the lower part of my body.

'Baba.'

'Sadia.'

'Fareeda.'

Nobody was around. Nobody could hear me.

~

When I regained consciousness, I was lying in the maternity ward of Lal Ded Hospital.

It had become such a filthy hospital in recent times that one experienced an acute feeling of nausea the moment you entered inside.

The ward I was admitted to was the dirtiest of all. All that I could see were dirty floors, paint peeling off the walls, filthy toilets and bloodstains, coupled with layers of dust on the big glass windows.

It was a five-bed ward. All the beds were occupied, some with two women lying next to each other on the same bed; I saw one woman's legs touching another's face.

Some women were crying because of the pain and the contractions. Some, holding newborn babies close to their bosoms, had a broad smile on their faces.

There was no sense of orderliness or discipline, and no medicines or senior doctors were available. It was more like a fish market than a hospital. Everybody was running around anxiously instead of walking.

I did see the head nurse for the first time since morning, when she came to examine my arm with the glucose drip. She wore a forced smile; I could see that the turmoil had taken a toll on her from her wrinkled face.

'How are you feeling now?' she asked while checking my drip needle.

'Dizzy and tired, I have no strength left.' I kept looking around my bed on both sides.

She pressed my arm fixed with the drip and whispered in my left ear, 'You have had a healthy baby, mubarak *ho*! You might soon be discharged.'

I had no idea when and where I gave birth to a child. I didn't even know the sex of my baby—something that everybody at Asad's home would be very curious to know. I was dying to see my baby.

The head nurse was examining my pulse. 'Is this your first child?' she asked me.

'Yes, after seven long years of marriage.'

'Lucky you. Five babies were born during the night, and they were all boys. Nature has its own way of keeping the balance in the universe's affairs. The security forces are killing dozens of our boys every day, but God gives them back to us. His compassion and mercy are all that is keeping us moving on.'

'You are quite right.' I was enjoying the philosophical talk and suddenly thought: *Has my boy replaced Fareeda's husband then?* I was looking around to see my baby.

The head nurse's words took away my tiredness. I felt a strange fulfilment inside me. There were no terrible memories. It was as if somebody had wiped them all out with the stroke of a brush.

Near the door of the ward, my youngest sister, Mehmooda, was carrying my baby in her arms, protecting him in the warmth of her bosom. She was smiling with delight and a flood of emotions was about to burst forth from her eyes.

'See what you have: the most beautiful boy, with your brown eyes and chubby cheeks. Look, he has long nails—it was because of his nails that you were itching all the time.'

My sister realized that I was yearning to take him into my arms. I felt a deep longing to touch him, smell him, hold him and, most of all, protect him.

Mehmooda was holding him as if she were carrying the most precious thing in the world. She placed my baby into my lap. My vision became blurry with tears.

His tender little pink face looked so wondrous and irresistible. It was for this single moment that I had waited seven years.

I felt at peace with myself. Never had I found such contentment and happiness. I prayed to God to allow this moment of pleasure to every woman in the world.

This little man in my lap was running his eyes up and down me, as if he was saving my picture in his mind's eye forever.

My eyes were fixed on the door of the ward. Perhaps Asad would come in and smile proudly at me. He would take our baby into his arms, cherish the moment with me and treasure it for the rest of his life. He would hold both of us in his arms and ensure our safety and protection. In the past, he had dreamt of having our own little family and future together. He had yearned for a life based on understanding, peace and harmony.

But when my dream was finally realized, he was nowhere to be found.

He had not come to see me even once. And he did not come to see our precious newborn child.

He broke his promise, and destroyed his home and future.

He robbed me of the moment I had been waiting for over seven years.

I was crying—my tears were welcoming my son to this new world and preparing him for the hard truth that we would have to be on our own, just him and me.

CROSSFIRE BABY

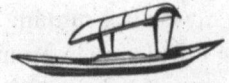

It had been almost a week since I had been lying on the same bed in the hospital. Its stench had entered my being through every pore in my body.

Everything was for sale in this government-run hospital. From bed sheets to X-rays, not even the most basic things were provided to the patients as a matter of routine.

The birth of a child cost a huge amount of money as one had to literally reward the staff for doing certain things—even though it was actually their duty and they were being paid to provide these very services for the patients. But the reality was that without bribes, they did not listen.

Most of the staff behaved rudely towards the patients and their attendants and vice versa. The corridor in the main maternity hall had turned into a pantry. Most of the attendants were cooking rice and boiling water, there being nobody to restrict them.

The 500-bed hospital now had around a thousand beds— ever since the eruption of the armed struggle, all its peripheral health centres had become dysfunctional or been made deliberately dysfunctional. Hundreds of patients and their attendants, including men, roamed in the wards in search of beds, cotton sheets, doctors, drips and nurses.

Women in labour cried not only with pain and contractions but also with the shame of being naked in the presence of strangers in the ward.

I was eagerly waiting for the doctor to come by, examine me and remove my stitches, so that I could go home and have a shower to get rid of the hospital stench. There was hardly any cleaning done. The bathrooms were wet and all the fixtures leaked, there was blood all over the floor and the foul smell was making my stomach churn.

Outside the maternity ward, people were running back and forth, as if heavy boots were after them.

After a while, the team of doctors entered our ward, followed by a group of soldiers gazing at every bed and attendant. Some doctors looked nervous and tense, though, trying hard to keep calm in the presence of the furious soldiers and worried patients. The soldiers could find nothing suspicious in our ward and entered the one adjacent to it.

The other ward was bigger, housing many patients and their countless attendants. The soldiers had been scrutinizing everything in the ward: cupboards, toilets, X-ray machines, corners, the patients and their attendants. After questioning the nurses, sweepers and technicians about the presence of some foreign militants in the hospital, they rushed to the other ward. Many women, covered only in dirty hospital sheets, started crying upon seeing soldiers in their ward. They felt ashamed, embarrassed and scared.

Presumably, the soldiers found nothing in the hospital. The women cooking in the pantry outside the ward would be cursing the soldiers, but would observe pin-drop silence once they walked past them.

Soon, the soldiers began leaving the main hospital building in a single file. Near the outpatient department, where they had left their vehicles, they suddenly came under heavy firing whilst boarding their vehicles. Some shots instantly came from the registrar's office, hitting their vehicles directly and leaving them crumpled on the ground. A lot of the soldiers were directly hit. A few of them fell to the floor.

The other soldiers watching over their vehicles were caught off guard. In an instant, however, they took stock of the situation and positioned themselves behind the vehicles to shield themselves from the incoming fire. The soldiers stationed in the bunker near the main gate of the hospital started firing indiscriminately in every direction.

Dozens of people waiting outside the outpatient department were caught in the crossfire, and fell to the floor, screaming and begging for help. The rounds and rounds of firing from both sides were hitting their heads, hearts, limbs and other body parts. Patients, attendants, children, women and soldiers were lying down, soaked in blood.

The carnage continued for some time. Bullet-ridden bodies were scattered all over the ground—eyes wide open, hands half raised, shoes scattered and blood flowing like stream.

It was an awful and indescribable sight.

Death was everywhere.

Time had stopped.

Some shots were still being fired. The soldiers at the bunker went berserk; they ran, frenzied, and ransacked the registrar's office, which was found empty, with no trace of gunmen.

The soldiers were prepared to blow up the building with heavy explosives, but the hospital staff begged them not to.

One more massacre had just been recorded in our history books.

So many violent incidents had happened in Kashmir that the last one was hardly remembered; and we thought the latest incident was worse than the last.

Everybody in my ward was lying flat on the floor—doctors, nurses and patients—in a position so as to save themselves from the bullets.

My sister and I were lying on our stomachs, on the bed, with my little boy under my bosom to protect him, so that if I ended up being hit, the bullet would not touch him. When I couldn't carry on in this position any more, my knees and toes in acute pain, my sister put my son under her belly without letting anybody noticing. It was like reliving our childhood, when we used to watch columns of ants carrying loads over their backs, swapping their burdens with the other ants.

Everywhere I looked there was chaos, smoke and tears.

We feared even getting up from the floor to see if it was safe to breathe outside.

In the midst of all the shouting, fired shots and wailing, the shrill cry of a newborn baby escaped from the maternity ward—a woman who had been in labour for over eight days had at last given birth to a baby boy.

All the frightened, horrified people lying on the floor stared at the door of the maternity ward. The jubilant attendant was telling his relatives that he had become the father of a healthy son and had named him 'Crossfire Baby'.

HOUSE

The peach tree touching my room near the big window had become naked and lost its original green colour. Only a few months ago it was in full bloom, laden with blushing peaches. I had never seen so many peaches on it. Had it lived its full life or had it started decaying earlier than it should?

Perhaps time had flown past and we had all aged together.

Days, weeks and months had passed without being noticed, or had life gone to waste?

Maybe I had lost sense of time. Or maybe this was the natural process of life that nobody had taught me and I was only learning it now on my own.

I could not remember my job or my life. I spent all my days and nights with Muna, my son. Though a lot was happening in our surroundings, I did not want to know. Outside Baba's house, every aspect of life was undergoing tremendous change. I could read Baba's face. I never went into the details of the sad events that transpired that day. Baba avoided mentioning anything related to turmoil. He did not even mention Fareeda, who had become seriously sick after her husband was killed by security forces.

Every moment I spent with Muna was a new experience, a new lesson and a new challenge. But every moment with him was enjoyable. I was making the most of motherhood, and it gave me a feeling of pride, dignity and contentment. I had shut my eyes to the outside world, which had lost meaning for me. Muna had become my cocoon and I wanted to hide with him.

Baba would keep himself busy by playing all day with Muna, who was growing up within the four walls of the house. It was Baba who taught me the secret skills of motherhood.

How ironic it was that my son was growing up in the same house I had grown up in. Baba had come into this house as a bridegroom forty years ago. All my sisters and I had been born and got married in this house. It was the same house where my mother was born, became a bride and then died. I had never thought that my son would grow up in the same house.

The whole world had changed—the people and our neighbourhood—but hardly anything had changed in this house. The small windows, wooden doors and the rooms with tall ceilings were all untouched. The house had a huge hall on the top floor, decorated with wood carving and panelling. It was my grandfather's house that had, later on, been given to my mother as a part of her dowry. The house had come to Baba after my mother died.

After my mother's death, Baba would not let us change even a brick in the house. He feared that by doing so, he would lose her memories. My mother's spirit was embedded in every brick of the house. We still felt her shadow everywhere. Her collection of copperware was intact in the glass cupboards. Everything was kept untouched and undusted.

'Baba, can we at least change the colour of the paint because this colour is no longer available in the market any more,' I would often tease Baba. He would turn his head towards the door to avoid the grin on my face.

Baba had become a silent worshipper of my mother. Though he hardly talked about her, even a mere mention of her brought tears to his eyes and he would stare at her photo for hours afterwards.

The house was not only a treasury of memories of my mother, it was also the secret holder of our life's moments. The foundation of the house was based on and strengthened by the love and contentment shared by two people.

Baba's admiration and respect for our mother had never diminished—not even after her death. He still spoke to her in his head. I would always wonder about their strong bond of love.

Baba's concept of a relationship was totally different from what Asad believed. Baba would say, 'It is all based on understanding and mental alignment, and that is what makes a relationship work. Oppression makes it worse.'

It was beyond my imagination as to why the current turmoil had changed the basic fabric of our relationship—or had it changed our marriage alone? Some people were so overwhelmed by the Azadi movement that they ignored their families. But when it came to subjugation, even mothers would not forgive their sons; they fought against it.

Kashmir has a unique character, so do its people. Baba always said that we have recorded a long history of not aligning with our oppressors, no matter who it is. Mughal kings or maharajas, Sikhs or Afghans, fathers or husbands, there was never any compromise with any of them on the matter of subjugation, no matter how powerful the opposing force.

Kashmiris consider the great Mughal king Akbar the first 'oppressor' in Kashmir's history, referring to him as 'Akbar the Oppressor' or 'Akbar the Deceitful', though he was 'Akbar the Great' to the rest of the country. He was the one who robbed us of our independence and led the way for others to subjugate us. Kashmir would never forgive him. Every time any political turmoil or debauchery is witnessed, most think of and despise Akbar.

The house I lived in had been witness to much suppression and subjugation, even after the maharajas had left.

We had been forced to forget about the trade agreement between the colonial power and Maharaja Gulab Singh in 1846, when we had been sold for seventy-five lakh rupees. It was not only the land that was the merchandise of the trade but also the forefathers of my grandfather—his ancestors, descendants, livestock, forests, streams, my past and future. This legacy of the trade of humans for land did not stop there. It continues till today in the form of crackdowns, forced labour and persecution. Every minute detail is carved on every brick of my house, no matter how much we tried to cover it.

Beyond the mountains of Pir Panchal, people enjoyed free will and a free atmosphere. Once the range of mountains emerges on the surface, the subjugation overwhelms, its fangs buried deep in the valley.

I made sure Muna learned every bit about our history, just as Baba had taught me. Our secrets, sale deeds, conspiracies and politics were written on every brick of the wall. He deserved to know the truth so that he could record the authentic history of my own time.

Most of my chronicles were false and had been written at the behest of my oppressors. I had left all my textbooks to decay in the storeroom, including my copy of *Aatish-e-Chinar*, Sheikh Mohammad Abdullah's memoir. But every time I would reveal the historical facts of my motherland to my son, I would get muddled-up thoughts like I did when I was studying my history lessons in school.

~

The government-run high school for girls was the first educational institution I attended after leaving my mother's lap.

The school was half a mile away from my home, but had many small, winding streets, like a python's curves. Baba would send us off either in twos or threes because he believed the neighbours' watchful eyes peering from their half-opened windows would give us the evil eye. When Baba bought a bicycle for my eldest sister, Sadia, the whole neighbourhood came out on the street, jealous, whispering and making jokes about her. Our neighbourhood was very close-knit and supportive in general, but when it came to our daughters' education, everybody targeted Baba. His actions were considered detrimental to peace in the family as well as neighbourhood.

Baba would often have a smile on his face while watching our mother get us ready for school. She would comb our hair, help us into our chequered uniform and hang the bags on our backs. She would keep watching us till we reached the end of our lane.

What used to make me cross with Baba was his taking of lessons at home, the content of which would be totally different to what we had learnt at school. At times, I would have to tell Baba to stop his history lecture because I wouldn't be able to find the relevant details that Baba was teaching me in the textbooks prescribed by the school. There was a total contradiction between what Baba taught us and the information given in textbooks—which sometimes resulted in chaos during examinations.

Baba would say that the Partition formula was based on the premise that Muslim-populated areas would go to Pakistan—and Kashmir was one of them. My schoolbook, in contrast, mentioned that Jammu and Kashmir was a part of the Indian freedom struggle, which resulted in the division of the subcontinent into two separate countries in 1947.

I had also heard that Kashmir was a state different from the rest of the states in India; it had enjoyed its special status even during colonial rule, due to which the last viceroy of India, Lord Mountbatten, had told Maharaja Hari Singh to opt for the state's independence rather than be a part of either India or Pakistan. The then-popular leader of Kashmir, Sheikh Abdullah, who rose against the Hindu maharaja, was influenced by Indian leaders so much that he made Kashmir a part of the Indian dominion, against the wishes of the majority of the population. Prior to the implementation process of Partition, the first prime minister of independent India, Pandit Jawaharlal Nehru, had become a close friend of Sheikh Abdullah's, and felt uncomfortable in the presence of the elite Pakistani leadership, especially with respect to the founder of Pakistan, Mohammed Ali Jinnah. For Kashmir, Abdullah was the father of the state—like Gandhi was for the country—so nobody had the courage to challenge his decision.

'Abdullah observed the intrusive approach of the government and started to lose his grip on power, whereas the government became suspicious of his political activities inside and outside the valley, which resulted in his removal and arrest on 9 August 1953. This was the beginning of the long freedom struggle of Kashmir against the central government, which had earlier pledged to the United Nations that it would grant the right of self-determination to the people of Kashmir in order to decide their destiny.' This was what Baba had taught me.

Nothing of the sort was mentioned in my history book.

So I preferred to remain dumb. Throughout my school life, I never had clarity about my history or political legacy because we were never allowed to know the truth about our turbulent past.

SOCIETY

The black clouds clustered on the sky were flying over the massive Pir Panchal mountains, leaving the valley swirling with pure, fresh mist after the previous night's torrential rain.

The valley looked like a newly-wed bride decked up in a lush-green chador. We rarely enjoyed the majestic beauty of our motherland. Rather, we were forcibly deprived of it.

Nobody wanted to stay indoors, but nobody wanted to come out and face the huge presence of the security forces either. Only in the small streets of the interior downtown area did people dare to come out for fresh air, whisper about politics and inquire about the activities in the neighbourhood.

As my maternity leave neared an end, I decided I had to force myself to return to work, partly because I wanted to force some fresh air into my lungs. I had turned pale by staying confined to my house. Baba had mentioned this to me several times.

There was no help available to look after Muna, except for Baba, who would chip in whenever he could. I felt guilty putting so many of my burdens upon him. Now he would also have to look after Muna during the hours I would soon be spending at work.

To leave Muna alone with Baba was heartbreaking. I was hardly prepared for this most hard of tests. I had no choice but to let my son develop a habit of staying at home without me. Negative thoughts would fill my head: *What if he goes close to the gas cylinder? What if he suffocates during sleep or if he falls on the stairs?* I would become restless and sometimes reluctant to cross the threshold of my house.

During my childhood, I often blamed my mother for not giving me her complete attention. I would complain, 'Am I a liability to you?' She would laugh, but become sad at the same time. I had no realization then of the domestic and societal pressures she had to cope with. I wished I had got one chance to ask my mother for her forgiveness.

~

All my sisters were huddled together in the big room. They had been strictly told by Baba not to make any noise, come downstairs, or ask for our mother, who had been going through severe pain for the past two days.

Being the eldest, Sadia was responsible for maintaining discipline and keeping the house in order, which she never did. It was our common belief that she was Baba's spoilt brat.

We knew our mother was very sick again; we felt sad for her. We knew she would produce another baby girl and most of our relatives would come to say they were sorry for her. They would all come and tell our Baba how unfortunate he was for being a father to so many girls but not a single boy. We knew they would cry over my Baba's bad luck and then mum would cry for days for producing yet another girl. For many weeks, the mood in the house would remain sombre and sad.

Aunty Boba would be upset again and scold her younger brother for not producing a male heir to continue their blood lineage. We looked at Baba's sad face; he never said a word to his sisters.

Baba was, as usual, waiting on the stairs for another aunt to rush out of our mother's room to call him inside to recite a prayer in the ears of a newborn girl. The prayer was meant to declare her a Muslim.

Aunty Boba kept coming out of Mother's room every few minutes to breathe in some fresh air. She had been inside the room for the last two days. All the windows were shut and the ventilators closed. Baba was not allowed to see his wife in such an odd situation. It was against our social values to comfort one's wife, even when she was suffering from labour pains and distress. And my mother had been through this every year— alone.

We were trying to make sense of all the gesturing and sign-language talk our aunts and Baba were doing.

For what would be the dozenth time, I saw our eldest aunt carrying water, towels, or things mum had put inside the big box the day Baba bought them. Those things were forbidden for us. We were not allowed to go close to the trunk.

The subject of the trunk always raised great curiosity in us. Sadia was under the impression that my mother was storing her wedding trousseau in it. A friend once told me that her mother had bought a similar big box, just like ours, to keep things prepared for her marriage.

My mother would often say, 'When you grow up, you will come to know which things are shown to children and which are not.'

Baba often had some sort of a packet or bag in his hand when he came from office. I would rush outside to take it from him, but my mother would snatch it away. Only after I saw my newborn sister in a boy's dress did I realize what those packets contained.

Every year, there would be an addition of one more sister to my family. I felt sad seeing my mother's shrunken face. Relief would only come when a newborn sister, in flesh and blood, would be placed in front of us. Our neighbour Moulvi Sahib would rush into our living room and decide on a name for a girl by looking at the first word of the sura in the Quran. He would randomly open any page and place his finger on the sacred word, his eyes shut the entire time. Mother would make us practise her name and demonstrate, many times, the proper way of holding our newborn sister.

I was sick of listening to the screams of my mum, sick of her being confined to one room and sick of Aunty's scornful looks at Baba. I could not bear it any more. My patience had run out, but my sisters were watching every move made by Baba's sisters.

For a while, we resented Baba. We did not understand why we got angry at Baba and not our mother.

I waited and waited to hear the sounds of our mother in labour accompanied by a baby's cry, as this would have meant the end of her pain and the end of our solitary confinement.

Earlier, we would get to see our mother carrying a little baby in her lap after only two days or so. This time around, the third day had passed without us catching a glimpse of her or hearing a baby cry.

The fourth day also went by, and our mother was still screaming in agony behind the closed door.

On the fifth day too we heard none of the familiar sounds.

Now my sisters were also getting impatient about the uncertain, gloomy situation in our home. Baba looked really worried and tense.

Aunty Boba and our eldest aunt were whispering outside Mother's room for a long time. Tiredness had shrunken their faces a bit more. I think they were suggesting to Baba that he take Mother to the hospital. But he seemed reluctant at the idea;

he never allowed her to get her routine medical check-up there. He probably thought the idea of involving the hospital went against family traditions, or perhaps he didn't want to run into people telling him to stop producing more girls in the desire of begetting a boy.

Suddenly, there came a loud scream from my mother's room. We all became silent, sad and fearful. I thought my mother must have died because no sound came after her big scream, neither did the baby's cry.

Aunty Boba and our eldest aunt hurried back inside Mother's room. Again, her crying, along with the 'push-push' exhortations, became louder.

Thank God! Mother was alive.

Baba was pacing the floor, back and forth, looking at the ceiling as if somebody was up there watching all the pain my mother was going through. I saw him raise his hands, fold them and pray, like he was pleading for something.

Is he praying for Mother, or does he have some other wish? I couldn't muster up the courage to ask Sadia. But she read my mind.

I peeped further through a crack between the door and the wall. Sadia pushed my legs away from the door and also kept looking at Baba's gestures.

We were both simultaneously giving our other sisters a running commentary of what we saw happening outside Mother's room.

'Baba is looking at the ceiling again. Aunty Boba has taken another bucket of water inside the room. The door has been opened again and Baba is moving towards the door. He is reciting Quranic verses loudly.'

I felt a pang of hunger. Nobody knew or was worried if any of us had had anything to eat.

Sadia said in frustration, 'She should stop producing girls now! How can she bear this pain again and again?'

'How can you say that? Our mother is on the brink of death and here you are blaming her!' I was on the verge of tears.

'It is not her! Baba forces her to produce more girls,' said my younger sister Mehmooda, pinching Sadia.

I snubbed them both.

Mehmooda started crying loudly and called for Mother. Sadia placed her finger on her lips, took Mehmooda on to her lap and started telling us the story of the merchant and the monkey. Because of our fondness for monkeys' tricks, which Sadia had an inherent talent of relating by making funny gestures, we surrounded her and started to listen intently.

~

It was just about midnight when a loud scream, along with the sound of a baby crying, came from Mother's room. We woke up in fright, staring at each other, and called for Baba and Mother in desperation.

A few minutes later, Aunty Boba came out of the room overwhelmed and excited. 'Congratulations, brother, you have at last become the father of a son! Oh brother, you have made us all proud!'

Baba's face turned red and he started blushing like a bridegroom. At the same time, he looked peaceful and praised God for this beautiful gift—the first male heir to further his clan, at last.

Is Baba thanking God for saving my mum or for the beautiful gift he has been bestowed with? I kept wondering that morning.

'Mubarak! Mubarak!' Sounds of congratulations were coming from inside my mother's room. They crossed the threshold of my house, reached Moulvi's kitchen, travelled through the alleyways of my neighbourhood and entered the living rooms and bedrooms of my relatives, who sent their congratulations to Baba.

We had not seen Mother yet. She seemed to have gone off to sleep, exhausted. Or had she died? I waited in anguish as I could not see her until she was being transferred to another room that had quickly been cleaned up by Aunty Boba.

The new addition to the family changed my home, my neighbourhood and my relatives. Most important of all, it changed my mother—which she never noticed. Only my sisters and I did.

~

Mother was over the moon after finally becoming the mother of a son. She kept her head held high while walking on the street and would confidently look relatives in the eye. All of a sudden, she had become a sweetheart to Baba's relatives. At weddings or funerals she was given a pillow to lean her back on, which had never been done for her before. She was no longer the untouchable in the family. She had regained her status of being the queen of Baba's household.

My mum spent most of her time with Bhai—our baby brother—than with us. She would not let us hold him, worrying perhaps that we would hurt him and she would become an untouchable again.

Baba did not spend his leisure time with Bhai. Rather, he preferred to stay with us. He would divert our attention by teaching us the Quran and the history of our subjugation. I would keep glancing at my mother breastfeeding my only brother.

My inherent interest led me to talk more on Sheikh Abdullah's 'Quit Kashmir Movement'. Baba had related the stories of this movement against the maharaja to us hundreds of times. He told us stories about the forced labour that Kashmiris were subjected to during the rule of the Dogra dynasty or the discrimination practices prevalent in those days. Upon reaching the climax of the Partition period in his narration, Baba would become bitter and his tone would get harder with anger and disgust. He would mutter to himself, 'In the end, Abdullah betrayed his followers.'

I did not understand the mechanics or essence of the Quit Kashmir Movement and would ask Baba repeatedly, 'Was Sheikh Abdullah's movement against the maharaja, or was he fighting to permanently become a part of India?'

Baba would stare at me and say in a subdued voice, 'I am confused myself, how can I tell you?'

To ease Baba's tension, I would ask, 'You won't get cross with me if I start a 'Quit Home Movement' against Mother?'

In response, Baba would burst into loud laughter and hug me tightly.

Baba did not teach Bhai the history he taught us. He kept away from him, though it was his son who raised his profile and prestige in the clan. Bhai never left Mother's lap—or rather, *she* never left *him* alone for a moment.

I despised my mother for ignoring my sisters and me and would skip dinner on this pretext.

Mother would quickly leave Bhai on the floor and whisper in my ear, 'If you do not eat, you will become weak. If you become weak, you will not be able to carry your brother, who gets fat by drinking milk.'

Listening to her, I would start eating big mouthfuls of rice.

My complaints of her neglect towards me would hurt her sometimes, though she would laugh loudly, and cuddle and kiss me. I would cuddle her back when she laughed—it was like a shower of flowers over me. When Mother laughed, she seemed like the most beautiful woman on earth. I wanted to catch that moment in the palm of my hand and never let it go.

She did not mind my complaints so much. But when Sadia complained, she would become serious and not talk to her for the rest of the day. Baba would then take Sadia in his lap to make me jealous. He would take her to the market and buy new clothes for her. I sometimes felt abandoned by both my parents.

Seeing Bhai in Mother's lap always, I would tease her, saying, 'He is turning into a bull.'

Quickly, in response, my mother would whisper Quranic verses and rebuff me, saying, 'If he is strong and brave, he will be able to protect his sisters.'

Mother would never let him out of her sight and would keep him surrounded with toys, without noticing that we were constantly watching her every move.

Baba ignored me when I complained to him that we did not get toys, only Bhai did. He would say, 'It is not like we do not love you, my daughter. All children are equal. You will understand once you become a parent yourself that every child is dear to his or her parents—regardless of whether it is a boy or a girl. Your brother is younger than you and thus needs more attention.'

Still, a chasm grew between our brother and us. We always thought that he was Mother's favourite—the loved one.

The bond between our brother and us did not grow to be as strong as the one enjoyed among us sisters. There was a problem somewhere that could not be fixed. Perhaps our mother did what society expected her to do. She was caring and loving, but the societal pressures she was forced to face were beyond her control.

I only understood her dilemma once I obtained my new identity of being a mother to a son, after Muna's birth.

During my pregnancy, my in-laws were more concerned about the sex of the baby rather than my well-being. They would make it a point, each time, to tell me to pray to God for a son, so he could continue Asad's lineage.

But I dreamt of giving birth to a daughter and wanted to buy girlie things for her. But once I made my desire known to Asad, he lost his temper and scolded me: 'Are you insane? You are the only woman in the world who wants a daughter.'

'What is wrong in having a daughter?—our prophet liked to have a daughter. Why do you think it is a sin to wish for a daughter?' I asked Asad.

'Because you are not thinking straight, like a normal woman does. I wish to have a son who will carry on my name and make a fortune for this family.' His tone was condescending and proud.

'I will pray to God for a son and you pray for a daughter. Let us wait and see whom he listens to,' said Asad with a confident smile.

I did not bring up the topic of daughters and sons with him after that day. And soon, I had to leave for Baba's house for my delivery. Often, at Baba's house, I would think about my mother, her pregnancies, her wishes, her dilemma and the pressure she faced of bearing a son.

~

I heard that Asad's family had been rejoicing for weeks, ever since my son had been born in the family.

Faiza told me, 'He was over the moon and gloating all the time, as though he had freed us.'

The great irony was that Asad had not even seen our son yet—though he boasted constantly to his friends about being the father of a male child.

SILENCE

It was my first day back in office after a year of maternity leave. I left the house in peace, armed with the knowledge that Mehmooda was at home to look after Muna. In the past year, I had crossed the threshold of my house only once or twice.

The feel of fresh air outside the house and the stroll by the banks of the Jhelum river calmed me. Earlier, during ordinary circumstances, walking past the busy market of Kukar Bazaar had never been easy. It was crowded and busy, and the villagers would spend days buying spices and herbs in the market. The bazaar sold every kind of wedding goods: from dry fruits to garlands and decorations; most of it was imported from other Indian states.

But now the market was devoid of any hustle and bustle. Most of the shops had closed down; some people were sitting outside the shutters.

Further down the road was the scarier sight of the historical city of Lal Chowk, where most of the shops were also closed—some burnt down, some half-opened. Lal Chowk had become a ghost chowk.

Many black-and-white posters were hanging across the high-tension electric wires dangling over the burnt, dilapidated buildings and shops. The walls were pasted with posters and pictures of those killed during the recent security crackdowns. It was difficult to figure out how exactly people had managed to put up these posters, even under the watchful gaze of the security forces.

There was hardly any traffic on the roads.

Army vehicles and soldiers were all that remained of Lal Chowk now.

The hawk-eyed security personnel seemed to have been placed on high-alert and were looking around purposefully in every direction.

Lal Chowk had lost its colour and vibrancy. It was the first time in my life that I was seeing the place so quiet and empty, like a lost town. Without the rush of people and their cacophony, the chowk seemed incomplete, like a soprano without her voice.

Much had changed in the past year—the history as well as geography of our motherland. Some complained that even our demography had changed, perhaps by design.

I stepped on to the congested link road, right at the start of Abi Guzar market, so that I could avoid seeing any more security bunkers or soldiers.

The area seemed to have been given a total makeover. Many old houses of mud and brick had been replaced by new concrete, modernistic houses. One house close to a school was half burnt, and the school itself, at the far end of the road, was razed to the ground. Some walls looked like they needed just a small push to crumble down. On the other side of the lane, the children's park—used for enthusiastic games of cricket after school—was now full of cow dung; it had been virtually reduced to a dumping site for garbage, prowled by dirty stray dogs sniffing around.

On the right side of the road I could see newly built houses with tin roofs and enhanced walls that served as fences, crowned with barbed wire at the top. Earlier, only security forces used to barricade their bunkers with tangled barbed-wire to prevent grenade attacks.

The houses had become bigger and were in an elaborately constructed modern style, but it seemed like nobody was living in these posh dwellings. Maybe they had moved out of the valley.

Our thinking was muddled up on account of the many contradictions all around us. Perhaps we were trying to live a normal life, or we were trying to put a lid on our emotions by indulging in pleasurable activities.

On the one hand, violent incidents consumed dozens of lives every day. On the other hand, the instances of the construction of big houses, spending money lavishly on wedding ceremonies and travelling to other parts of the world had increased.

Money was being spent like water. Did we not care what was happening around us, or were we taking refuge in pleasurable tasks that kept our minds off the sufferings we were experiencing?

The frequent strike calls, curfews and relentless violence had shattered our economy. Despite the fact that tourism and trade was in a shambles, some people had managed to become wealthy—and nobody knew where the wealth came from.

I reached the small lane in the locality where vendors were selling rotten vegetables on their carts. A lot of people had gathered around them. The scene was different from that on the main road. Here, people were sitting outside their old, small houses, talking for hours about the prevailing situation. Thank goodness people still enjoyed huddling together, even in the presence of patrolling soldiers. It seemed that people had developed some sort of a bond with the soldiers. At least there was some life left in the small lanes and streets.

~

My office was just a few yards away. I sensed an eerie silence all around me, which became scarier with every step I took towards the metal gate covered with barbed wire.

The soldiers in the bunker were watching me and were perhaps suspicious of my evident nervousness. I mentally prepared myself to confidently answer any questions they may ask me. Being the mother of a son had boosted my confidence, and I walked with my head held high, just like my mother did after my brother was born.

I walked past the bunker, looking straight at the soldiers. They did not bother to question or look towards me. I resumed my normal pace after I reached the gate.

At the entrance, I took a deep breath. The only colleagues present were those who had permanently shifted into the office to live on the upper storey of the building. It had been recently turned into emergency residential accommodation for the staff.

I was expecting a warm welcome from my colleagues as, after all, I had now become the mother of a son. I thought they would ask me a lot of questions about Muna—whether he has started walking, talking or recognizing faces, how I cope with everything, and so on. But there seemed to be no time for exchanging pleasantries or catching up. My colleagues had not noticed my absence the whole year. They left me in my office after the customary greetings. This upset me.

My room had remained closed for almost a year. The dust and dead mosquitoes were testament to it. The windowsills were covered with dust, and there were spiderwebs everywhere. Dry and decayed chinar leaves had found their way through the broken glass and lay scattered on the dirty carpet.

Nobody had entered my office since I had left. The files, telephone, penholder and stand—all were exactly how I had left them a year ago. The room was cloaked in layers of dust.

There had been no work, no funds allotted and no broadcast to produce. Most of the programmes that were being transmitted now had either been previously aired or been developed in Delhi.

Members of the staff now hardly bothered to come in to work. One of my colleagues told me that the head of the station had strictly advised them to stay at home, and that they would be called in only if their services were required.

I had stayed indoors only for the birth of my child.

My colleagues used to call me a workaholic. I was always in search of exclusive, challenging stories, looking to make strides in new, experimental broadcast journalism. I dreamt I would achieve big things in my career.

I walked across the long corridor leading towards the studios. Outside every room was a nameplate, hanging like a scarecrow in a plundered rice field. Some had only one hinge remaining, others had lost most of their letters. A lot of the members whose nameplates were still hanging outside their office rooms had left the valley. And those who were still in office had their nameplates missing.

The huge building of the radio station appeared as lifeless as the few remaining musical instruments in the studio. The recording machines lay unused for a long time. A thick layer of dust covered everything.

The drama department used to be filled with people in this gigantic building. The rooms used to be filled with artists, rehearsals, scriptwriting and loud laughter. But now there was nothing left except a photo of Shiasta's mutilated body nailed to the wall. It was the same photo that had been published in almost every newspaper after her body was found in the gutter.

Last December, we recorded *Othello* in that corner of the studio. Shiasta was Desdemona. She had wept bitterly when recording the murder scene.

'This scene has become my nightmare. Every night, I see myself being killed by somebody. My mother threw the script away last night when I was screaming in my sleep.' Her sobbing increased.

'Oh! I never realized you were so weak of heart. You are only playing Desdemona, you are not like her,' I said, in an attempt to comfort her with a bit of sporting sarcasm.

'That is true. But I don't know why this scene scares me and makes my skin crawl. I feel like somebody is going to kill me.'

I snapped back to the present. I was sweating; my eyes were full of tears.

I felt suffocated and wanted to leave the drama section immediately. My feet felt as heavy as lead. *Shiasta was blaming me because I had written her death warrant the day I gave her the role of Desdemona*, I thought desperately. I could hear her say, 'Why didn't you realize I would be declared an outcast? Why did you make me act in plays that were considered un-Islamic and unethical?'

I ran out of the place like a lunatic, towards the gate and on to the road. My frantic running must have seemed suspicious to the security forces, because they kept looking at me until I walked past the main road.

That day, I vowed to myself that I would never ever enter the drama section again.

APART

Shiasta's killing had left a deep scar in my heart. I tried to forget her, but I could not. She was all around me.

I was frightened. The storm within me was robbing me of my sleep and peace of mind.

I had nobody to share my grief with.

Asad had forgotten me. He never came to see our son and me. Not a single member of his family had come to inquire about our welfare, except Asad's youngest sister, Faiza, who would discreetly visit us from time to time.

Anger and bitterness were eating me from within. I had become a mute spectator to my surroundings. Baba took me to a psychiatrist to try and find a cure for my muteness. The psychiatrist diagnosed me with severe depression, but prescribed no medicine. Depression was not considered a disease; it was seen as a spell cast by neighbours or relatives with the evil eye, for which witchcraft was needed. And the obvious reason for people envying me was because I had given birth to a son.

Nobody mentioned Asad; even my sisters remained silent.

Insomnia, exhaustion and Muna's constant crying on account of his teething had made me jumpy and nervous. I needed more help and support. Baba's shoulders were not strong enough now to carry me. My sisters were worn out because of their own harried lives and juggling problems and priorities.

Once, when Faiza paid me a clandestine visit, she said, 'Asad was over the moon at the news of becoming a father and celebrated by distributing sweets among relatives and neighbours. He had made preparations to send his family to go and greet you, but on the day they were scheduled to leave, two of his close friends were killed by the security forces during a search operation in the neighbourhood. Asad was devastated. He wailed and cried, "I would have preferred to father a girl instead of a boy because I know what his fate will be."'

Faiza said he would not come out of his room for days.

What Faiza had said did not make any difference to me. That was no excuse for ignoring my son or me.

CHINAR

The valley had experienced a long rainy season this year. Spring had been swept away by rain and floods. Summer came abruptly with a heatwave that was very unusual for Kashmir. Then there was an acute shortage of water and the electricity was almost cut off.

In Kashmir, the seasons went unnoticed—they started either too early or too abruptly. No longer did people count the days of *chilakalan* ('old man'), *chila khurd* ('youth') or *chila bachcha* ('child'). Earlier, we had knowledge about nature and the severity of the different seasons, the names of which were based on the typical general characteristics of particular age groups in people. For example, we knew the chilakalan would be very harsh and cold, whereas the chila bachcha was noted for giving us rain and sunshine at the same time, like a child crying and laughing simultaneously.

But the seasons too had changed their ways; it seemed as though every part of Kashmir was under some kind of metamorphosis, even the climate and nature.

It was torturous to stay inside the house in the hot summer; at times it got unbearable.

Outside, the soldiers kept constant vigil from the bunker, which proved to be too humiliating and degrading; we felt we were being watched like criminals.

To get a little bit of respite from the sweltering heat, Baba had cleared the backyard garden so we could sit comfortably under the chinar tree. Fortunately, the summer had proved to aid Baba's recovery. He had suffered a severe asthma attack that had left him a frail and diminished man. Still, too much heat hampered his breathing.

Baba spread the durrie under the shade of the chinar—the only remaining witness to his vicissitudes in life.

He would say with a broad grin on his face, 'The day I came to this house as a bridegroom, my father-in-law planted this chinar sapling. So both, the tree and me, became members of this house on the same day.'

'So you both were infiltrators in this house on the same day,' I teased Baba, who laughed in response.

This chinar was Baba's long-time confidante and keeper of secrets. When he took a nap under its shade, he felt tranquil, at peace. He would keep smiling to himself as if remembering the treasured moments of his life.

It was hot that day too. Since dawn, Baba and Muna had been sitting under the chinar's shade. Muna picked up the leaves and gave them to Baba to pile up. Baba placed the leaves on his palm to measure their shape and size. Sometimes, both grandfather and grandson would hug or kiss each other.

I was watching them through the kitchen window. Someone wise had correctly assessed that there isn't much difference between a child and an old person. Sometimes Baba looked like a child, while Muna looked old. I forgot to put the kettle on as I got lost going back to when Muna was born, wondering how the time was flying past.

Baba's voice jolted me out of my maze of wistful thoughts: 'Daughter, can we have some tea?'

I quickly made the tea and placed cups on a tray to take it outside, so that we could enjoy a little impromptu picnic.

Baba was looking better after many days of illness. There was a strange expression on his wrinkled face; perhaps he was enjoying Muna's company the most.

We were both absolutely thrilled when my son took his first step without any support from us. He stood up for a few seconds before he took another step. This little man had changed the course of my life. His every action and gesture was making me delirious with happiness. Joyful tears welled up in my eyes. Baba was encouraging him to come towards us without falling down. Enjoying his first wobbly steps, Muna kept laughing and kept making us laugh in turn.

Oh! You Devil! I felt a sudden unease.

Muna took one more step but soon crashed to the ground at the sound of a loud bang that came from our backyard gate. The soldiers had stormed our house from every direction and barged inside from the back door, which usually remained closed. They entered into every room, looked under the beds, closets, kitchen cabinets and bathrooms. The rage in their eyes terrified us. We were mute spectators of our own helplessness. We prayed to God to protect us.

Muna was frightened and hid inside my pheran.

I could not hide my shock at seeing the soldiers encircling us menacingly, as if we were criminals about to flee. One of the soldiers, his finger on the trigger, was asking Baba for information about some foreign militants.

'How many guests did you entertain recently?'

'Did you see any strangers in the vicinity?'

'Give us the names of those who have recently visited you!'

Baba was speechless initially and did not find the words to respond to their angry queries. After a lot of effort, he managed to convince them that he had no knowledge of anything happening outside his house—he only knew about his own home. Seeing Baba and the soldiers busy talking, my son emerged slowly from his hiding place, crawled close to a soldier and placed his finger on the gun. The soldier took a step back in surprise.

Muna was frightened again.

Baba was experiencing breathlessness, but was pretending to keep calm in an attempt to prevent Muna from getting scared.

Meanwhile, the sun had shifted its course and we were now directly under its scorching rays. The place became too hot. Baba mustered up his courage and requested the soldier to allow my son and me to go inside the house. The soldier guarding our doorstep nodded roughly; we felt interrogated by the sun as well.

I looked straight into Baba's eyes to reassure him that it would be over soon. He seemed to be in great distress and agony. Our neighbour came to the house to comfort Baba and tried to reply to the soldiers' further queries.

One of the soldiers came out of the house showing everybody Baba's woollen hat, which was fashioned in the Afghan style. He went closer to Baba and started interrogating him about the hat's owner, seller, and so on. Baba tried convincing him that he had bought it at the Sunday market where second-hand merchandise—thought to be charity goods from European countries—was sold. The soldier remained unsatisfied and went to his commander for advice on how to deal with the situation.

After an hour or so, the soldiers left in a single file, one by one, failing to find any militants, or their guns, hiding in our house. Muna followed the soldiers outside; one of them moved a gun close to him. Muna was trying to touch the gun and keenly looking at it from every angle. One of the soldiers, smiling at his curiosity, said, 'Your son seems interested in the gun. Make him a soldier, not a terrorist.'

I shifted Muna away from him. The soldier did not like the expression on my face.

In the evening, Moulvi Sahib came to inform us that every house in the mohalla had been searched and the regular army had been called in to look for some Afghan militants who were thought to have taken shelter in our neighbourhood.

1991: On 23 February, the army launched a search and interrogation operation in the village of Kunan Poshpora, located in the remote border district of Kupwara. The local population accused the army of gang-raping as many as 100 women during the operation.

BOMBSHELL

Muna had just started to speak a few words when his father came to see us at Baba's house. Baba had told me earlier that Asad would be coming to take me back to his house, because he had realized at last what he was missing in his life. I was looking forward to seeing him, but at the same time I was bitter about his extremely belated visit, which also happened to be suspicious.

I saw him from the bathroom window as he stepped inside the gate. He was not the man I had married nine years ago. He had totally changed. A thin, skinny body, sunken eyes and a face full of wrinkles—this was all that remained of Asad.

He used to be proud of being handsome and smart in the family. Such a pity that he had lost everything in the wilderness. He was everything but his own self today.

Apart from having lost weight, Asad looked very pale, and his hair had receded too. His condition reminded me of a Pakistani soldier from the Bangladesh War, who had returned after losing everything on the battlefield. At that time, Baba had wept bitterly when a column of soldiers—or what remained

of them, covered in shame and humiliation—were waiting
to be released after India and Pakistan entered into the Simla
Agreement. I wept because Baba was in tears, though it haunted
me later on, when I wondered whether Baba was crying due to
Pakistan's defeat or because Bangladesh had been liberated.

This time, as I looked at Asad, I had no tears left in my eyes.

He did not dare to look straight into my eyes, but fixed his
gaze on Muna, who was silently watching him. In a calculated
manner, Asad came close to him and retrieved a chocolate from
his pocket. Muna took a few steps towards him. Asad placed the
chocolate in his own hand. Muna wanted to reach out and take
the chocolate, but Asad put it back in his coat pocket.

Muna jumped back towards me and Asad started playing
chess with him again.

Muna succeeded in taking the chocolate from Asad's hand,
on his third attempt, and quickly unwrapped it. Asad offered to
remove the wrapping of the sweet and made him sit on his lap
while Muna enjoying eating it.

After only a while, both were talking and laughing, as if they
had known each other their entire lives.

Devil! I kept muttering to myself. Asad had won his first
war against me. At that moment, Baba came into the room.
He gave Asad a warm welcome, as if nothing had happened,
behaving as if Asad were an angel sent by God to save us from
all our troubles.

I wanted to ask Asad why he had left us at Baba's mercy,
and why he hadn't come to see our son for two years. But I
could not. Baba and Asad were talking non-stop, catching up
on everything they had missed over the past two years. I wanted
answers from Asad, but he, and even Baba, seemed indifferent
to my agony.

They were talking about crackdowns, arrests, undeclared
curfews and also exchanging jokes. They discussed Pakistan's

offer of talks with India as well as the tough stand the latter had taken to curb the armed movement.

'The government is not taking this movement seriously and has used all its resources to curb it,' Baba said, sounding distressed.

'But it is not going to win this time. More than fifty thousand boys are fighting with guns, and they have the strong support of the people across the valley,' responded Asad, still condescending.

'The people's suffering is hellish. The hospitals are stuffed with the dead and the injured all the time due to this never-ending violence. There is no medical help available. And the schools have been closed for almost a year now—we are going to breed a new generation of illiterates,' Baba bemoaned.

'Baba, when our honour and dignity is at stake, why should we care about the children's education? The security forces have been given carte blanche to kill us—should we care for life or education?'

'Both, I think, because without education we are not going to get anywhere and progress.'

'They have no mercy while killing our boys, raping our girls and destroying our property! When we have no safety and live in fear, why bother about other things in life?' said Asad, sounding sentimental.

For a long time they continued talking; sometimes they were serious and sometimes laughing.

But it was all very irritating to me. I was finding it hard to wait further.

Their conversation had not one mention of me, my son, my pain or my future. Perhaps I didn't mean anything to them. It was true that we all had lost touch with each other and there were no more family gatherings or get-togethers, but I felt they were deliberately ignoring me and my child.

They mentioned the killing of Fareeda's husband. They felt sorry for her and talked about how she had been coping. They did not realize that in their very midst was a married woman who had been living like a widow for the past two years. They did not care to mention how I was managing to bring up my son in the absence of his father.

My son and me did not figure in their conversation at all.

Hypocrite! I lost my patience. My heart bled and my humiliation ate at me from within.

In utter frustration I left the room, leaving them to discuss Kashmir politics, for which they were ready to spend another sixty years of their life.

It was only when they both ran out of saliva that eventually Asad came to my room. Muna was sitting lovingly on his shoulders and was holding on to his ears for support. Asad pretended to drop him and then put him in his cot. Both were laughing and had already formed a bond within just a few hours of having met.

Asad faced the window with his back towards me as usual.

'Did you not miss me? Did you not miss your home? How can you forget your home and your husband?' The words came out of his mouth like a stray bullet. I was taken aback. I felt like slapping him so hard. *How audacious of you to say that!* I wanted to scream at him. Instead, I felt nauseated and remained tight-lipped.

'Why are you looking at me like that? Why don't you talk?'

'What should I say? You never gave me a chance to talk; your every action suffocated me. And still, always, you play the victim.' My tongue felt more and more dry with every word I spoke.

'What do you want me to do now, fall on my knees and beg for your forgiveness?' Asad's sarcasm was obvious even in his gestures.

'You never gave me peace of mind, a home and respect. Instead, you humiliated, insulted and degraded me. And you claim I did not miss you or your home. How very audacious of you. You did not even come to see your own child, which was the very least you could have done. What should I expect from you?' I said bitterly.

'Yes, I made some mistakes, I accept that. I put you through a lot of stress. But have you ever realized what I have gone through, because you know nothing about it. You never asked or cared. Did you? And it was always "you" that mattered the most.'

'Excuse me, but you deprived me of that right. You never let me talk. Instead, you continually ridiculed me in front of your family,' I countered.

'Well, I never start the arguing, but you have a strange tendency of questioning everything. You play journalist at home too. I told you that we have no custom of arguing with women, but you never listen.'

'But you exploit my journalism when it suits you.'

'Now, I am not here to argue or go round in circles. I want you and Muna to come with me,' said Asad in a tone bereft of any emotion.

Whether his offer of taking me home with him was true or false, I could not tell, but it certainly was of some comfort to me. I did not show my emotions though.

'When I realized that I was losing everything I have in my life, I wanted to come to see you. I do not know what happened to me, what made me neglect you and my own child. Maybe I was overwhelmed by something unknown and lost control of everything. I need you and Muna, I cannot see my own son growing up without a father. Can't we forget everything that happened and start afresh? Make our home again?' Asad said gently, sounding unlike himself all of a sudden.

'How can you reassure me that you will not behave inhumanly again, like you did before? I cannot bear the shame of being humiliated by my own husband. Can you make me trust you that it is not just another act? I have no strength left. I cannot take it any more. My patience has run out,' I said, finally opening my inner self to him.

He stared at me, saying nothing for a long time. I did not know what went on in his mind, but he seemed wrapped up in his own turmoil.

We both remained silent, absorbed in our inner chaos.

'Have your brother and Bhabhi gone back to their village? Who else is staying with you now?' I said, breaking the long silence by asking about his brother, whom I had managed to get released earlier when the security forces arrested him for sheltering the militant leader Momin Khan.

'No, they are still with me. They say they cannot face their neighbours, who now suspect their loyalty, and feel threatened. They are planning to buy a house in the city and settle there for good.'

'Have the villagers left now or do they still feel threatened?'

'Yes, they have left. There is another serious problem that I have been unable to handle. That village girl Pasha has become a shame for the whole family—she is pregnant,' he said, going closer to the window.

The news came as a bombshell, creating a deep crater in my heart.

'Pregnant? How? Who is . . . ?'

'Don't ask questions; think of some solid solution if you want to help.'

'Get her married to the bastard who impregnated her.'

'What? Are you crazy? How do I know who he is?'

'Why, she lives in your house, under your protection, how can you say you know nothing?'

'It is not that simple, it is a lot more complicated than you think. Everybody I spoke to has pleaded innocent to the crime. I am helpless . . .'

'You are not the culprit, are you?' I did not know why I asked him that question, but something made me.

'Have you lost your mind?' he said, but did not look at me directly.

'You might know who is responsible. Why don't you disclose his identity?'

'I told you it is not that easy. I cannot repeatedly ask my family who slept with her; do you think I would take the liberty and dare to ask the others in my house about it?'

'Why not? Anyway, you follow them like a shadow wherever they go. You might know who did it. You ruined your own family for them. Can you not ask them if they are responsible? Or somebody in the family?'

'Do not act like Sherlock Holmes,' he said, and went further away from me.

Shameful.

I knew that Asad knew who the culprit was, but he was protecting him. Also, he was irritated by my pestering.

In a fraction of a second, he lost his temper. He started blaming *me* for leaving home and not taking any interest in his family's affairs, which, according to him, had led to this complicated situation involving Pasha: 'Had you not left home, the situation would have been different. But you were only worried about yourself. You never cared about me and my family.'

Asad was so infuriated that his voice was full of venom when he spoke about my father, sisters and son. He didn't realize that my father, in the adjacent room, was listening to every word.

～

Baba's eyes were still moist—he had wept without shedding a tear. His face was still swollen. His silence tore me apart. He did not even lift his head to look at Asad when he left in a frenzy after dropping the Pasha bombshell and verbally abusing my family.

Baba had heard everything about the village girl. He had warned Asad, even before the bombshell, to never come and see us again. 'Your marriage ended the day I took away my half-dead daughter from your house. I knew you were not a noble person. You and your family have no respect for anybody. Your family could not even protect a poor girl who took refuge in your home. I wonder how you protect your own sisters,' Baba spat out in anger.

I had never seen my father that furious before.

Baba had also heard that Asad was making arrangements for Pasha to marry her distant relative, so the secret could be buried forever. What Asad did not realize then was that this secret would not let me enjoy even a day of normalcy any more. Time would show that it would not only destroy my reputation in my own family, but it would also make me an outcast in the neighbourhood and at my workplace. If my colleagues caught even the slightest whiff of the scandalous news, I would be immediately declared a pariah and would not be able to carry on my job any more.

An innocent, helpless girl had sought refuge in the household where she had been robbed of her dignity and chastity by her very own protectors.

Shameless.

My heart was boiling with rage. I felt sick. Scenes of Pasha with Asad, Pasha with my brother-in-law and Pasha with the gunmen kept playing in my mind repeatedly. I imagined her being assaulted in my bedroom by every member of the family.

Everything looked filthy in my bedroom: the wood-carved bed, imported quilts and the books she might have touched.

I did not know why I visualized in my mind's eye how Pasha might have felt in Asad's arms. He must have dragged her towards him by her hair, passionately stroking her face and pinching her breasts. She must have made every effort to escape from his clutches and kicked him in the face, but his long, bony arms would not have let her go without satiating his lust. She must have seen a monster in his eyes, ready to swallow her whole in one gulp. His smirk must have pierced her heart. After a lot of fighting and struggling, she must have given up in the end.

Then I imagined her with Asad's brothers, then with a gunman. I was losing my mind trying to figure out who the culprit was.

I was numb with intense disgust. My tears mingled with beads of sweat, my heart was pounding fast. I felt excruciating pain in my chest and wanted to cry out loudly, but I could not, as my son was sound asleep on a mat beside me.

He had been happy to see his father and was perhaps dreaming of seeing him again.

I thought I would talk to Asad's elder brother and ask him to send Pasha to my house, so that I could find out who the culprit was and potentially save her from shame and humiliation. But I did not dare contact him.

I left Muna sleeping and ran out into the open. My breathing was becoming more and more laboured with every breath I took.

Outside my house, I saw the soldiers playing with stray dogs. And I feared neither the soldiers nor the dogs that day.

DISREPUTE

Baba left early to buy some groceries and vegetables that would last us another week. Earlier, he would buy bread and milk every morning, but the custom had changed due to the present circumstances.

Baba came back empty-handed and rushed straight into the kitchen to drink water directly from the tap at the sink, which was very unusual of him. He had become pale, his eyes had shrunk into their sockets too deep and beads of sweat were shimmering on his forehead. He was finding it hard to hold the glass of water. He was avoiding my gaze. I knew something serious had happened.

I could read his face. He had either met somebody in the market or had received some very unpleasant news from Sadia.

'What is wrong? You didn't buy any groceries,' I said, breaking his silence.

'No, I didn't. We won't die if we don't eat for a few days,' he said, unusually agitated and shaky.

'Why are you talking like this?' I asked him.

'How should I talk now? I am ashamed of myself. Asad has not only ruined you, he has also ruined me, my honour and my life.'

'What has he got to do with us? He does not belong with our family any more.'

'You could say that. But he is still your husband and the father of your child.'

'He is no longer my husband. He lost that right a long time ago.'

'He has destroyed everything I had earned in my life: the respect and trust of people.'

'Baba! Asad is history, we have nothing to do with him. He has destroyed everybody—even the young village girl was not spared in his house. He is a sinner. His whole family has sinned, why don't you accept that and leave him to burn in hell?'

'He is marrying that village girl. Moulvi Sahib has been called in to fix a date for the nikah. The matter has been decided by the gunmen who told him to marry her.'

'What he does is none of our business now. We should not worry ourselves,' I said, sounding calm and unperturbed, to my own disbelief.

'He has no respect, no shame and no honour. He has become a disgrace. How can I show my face to the neighbours?' said Baba, crying and cursing Asad.

Soon, within me, I started experiencing a strange feeling. What Baba was revealing was a lot to absorb. I had never imagined that Asad would stoop to such a level.

'Baba, he is done with his first marriage, let him have another one. We should try to forget him.'

'He proved to be a failure in taking care of you and your son. How can he take Pasha's responsibility? He cannot destroy another family. I will not let him.'

'Let him rot in hell!' I exclaimed.

All of a sudden there rose a chaos in my heart. But I had the feeling that maybe the gunmen had given him a hard time. It did not matter that they had not succeeded in freeing us, but they had played a role in freeing me from Asad at last. I felt some relief from imagining the scenes of interrogation Asad might have been subjected to by the gunmen; their interrogation procedure was much more severe than what the security forces indulged in, and I wish Asad had met the same fate as some of the politicians whose mutilated bodies were found in random nooks and crannies in the valley.

I wondered how the gunmen had become involved in Pasha's sexual abuse. Why would they take notice of this personal affair, and why were the police silent over this matter?

I was pained to see the distress and shame in Baba's eyes. He couldn't bear to look into my eyes. He always found himself helpless when dealing with my estranged husband.

I wished Asad would disappear from the earth like the other hundreds of boys who went missing every other day in the valley.

PROTEST

After crossing the half-burnt Habba Kadal Bridge, a huge procession of burka-clad women and young girls were marching towards Lal Chowk. It was the first big demonstration by women. They were shouting and raising slogans against the atrocities of the security forces, who were being accused of the gang rape of a girl in Kupwara a few days ago. The news about the protests in Kupwara that had left two persons dead and scores injured had reached Srinagar; Kupwara had been placed under strict curfew since Tuesday. But the local people had tried to defy the curfew by remaining outside their houses as a form of protest, and demanded the arrest of the rapists.

'We want freedom! Punish the rapists, stop the torture!'

The slogans got louder as I neared the procession. The vehicles of the security forces were all over the place.

I was stuck in the middle of the crowd. The paramilitary forces had encircled the demonstrators and were not allowing anybody to move further or return. The procession was almost under siege now. The women were infuriated and agitated—and perhaps ready to become martyrs.

The woman beside me was carrying a poster of the victim: a young girl who had been gang-raped by the security forces after being arrested during a crackdown in the town. Her poor father had committed suicide upon seeing her mutilated body at their doorstep.

She seemed to be the same age as Pasha, the village girl whom Asad had been asked to marry to pay the price for the lust of some unknown person who had raped her and whose seed she was carrying in her womb.

The woman with the blue scarf was relating the incident to the crowd, 'Five soldiers raped her in front of her neighbours. Has anybody seen this sort of brutality that the armed forces have been committing against Kashmiri women in any other part of the world? Why are people silent over this heinous crime? Why is the world so mute over our constant suffering? How long are we going to suffer this subjugation? Perhaps the leaders think they can weaken us, weaken our resolve. Let me tell them, we are fighting for our freedom and we will fight for another hundred years. We will never give up our right of self-determination.'

The other women encircling her clapped and shouted loudly: 'We want freedom! Rapists go back!'

The rays of the sun glittered and fell directly on my face. My vision was blurred. The woman with the posters in her hand walked closer towards me, making some gestures—perhaps she wanted me to take some posters along to distribute to the other protestors.

The people were raising slogans in strong voices: 'Punish the rapists! Punish the forces! We want justice!'

I took some posters from the woman and began distributing them and shouting slogans. My voice became louder and more frantic than the rest. Intentionally or unintentionally, I found myself shouting, 'Punish the rapists! Punish my family and punish Asad!'

Most of the posters were distributed quickly. The young victim's picture on the posters was making the atmosphere highly charged.

The women around me were listening keenly. Some were looking at me in surprise and embarrassment. A girl standing behind me came up and placed her hand on my mouth to stop me from shouting. But a middle-aged woman pushed her back and told her to raise the slogans louder and louder.

'Punish the rapists! Punish Asad! Punish my family!' The crowd surrounded me, shouting, 'Punish the rapists! Punish Asad! We want justice!' A few people were staring at me in astonishment. My voice, demanding punishment for Asad, was reverberating all around.

I suddenly came to my senses and became aware of what I was doing, what I was asking the crowd to shout. They were proceeding further without taking any further notice of me. I placed my hands over my ears. Slogans naming and shaming Asad and his family were being raised throughout the procession. The protestors had identified Asad as a rapist.

My acute mortification overwhelmed me. I wanted to run away. Instead, I cried loudly and stayed ensconced in the crowd until the security forces dispersed the procession by throwing tear gas and then firing into the air. Amid the shots and the slogans, I found myself lying in the middle of the road, drenched in shame.

WHISPER

Autumn had crept into my life and I had hardly realized it. The nights were falling earlier these days. The days were shorter, and the nights longer and darker.

The frequent power cuts had plunged the valley in utter blackness. The human traffic on the roads was minimal, whereas the dog population had increased manifold. Their constant barking was giving most of the neighbours' sleepless nights. It was only the soldiers who put their leftover food near the security bunker who fed the dogs properly.

Due to the untimely heavy snowfall in the upper regions, the main highway linking our valley to the rest of India was closed for many days. The shortage of essential food items, which would be able to reach us only through this highway, made our living very tough. We would unintentionally pray for the closure, but were unable to put our hearts into prayer.

Well-off Kashmiris left the valley along with the state administration once autumn arrived. This tradition was a reflection of how the maharajas of Kashmir moved their entourage to Jammu during the winter. We did not give up his

tradition even though we had fought against the last Dogra ruler
Maharaja Hari Singh. He had gone on, in retaliation, to make
Kashmir a part of India after the partition of the subcontinent
into two independent nations. Baba says, 'They achieved
freedom the day we lost it.'

When people faced the hardships of winter in Kashmir, the
state government and administration stayed put in Jammu. And
when Jammuites faced the scorching heat and acute shortage of
water during the summer, the government continued worked
in the pleasant weather of Kashmir. This custom had continued
without interruption, with the state footing the bill for every
annual 'move of the durbar'.

We were facing a famine situation this winter. The
shops were empty, the ration depots had disappeared and the
government was invisible.

All three gas cylinders were lying empty in my house, there was
hardly anything left to cook. Baba kept looking out of the window
repeatedly, pondering over whether he could borrow some eatables
from Moulvi Sahib, who seemed to be confined to his house as his
daughter had been seriously sick for the past few days.

Moulvi Sahib had tried hard to get her out of her pain and
trauma. She was also working hard to sort her life out, but she
just could not sleep. Fareeda complained, 'The sight of my
dying husband keeps appearing in my mind each time I close
my eyes.' She would sometimes start crying and shrieking in the
dead of the night.

Fareeda was not the only one suffering though. We had all
reached the starvation point, mentally and physically.

I was overwhelmed to see Moulvi Sahib coming towards
our house. He was carrying a gas cylinder in one hand and in
the other there was a bag filled with groceries and eatables. Tears
rolled down my cheeks and I quickly dabbed at them with my
dupatta so that Moulvi Sahib could not see.

I took the cylinder from him and quickly fixed it to the cooker. I wanted to make some tea for Baba, who had not had any since morning.

Baba took Moulvi Sahib into the living room, thanking him all the way for his generosity.

They went to sit in the far corner of the room and, within a few minutes, I could see them with their heads together, whispering. I had a strange feeling about their postures, how they were facing one another. It was a sort of amusement for a bit in the past—they used to sit like this when quietly recalling the secrets of their youth. They would laugh and blush at every joke and memory. Their hair was not as grey then as it had now become. But this time around, it did not seem like they were having a pleasant discussion, they looked serious and in despair.

They were trying to resolve a matter that seemed to be getting more complicated. Perhaps Fareeda was in a critical state. Either they were planning to take her to a dervish, or maybe something serious had happened in the neighbourhood.

While pretending to make tea, I observed them. They were constantly talking, their faces contorted with emotions: anger, guilt and shame.

Once they saw me approach them with a teapot, they quickly ceased their conversation.

'Moulvi Sahib, this is the tea you brought. Please feel free to drink it.'

'My daughter, the tea is neither mine nor yours—everything belongs to the Almighty.'

'Thank you so much, Moulvi Sahib! You are very generous and a true friend, because nobody helps others out in such circumstances,' I said, acknowledging his kind gesture. I was keen to find out more about Baba's and Moulvi Sahib's frantic whispering. While pouring the tea, I asked them why they looked so worried.

'It is nothing, my child. I was telling your Baba that all this is a test of our patience and endurance. Unless we help each other, we will turn into monsters. The government does not care whether we live or die—it wants to destroy our generation.'

Baba was listening with keen interest and nodding his head at every word Moulvi Sahib was speaking.

'Moulvi Sahib, we have to understand the situation, we can't carry on like this. Sometimes, we have to make compromises in life. Resistance and guns makes it worse. It has never been a solution to our problem.'

'Nobody in the whole world cares for us.'

'Moulvi Sahib, there are so many movements in the world— who considers them right or legitimate? People take to guns in utter desperation. Who would have imagined that Kashmiris would take to arms when once it was believed that they couldn't even slaughter a chicken? Still, I do not know if the gun is the appropriate way of demanding one's rights, because we have seen the worst of it.'

'This is really a bad time, my brother. The security forces are hell-bent on killing us all. Nobody raises their voice against it. If our gun suppliers had learnt to raise a sane voice in international forums rather than giving guns to our boys, things would have been better and different.' Moulvi's face went red with fury.

'We have reached starvation point. How can we fight a mighty power when we do not even have enough vegetables to sustain us? From matchsticks to lentils, we have to beg for everything.'

'The national highway has been closed for a week now. Nobody cares. The valley is in the grip of famine. But the administration is in slumber.' Baba sighed deeply.

I left them alone to carry on with their discussion. But the moment I exited the room, they started whispering again. The two old men sitting close together were definitely up to something, and they made sure I did not get a whiff of it.

SHORTAGE

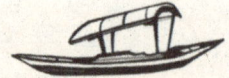

The state of Jammu and Kashmir was divided into three divisions on the basis of religion, language and weather. Each division had a limited capacity to grow crops or attain fresh food. Rice was the main crop in the valley, wheat in Jammu and apricots in Ladakh. Our staple food was rice, distributed only through government channels and rationing. The rice crop was either available to just a few families or otherwise exported to the other Indian states.

Except milk, all the other essentials were sourced from the rest of India. There was no reason to believe that milk would also become scarce in the market, because milk was the one commodity produced in the valley in large quantities. Pulwama, one of the districts in the valley, had the greatest number of cows and was the main producer of milk.

It was now the third day that we were drinking black tea because there was no milk.

Moulvi Sahib helped in every possible way to sustain us during the long curfew days. It never occurred to me the day would come when I would be compelled to beg Moulvi Sahib for a cup of milk as well. It was not only embarrassment for him to nod his head, but so horrible for me to beg to him for every little thing we needed. I wept for hours in the bathroom. The situation had become especially bleak because Moulvi Sahib had also run out of milk. This had never happened before.

For the last few days we had had tea, but without milk. We did not complain about it. It only became a serious issue in my house when, one day, Muna too did not get a single drop of it.

Muna's main diet was milk. He would eat rice and vegetables, but only when it was mixed with milk. He had been looking in every utensil for it, but there was not a drop to be found anywhere. He would sleep without eating anything.

All the milk shops had opened, but they were not selling milk, curd or cheese. Due to the curfew, milk vans had yet to reach Srinagar.

On account of inclement weather, the only access route to the national highway would let us down more often than not, and its closure for weeks created a famine-like effect throughout the valley.

From toothbrushes to rice to building material, the valley was totally vulnerable. Before Partition, there were other routes connecting the valley to Pakistan, but these pathways had been sealed off by both nations after Independence.

When the enthusiastic youth of Kashmir had conjured up the armed struggle, a certain crucial question—of how to sustain the people if the only connection with the outside world remained closed—had never arisen in their minds.

Baba was pained to see Muna helpless, craving milk; he left early to see his old friend, who used to own a lot of cows and supplied milk to his close neighbours, near the banks of the Jhelum.

Muna ran after him, hanging on to Baba's pheran, not letting him go. Baba lifted him up in the air and then put him on my lap, telling him that he would buy milk from the market.

What Baba said was beyond Muna's comprehension. He merely wanted to stay close to Baba and have milk to drink at the same time too.

I urged Baba to go quickly to bring some milk for my son.

~

Night fell earlier than usual or so it seemed.

Waiting for Baba for long hours had made me anxious. The day had passed, the shops were closed and the birds perched on the tall poplar trees around our house were chirping, or crying, loudly. Baba was nowhere to be seen.

The dogs outside the security bunker had resumed their barking, but still there was no sign of Baba.

I peeped through the window looking out repeatedly at the road. Muna called for Baba again and again. He did not come.

Baba seemed to have vanished into thin air. I prepared myself for the worst.

Muna went to Baba's room to see if he was hiding from him intentionally, which he used to do more often while playing with Muna. Seeing his room empty, he threw Baba's spectacles, books, socks, gloves and other things here and there in desperation. And when he ran out of things, he left most of his toys dismantled on the floor.

My guilt had taken the shape of a monster that was tormenting me for letting Baba go out of the house. I kept my eyes on the clock and peeped constantly through the window. My prayers for Baba's safety, prayers for my own safety, being alone in the house, and prayers for Muna's safety, who felt restless because the security forces were on patrol outside our house, had not made an impact.

Time seemed to have stopped. The moment had become dreadful and darker. Seconds seemed like hours and hours longer than days. My heart was sinking with fear and my mind became entangled in horrible thoughts.

'Baba is gone.'

I was so terrified I could not move to phone my sisters to tell them. I sat still in the corner waiting for Muna to fix the toys back into working shape again in order to pass the time.

Suddenly, there was a quick knock on the door followed by banging. My heart skipped a beat. I felt hot sweat all over my forehead and seeing innocent Muna made me vulnerable in my own eyes.

I was unsure about what to do. Should I open the door? The person kept knocking at the door continuously.

I took a deep breath and pulled myself together. First, I peeped through the keyhole of the door and then opened it. My youngest sister, Mehmooda, was standing there, a small bag in her hand. It was a relief to see her, but I thought perhaps she was the messenger of bad news.

'Where did you come from? Is everything all right?' I asked before she stepped in.

She seemed exhausted. Her hair was dishevelled and her eyes puffy, as though she had been weeping all day. Still, she was calm, trying to hide her distress and tiredness.

'I am coming from the hospital. Baba was admitted this morning. He is all right now, but the doctors want to keep him under observation,' she said in one breath.

'Why, what happened to him? He was all right when he left,' I said, trying to hide my guilt.

'He was caught in a cross-firing after a grenade attack at the patrol party near the State Bank building on Residency Road.

He was in the milkman's shop at that time. The milkman died
on the spot. Baba was lucky to escape the attack, but he's got
a few splinters in his leg and bruises on his face. The doctors
were surprised at how he had escaped unhurt. It was a miracle.
He will be discharged in a couple of days. Can you give me
something to eat? I have been starving all day. Look at me—I
am not hiding anything from you. He is all right, there is no
need to worry now,' she went on and on without giving me a
chance to ask her what was on my mind.

'How did you come to know about him?'

'Baba gave the doctors my phone number. When I got a
call from the hospital, I thought maybe Baba had died. When I
rushed to the hospital and saw him taking care of other injured
people, I was relieved.'

'I had told him not to leave the house in the morning. I
knew something bad was going to happen. Muna was behaving
strangely today, throwing his things out of the window.'

'Come, let me eat something.'

*How much had happened during the day? And why was
Mehmooda playing so cool and calm?* I thought she was hiding
something.

Maybe she did not want to frighten me as she knew I had
nobody except Baba. He was the one I had to keep close. Maybe
she was preparing me gradually for the bad news. Maybe Baba
was already dead.

~

Later on, even if Mehmooda had related the story of the blast
dozens of times, I was still finding it hard to believe that Baba
had had a miraculous escape. This was a blast that had killed
more than two dozen passers-by along with three security
officers—how could Baba be unhurt when his milkman friend,

whom he was sitting close to, had died on the spot? I could make neither head nor tail of the matter.

At a distance, Mehmooda was watching me through the half-open door. She came close and hugged me. While stroking my hair, she was, I thought, finally preparing me for some bad news.

'Do not worry too much. I have told you many times that Baba is fine. Neither is he dead nor is he in danger. You should concentrate on your own problems and find a way to move forward. Don't get lost somewhere you have no chance to return from.'

'What are you talking about?'

'You and your future. Better be strong and brave to take some final decision about your life. Little adjustments here and there could make life a bit easier.' She seemed to be suggesting something I was unable to understand.

'I told Baba to not go out, but he never listens to me,' I tried to explain, but she diverted my attention from Baba to my personal life.

'We have learnt to survive by eating grass in the past, we can live without milk too. It is not a big deal for us. What is the big deal when you will realize one day that you have lost yourself in the wilderness?' she said, sounding a bit sarcastic.

'Why didn't Baba listen to me?'

'Your life and your future are more important than milk. I am talking about your future, Muna's future, and so on.' She seemed to be bent upon discussing my troublesome marital life, whereas I was trying to avoid its mention.

'Put on a brave face for Baba when he returns from the hospital and never give him the impression that you cannot survive without his support—it breaks his heart. Look, my sister, try to restore your confidence and sort out your problems. It gets tough sometimes, but a little bit of compromise can make it simpler. Learn to stand on your own feet and demand what is your right.'

I still had no clue what she was leading me to.

'You have been an intelligent and confident person. You used to be an inspiration for others. Why have you become so timid and meek that you cannot stand up for your rights, desires and dreams?'

I was totally lost in Mehmooda's words. She seemed to be suggesting something.

'You might think that everything is rosy in my life. Well, it is not. I compromise on everything. Sometimes, even with my pride and self-esteem. Still, I walk with my head held high because I have not let myself become a topic for random gossip, even if I feel deeply hurt and bruised inside.'

I could hardly make sense of her pep talk. My looking deep into my sister's eyes made her a bit uncomfortable. She did not want to reveal the ocean of secrets hidden inside her heart. We had lunch gatherings at Baba's house and shared secrets, but we kept our personal marital matters to ourselves. It was not because we were dishonest, but because we were egoistic and full of pride. And our culture had taught us to be discreet about our personal matters.

Mehmooda left me there and went to Baba's room to clean it. She arranged his scattered clothes on the shelf and made his bed. As usual, she was working like a machine to keep everything neat and tidy for Baba's return from the hospital in the morning. In fact, she was trying hard to keep herself busy, so that she had not even a moment to think about her own problems.

PLAN

Later in the afternoon, the sky had turned dark grey and clusters of clouds hung over our heads. The long, thin poplar trees, bereft of all leaves except a few, were only waiting for a small gust of wind to blow them away in different directions.

Mehmooda wanted me to feign being brave in the presence of Baba, but I proved to be the weakest of all. Baba's fragility and vulnerability was too frightening. He was going to die. It was written all over his face.

He was covered in a white blanket and bandages. His face had bruises, with a blackish-red patch on the forehead. His left arm was in a plaster and the thumb of his right hand was covered in thick Band-Aid. The shirt he wore at the time of the blast seemed to have been soaked in blood. He was shaking. And I was shaking with guilt.

Mehmooda helped him lie down on his bed and kissed him on his bruised cheek. She said, 'Baba, you are a tiger. I can vouch for it,' trying to raise his spirits.

She went away quickly to bring him a hot drink. Baba was trying very hard to smile at me, but he could not. His face had stiffened due to all the bruises he had sustained.

Countless people came to meet Baba and were offered kahwa; they were also given shirmal, a sweet traditional saffron-flavoured flatbread, which had been specially ordered for the occasion from a bakery in the saffron town of Pampore. Pampore was the biggest producer of saffron and was home to special bakeries producing remarkable baked goods that were presented to guests on special occasions; it also housed the graveyard of sixteenth-century poetess Habba Khatoon.

Due to the influx of guests, I could hardly find a moment to rest. I felt exhausted and worn out.

Even weeks after the deadly blast, Baba was shaking at the mere mention of the death of his friend. He had become timid and weak. Most of the time, he remained silent and stared at the ceiling. Sometimes, he locked himself in and read the Quran for hours. I would take him tea from time to time, but he would not open the door; he did not bother even to take his medicine.

My heart sank every time I saw his face.

I was also going through some bodily changes. My body would become hot with perspiration and start itching. I felt dizzy and nauseous. My restlessness was very disturbing for Muna, who kept dabbing the sweat away from my forehead.

I did not get a chance to drink enough water, which might have been one of the causes why my body was malfunctioning, or maybe I had some internal ailment.

When I was a child, Baba used to make lassi for us by mixing curd with mint and salt. It was our mother's best prescription for dehydration and fatigue.

We used to call it a wonder drug. I tried some to combat my condition, but the wonder drug did not seem to work this time. I was in pain, mentally and physically. There was no name for my ailment.

Every time Baba left home, I would start pacing the floor. How hard I tried to dissuade him from leaving us alone in the house, but he did not listen. For the last few days, he had been leaving early in the morning with Moulvi Ṣahib to go to some unknown destination on an unknown mission. He did not discuss family matters with me any more. I did not want to worry him with my health problems.

I would talk to Muna. Whether he understood me or not, I hardly cared.

DILEMMA

Early one morning, Baba barged into my room. He looked seriously disturbed, something was wrong. His bloodshot eyes were an indication that he was struggling with something agonizing.

I felt so bad that he was in such a condition. He lacked confidence, which ate at me from within. I felt I was responsible for making him meek and submissive.

The near-death experience had not only changed Baba, but had left him shaken and frightened as well. Was he worried and scared that if he had also been killed that day, along with the milkman, what would have happened to my son and me? Or I had become an unbearable liability for him?

My so-called protector had left me in the lurch. He had not come to see his son.

Baba was pacing the floor in a frenzy. I could not bear to look at his serious face.

'You have to leave tonight and return to your home. I want you to settle down in your house before my eyes close forever,' said Baba, revealing what he had been struggling with. I could feel the pain Baba was going through and realized how much courage he must have mustered up to say those words.

'I can't look after you and your son on my own. I am an invalid and too crippled to carry on like this. You will have to make compromise on your situation,' he said gently.

I did not know how to react.

'We are all cards in the hands of fate. The sensible thing is to accept reality and find ways to adjust, not run away from it. Or people will ridicule you for the rest of your life,' said Baba, sounding simultaneously strange and outrageous. What he said was devoid of coherence. How could he talk about compromise? It was only me who had compromised on *everything* in my life: my relationship, my self-esteem and my future. Yet, he said I would have to compromise.

How cruel of him, I thought. I was taken aback by his attitude.

He was looking at me from the corner of his eyes. I saw tears rolling down over his beard. The more he tried to act tough and make me fear him, the harder it became for me to accept his verdict. What had forced Baba to concede so much to Asad? I tried to figure it out.

It did not make any sense to me how Baba had forgotten everything Asad did. Asad disrespected and humiliated me to such an extent that I felt rotten inside. He insulted my motherhood by leaving me after Muna's birth and never came once to see me. He hadn't bothered to find out whether we were alive or dead. Yet, in spite of knowing everything, Baba had still surrendered before him. What a shame!

I pulled myself together, gathered some courage and asked him, 'How could I live under the same roof with that village girl whom Asad is marrying soon? Why would you put me in such a humiliating situation?'

'The village girl has left your house for good. Neither Asad nor his family have any connection with her any more. Why would Asad marry her when he has nothing to do with her? He can be ruthless, but he can't be characterless. I accept that Asad made mistakes, but why are you punishing yourself and your son? That is your home and you have every right to live and enjoy it. If somebody deprives you of it, you have to get it back. It is not just your right but a moral responsibility too. How long will you suffer and make your son suffer? Why would I let others hurt you—why? Baba wanted to hide his face because the flood of tears had burst from his eyes.

'Baba, you have taught me to hold my head high. Asad wants me to walk with my head down. You tell me whom I should follow. He never treated me as a wife, a partner, who needs love, affection and support. He humiliated me. What right or home are you talking about that I should claim from him?'

'My daughter, make him love you. Demand your right and confront him with your issues. He is a human being, he will learn. Give him a chance to learn from his mistakes and make an effort to make things right with him.'

My blood boiled, but I had no courage left to keep talking to Baba because I knew he was not going to give up on his decision. Moreover, I had lost the right to argue with him ever since I got married and was sent off to my in-laws' house. It was the law of society rather than the law of nature.

I wanted to question Baba as to how he thought he could make a decision on my life and death in a matter of seconds. How cruel he was to send me away to a man who had abused me and had not even bothered to come and see his son in two years? How could he beg Asad to take me back?

This was too much to endure. *Why am I alive, why don't I die? So many people die every day in Kashmir, why am I not among them? Am I a piece of dirt or filth that everybody wants to get rid of?* Destructive thoughts filled my mind.

I loathed myself for being a woman. I despised the life of the poor and destitute village girl. Why had my fate entangled with hers? She was disgraced for being poor, while I was ashamed of being timid and helpless.

I felt nauseous and wanted to vomit my stomach out.

Baba had named a high price for my self-esteem and dignity. He had shamed me of my own existence.

Asad had paid some money to the village girl and sent her back home. He had decided to buy me back, as though I were a doll in a toyshop.

The irony was that my father had also played a role in my being demeaned.

This was a man's world for sure, and women were made to endure and obey.

'The taxi will be here in two hours. Get your bags ready so that you can reach your home before it gets dark.' Baba's order was like the verdict given by a judge who knew that his ruling was unfair and unjustified.

How can I face Asad and his family after all that has happened over the last few years? I was in despair.

My son was running after Baba to show him the painting of a soldier pointing his gun at a woman. Muna seemed to have understood my dilemma.

Baba did not look at the painting. He left Muna crying in the lounge.

I had no choice but to return to Asad's house.

Baba had done the same thing that he had seen being done by his family. He seemed to be no different from his sisters.

I asked the taxi driver to come by later, so that it would be dark when I reached Asad's place. I did not want to see anybody's face nor Asad's triumphant smirk, both of which would tear me apart.

I stayed locked inside the bathroom for about an hour in order to muster up the courage and strength to face this new phase of my life.

SURPRISE

It was a scene I had never expected. The house was illuminated with colourful lights and balloons. Asad's house looked unbelievable. All his brothers, sisters and their families, in their new and colourful dresses, were eagerly waiting to welcome me to the home in the same way they had when I had first entered their household as a bride.

The neighbours were watching from the windows of their houses; Asad's sisters showered flower petals on me as I stepped out of the taxi.

In the air lingered the fragrance of wazwan, delicate and tantalizing. I started salivating and my taste buds started itching. It was something I had not tasted for a long time.

Children, elders, women and men followed behind me, waiting to get seated in the hall for the grand feast.

My homecoming celebrations were unexpected and overwhelming. I became sentimental and prayed to God to give me the strength to control myself and not give way to tears.

Everywhere I looked, I saw flower arrangements, colour lights and balloons. It must have taken days to prepare for the event. For a moment I thought that all this was perhaps for Faiza's wedding celebrations. But when I saw her, she was, as usual, looking after the elderly guests in the hall. Moulvi Sahib was seated right in the middle, busy in talking with Asad's elder brother.

I now realized what Baba and Moulvi Sahib had been whispering to each other in our living room. They had been planning this day for months.

I felt strange but calm. My heartbeat returned to normal, but still I did not have the courage to look into their eyes.

Muna was playing with children he had never met before, but he seemed to like their company. Earlier, he had felt a bit uncomfortable by the hugging and kissing his aunts and uncles subjected him to, but he soon settled in by playing with the other kids. Dozens of toys were scattered all around him.

I could barely walk after the sumptuous, heavy dinner. Listening to the complaints and grievances of the relatives made me feel guilty rather than like a victim of their indifferent attitudes. I did not react and listened patiently to everything they had stored in their minds. Most of the guests had left the hall; only close relatives remained now, gossiping in groups. Faiza took hold of my hand and showed me the room that had undergone a total makeover during my absence.

The bed, cupboards and shelves were all newly built. The walls were painted parrot-green, Asad's favourite colour when he was feeling romantic. The windows had new curtains. Dozens of musical toys were hanging over the top of Muna's cot, which had been placed next to the king-sized bed.

The room had been refurbished and decorated beautifully. It contained no traces of my past seven years spent there. My leftover garments were nowhere in the room. The cupboards were full of newly tailored dresses, pherans and male suits.

Perhaps Asad had changed his dress code again. There were no more Khan dresses in the cupboard.

Faiza whispered in my ear, 'This is a new beginning in your life. You are starting a new life today, so everything is fresh and new in this room. Don't feel nervous, it is your home and everything here belongs to you. Be brave enough to tread on this new path and make its foundation strong. What happened in the past is over. Either one can forget and move forward, or one can get stuck, making one's own life miserable.'

Faiza looked like my mother, whose every move forged a new foundation in my life. With a big smile on her chubby, angelic face she left the room. Near the door, she almost collided with her brother who was carrying Muna on his shoulders.

Asad placed Muna on a cot; my son was staring at me with his sleepy eyes. He was standing close to the window with his back towards me. I could sense a triumphant smile on his face. I wished Asad would hide his own face, at least for a while, but he seemed at ease with himself—calm, peaceful and confident as ever—even if he was the culprit.

For me, all this was beyond my expectations.

Asad sat beside Muna on the cot, and ran his hand through his curly hair and kissed him on his forehead. I was watching his every move and gesture. Muna fell asleep instantly. Asad's presence made me uncomfortable. I wanted to run away, but I had no place to go to.

'I am so sorry for everything that has happened. I did bad, wrong things in my life and put you under a lot of stress and pain. I wish I could undo all that, but I can't. However, I can promise you a new start from today.'

There was a bit of remorse in his speech. 'Asad' and 'remorse' were two words I had not expected to hear in the same breath.

I could not bear to see his phoney apologetic attitude and display of being timid, when he had acted and managed the whole drama.

'I am not sure if I will be able to forget everything and make this relationship work. What you have done is inexcusable and unforgivable. You played with me and my emotions. You ruined my life and humiliated me. An unfortunate girl sought protection in your house and you let others play with her and her emotions. How you managed this whole charade of bringing me back home is beyond my understanding, but had my father not helped you, you would not have succeeded. I was forced to come back to this house. I had no wish to come here or to see you again,' I said. I was so open and honest about my emotions, I could hardly believe it myself. Where did I get this courage from?

'I realize the pain you have endured. Please forgive me and let us give our relationship another chance to work. Let us give our son a better future and bring him up like other children. I can only do it with your support and love,' Asad said, looking deep into my eyes.

My mind and my heart, both, were in turmoil.

Was he really being honest and regretting his inhuman actions, or was he trying to hoodwink me again? I failed to read his mind.

From the grand welcome and decorations, the humility and the apology, I could not believe it was all real. I pinched my arm to reassure myself that I was not dreaming.

I was silently watching him, his changing expressions, his sighs and his wrinkles. He was playing with Muna's hair, kissing and cuddling him. Muna was sound asleep.

I glanced at Asad, but he was trying to avoid making eye contact with me. His overgrown silver hair was hanging over his right ear. He seemed to have really aged.

I came close to the long mirror fixed along the door of the wardrobe and looked at myself—perhaps for traces of silver hair. I found none. Instead, I saw a wrinkled face that had lost its youth. I hardly recognized myself.

I had lost everything and I had remained unaware of it. There was no colour in my cheeks and no glitter in my eyes—I had lost my youth.

Baba's words were reverberating in my brain repeatedly: 'Do not ruin your life or Muna's. Demand your right if it has been snatched from you. Make him understand what he is bound to lose, or people will ridicule you, even if you are the victim.'

Faiza's words were mixing with Baba's: 'It is a new start today. Give it your best shot.'

I lost my words and my grip on everything and started sobbing like a child. My tears rolled down my cheeks like rain at the beginning of spring, which would often bring devastating floods.

Asad came close to me, took me in his arms, cuddled me and stroked my hair, the way he had just been doing with Muna's.

I do not know for how long time stopped in this moment. My sobs became uncontrollable. Asad was holding me in his arms, which were soaked in an ocean of tears. When my eyes ran out of water, I looked around. The room had changed its reflection and so had my life.

I settled myself in a routine again as if I had never broken away from it.

1990–2000: Renegade militants supported by the security forces are used for extrajudicial executions of militants, extortion, intimidation and harassment of common people mostly women and girls.

Amnesty International.

OFFER

Until recently, Faiza had been a silent and shy girl. Now she spoke with such confidence and authority that she sounded like Aristotle's mother.

A tall, slim girl had blossomed into an intelligent, wholesome person. It was indeed the contribution of the books she had been reading. She had this urge, a habit, to keep busy in some productive activity or the other. If she was not reading a book or doing household chores, she would be decorating the house with fresh flowers. How long she begged her brothers to let her take a course in interior designing, but they were all annoyed and agitated over the idea. I did not help her fight her battle this time because I knew this was too much to ask from a family where all the girls except Faiza were barred from leaving the house without a chaperone. She was forced to bury her dream of being a designer for the rest of her life.

She had immersed herself in the world of philosophy. Inspired by and loosely based on the poetry of ascetics Nund Rishi and Lal Ded, she had a dream of recording Kashmiri philosophy that would depict the secular character of the valley.

It was only Faiza who realized the precarious situation I had been put in. Being more sensible and considerate than all her other siblings, she kept me reassured that things would become easier over a passage of time. She became my confidante and sometimes my guide too.

The day I returned, she had helped me a lot in my resettlement. Once again, she became my source of solace and comfort.

Faiza became Muna's godmother. My Muna also got so attached to her that he would not leave her. In my absence, during the day, he stuck to her, playing hide-and-seek, drawing pictures and riding on her back as though she were a horse.

The only task she dreaded was cooking grand feasts or serving dozens of guests at a dastarkhan, but I took on this responsibility wholeheartedly, in return for her looking after Muna.

Faiza was fond of solitude, like I had been as a student.

The only time she spent with the family was at dinner time, when she started continuously chattering about what she had read in books or seen on television. We had to swallow her every word along with every morsel we ate. Most of the time she said sensible things, but being the youngest in the family, nobody took her seriously or responded to her. It was not in our custom to listen to young girls.

The day she completed her graduation in college, her brothers started looking for a suitable match for her.

Asad and his family were desperate to get her married as soon as possible, because they believed Faiza had crossed the proper age for marriage, which was unacceptable to my traditional family. It had been an arduous task to find Faiza a suitable match under the prevailing circumstances. Some proposals did come in from distant relatives, but they were not considered appropriate for one reason or another. Most boys were unemployed, some had links to militants, while others were too old.

Faiza was not remotely interested in getting married or finding her Prince Charming.

All her siblings had been married off at a very young age. Faiza was much older than what her sisters were when they got married. Her youth had begun to fade and dark circles had started appearing under her eyes.

Asad and his brothers were looking forward to making Faiza's wedding a momentous event—once the match was found, of course. This would be the last marriage among the siblings of the family.

But the family had to face a grave problem. Since the Ikhwanis, or 'renegades'—referring to those militants who, after their arrest, are recruited by the government as informers—had, along with the security forces, rented the empty Pandit house in our neighbourhood, many families were being forced to move out of the vicinity. The street had turned into a hotspot for looting, hooliganism and plunder. Most of the girls were confined to their houses due to the increasing incidents of teasing, extortion, bullying and even sexual abuse.

The locality became stigmatized in society. Girls from this area, earlier considered amongst the finest in the valley, were now being turned down by suitors for marriage. It had become very dangerous to get away with Ikhwanis' attention.

We became very concerned ever since the leader of the gang started visiting us more frequently. He asked for money or food, and sometimes deliberately threw a football into our garden, as an excuse to enter the house. He would keep staring at Faiza. She complained about his behaviour to her brothers, who decided to tell him off at an appropriate time.

The renegade kept wandering around on our lawn, trying to get close to our windows; he even sat outside our main gate for hours to play *carrom* with his friends. He started asking all our family members a lot of questions about Faiza. The situation got out of hand when, in broad daylight, he came to our house and went to Faiza's room to talk to her. Faiza was so terrified that she hid herself in a bathroom until Asad's sister-in-law convinced him to leave the house. There was no male member at home at the time. Even then, her brothers could not find the courage to stop him from making further advances.

My family grew more and more terrified of his constant presence and growing interest in our internal affairs. Nobody dared to stop him until, one day, he silenced us all.

Seeing the Ikhwanis always hanging around our house, our neighbours too became suspicious of our family. They thought we were hand in glove with the renegades and had adopted the anti-freedom movement. Some of our neighbours even avoided greeting us when they ran into us on the street and considered us traitors.

Not having seen Faiza for a few days, the Ikhwani who had taken a fancy to her was so frustrated that he came over along with three armed men and forcibly entered our living room. Asad, his brother and Bhabhi were discussing dismantling the old kitchen beyond the backyard and building a new, more spacious one to accommodate the growing size of the family.

The Ikhwani bluntly stated that he wanted to marry Faiza.

Everybody in the room froze. Asad's brother was unable to breathe. He was so terrified that he started coughing. Asad struggled to talk, but his mouth went dry. Silence and terror ripped us apart.

It took Asad a few moments to regain his composure. Very politely, he told the Ikhwani that he would discuss the proposal with the rest of his family and would come back to him in due course of time. He thanked the Ikhwani for his proposal too.

The Ikhwani was desperate to get the matter decided quickly. His friends advised him to leave and give the family some time to deliberate: 'You have to give them some time to take a decision, according to Shariat.' Thanks heavens, his friend came to our rescue at least.

The moment they left, Asad and his brothers started cursing the Ikhwani for being so audacious as to ask to marry Faiza.

Though the disaster had been temporarily averted, the whole family was, however, completely shocked. No one in the family could bear the thought of Faiza marrying an Ikhwani whose hands were stained with the blood of so many innocent people. He was considered a vagabond, a traitor, a loose cannon.

'Who could bear to marry their daughter to him? They might as well throw her into the Jhelum,' Asad whispered to himself.

The family was shredded into pieces. Faiza's condition was pitiable, and her philosophy had provided no answers to deal with this calamity.

The ensuing discussions and arguments among our family members over the Faiza–Ikhwani issue had turned our house into a zoo with the wild animals left loose. There seemed no way to get out of this mess, and everybody was thinking about a plan to avert the danger. Egos were soaring, tempers ran high and the whole household seemed at the brink of collapse. I felt sorry for Faiza, who kept crying all the time. Muna tried to comfort her, but she felt very insecure and frightened. I hugged her. Perhaps God did not wish me to be happy. Every time I come close to somebody, they became cursed or were snatched away from me.

The whole family stayed awake under the faint light of the kerosene lamp. Baba was summoned for his thoughts and advice on the issue.

Asad's brother came up with the idea to flee the house at night, leaving no traces behind. The solution seemed unrealistic to implement though. 'It is impossible to move the whole household, thinking nobody would notice our movement. The Ikhwanis would surely butcher us the moment they found out,' said Asad, snubbing his brother.

The brothers were engaged in discussions till dawn. Asad said, 'How can we leave everything here and run like cowards? We better face his gun and die with dignity.'

'Baba was correct. You should take Faiza to Jammu and leave her there with Muna's uncle. I am sure that the Ikhwani will not find out,' said Asad's elder brother brusquely. Asad looked at Baba for his approval.

In the end, it was decided that it would be best if Faiza stayed with my brother and Bhabhi in Jammu—this would hardly occur to the Ikhwani. But I was plagued by the fear that if the Ikhwani got wind of this information, he would definitely not leave my brother alive. We were facing the worst nightmare of our lives.

Asad's brother managed to get a night-curfew pass from a local police officer. Early in the morning, when the taxi arrived in our garage, Asad and Faiza boarded it and drove way.

We all pretended to act normal.

~

To get any information about Asad and Faiza was out of the question, and nobody bothered to ask as long as they were far away from the Ikhwanis' area of influence.

I kept counting the hours until the time they would get past the Banihal Tunnel, which had been closed recently due to heavy rains. Would they be safe beyond the control of the Ikhwanis? What if they were delayed due to the military convoys on the highway? I was muttering to myself and, at the same time, keeping an eye on the Ikhwani's movements to make sure he did not notice anything unusual.

I was relieved to hear that the curfew had been imposed again in most parts of Srinagar, after the protests in Lal Chowk, against the killing of a marriage party, had turned violent. The streets became silent. We did not face the renegade on the street. The valley was drowned in darkness. The power supply had been totally shut. There was no connection to the outside world due to the erratic telephone system. The national highway had been blocked again, and the complete blackout of news and information was choking us all.

The government-controlled media broadcast patriotic songs, so we were forced to switch the radio off.

Muna kept searching for Faiza in every room, and we kept watching him in silence, until he fell asleep on the floor.

AWFUL

It might sound cruel to call it a miracle, but my family did. The miracle happened because it saved my family from a disaster. And most of all, it saved Faiza from certain self-imposed exile.

Due to reasons unknown to us, the security camp in our backyard received orders to be redeployed somewhere in Kupwara along with a group of renegades, including the one who had proposed marriage to Faiza. Before its departure, the Ikhwani and his group had been asked to report swiftly for a crackdown and identification parade in the Shaheed Gunj area, where gunmen were engaged in an encounter with the forces. The encounter and crackdown operation continued for a couple of days, so the redeployment was delayed.

During the encounter between the militants and the security forces, a grenade was hurled over the army vehicle, killing three soldiers and three Ikhwanis on the spot, including the one who connected with Faiza.

The grenade sent the Ikhwani vehicle flying in the air, and the body parts of the men inside the vehicle were found hanging on the dangling wires of the electric grid station. Their feet, hands and entrails were all that were left, scattered everywhere. When the details of the incident were related to my family, a chill ran down my spine. I could imagine the magnitude of the attack when I peeped through the window to see the chaos outside my gate.

There was crying, wailing and anger at the gate of the security camp. Many dead and injured soldiers and renegades were being brought in tatters. Some soldiers were placing the Ikhwani's remains in a coffin to make it look like a dead body that was being sent to his ancestral village for burial.

The scene reminded me of the deadly air crash involving Pakistani dictator General Zia-ul-Haq, whose jawbone was the only remaining body part that could be extricated from the debris at the crash site. Kashmir went up in flames after his death, when pro-Jamaat-e-Islami activists attacked the secularists, blaming them for things that had been planned somewhere else by somebody else. Yet, many mourned General Zia's death, regardless of whether he had allegiance towards Jamaat-e-Islami or the secularists.

Should I be jubilant or sad over the gruesome death of the Ikhwanis, the pro-government militants? I did not know. But I smiled and wept at the same time. Perhaps I had lost control over my mind.

After a while, Asad's eldest sister in-law invited us all into the living room to drink some kahwa. She contacted Asad on the phone, asking him to bring Faiza back. The tears rolling down her cheeks looked very strange alongside her grateful smile.

I could not drink the kahwa. It tasted bitter to me instead of sweet. I left the glass untouched and rushed to my bedroom.

The Ikhwani's death had been dreadful, but more dreadful was the fact that my family was celebrating his death by drinking kahwa. I could never have imagined that Kashmir would turn into such a dreadful place.

VEIL

For the last three years, my colleagues and I had hardly met in the conference hall of the radio station where we used to have our brainstorming sessions for creating new programmes and new adventures in journalism. The volatile situation remained unchanged and the counter-insurgency strategy initiated by the government had not borne any fruits, but the initiative of winning the hearts and minds of the people through radio programmes was finally being taken seriously by the authorities now.

It was after a long time that we had been called by the station director to report for duty and assemble in the conference hall for an emergency meeting. Some programme officers who had come from Delhi at the orders of the information and broadcasting ministry were also present. They seemed to be under a lot of stress as they had witnessed the encounter between the forces and militants near the gate of the station. Terror was written all over their faces and one could tell they wanted to leave Kashmir as soon as possible. All of them were silent and kept staring at the walls.

There were only a few Muslim employees in the office who were thought to be pro-Pakistan or spying for the mujahideen by the programme officers who had been sent in to support us.

The meeting was convened to discuss the launching of a new programme on women's counselling, aimed at helping the women victims of the militant violence. Nobody had any idea about the format and the structure of the programme. And there was no mention of those who had suffered at the hands of the security forces and whose number had increased manifold.

The objective of the programme was to win the hearts and minds of the Kashmiri women. Perhaps the authorities had lost confidence in the Kashmiri male population.

It had made me laugh—not at the stupidity of the politicians, but at my colleague Saira, who was overexcited about producing the women's programme. She had no idea what she was getting into.

Kashmir, in fact, had become like a mistress of the country that wanted to keep her close but never tried to win her heart. The two never accepted each other even after seven decades of bonhomie.

Saira had told us that she knew some victims of violence and wanted to get some financial help for them, for which the programme might prove helpful. Her proposal had been approved by the station head and she had been asked to present the pilot project of the programme in the meeting before it was allotted airtime in the evening transmission.

We had been waiting for her for quite some time. We started staring at the walls. The silence was making me restless.

It was not unusual for us to wait for a few more hours in such circumstances; we had become used to it. Most of us were aware of the difficulties one had to face making the journey from home to the office and back. Many search operations, the stopping of vehicles by the security troops and protest demonstrations had become routine hurdles. So we waited. The officers who had come from Delhi were restless and left the conference hall one by one after a long wait and continued silence.

I could sense that Saira was in big trouble and had a lot of explaining to do to the station head.

Although Saira was definitely late, I knew she would not have kept the outstation officers waiting for so long. 'Maybe she is trapped in some search operation or has been caught up in cross-firing. She has never been such an irresponsible officer,' I said.

I was the last to leave the conference hall after spending a few hours sifting through her programme layout file. I made some small corrections and left the file on her desk.

The moment I stepped out of the station premises and was about to get into an autorickshaw, I saw Saira coming from the opposite side of the road towards me. She was pushing everybody out of the way, trying to make room to pass through.

She had covered her face with some sort of a black scarf, which was not her style. She was drenched in some sort of paint that was all over her head, hands and clothes. Seeing her dripping in paint made me laugh, but I controlled myself and pretended to be angry with her for being late.

She grabbed my arm, getting some paint over my clothes in the process, and took me back inside the office. Once she took the scarf off her face, the tears poured down her yellow-painted cheeks. It was a chilling sight. I was still unable to make sense of her bizarre condition.

'What has happened to you? How did you get this paint all over you?' My curiosity was killing me.

'I was waiting at the bus stop. Some burka-clad women encircled me and asked me why I was not wearing the hijab. I tried to reason with them, but instead of listening to me, they threw paint on me for being anti-Islamic and against the movement. They abused me, called me promiscuous, a person of loose character and a harlot in front of a huge crowd.' She started crying loudly.

There had been rumours for the past few days that some reformist women groups had begun a campaign to make girls wear the hijab or the burka. They supported the idea of converting Kashmir into a puritanical state once it was free. However, nobody expected that things would go so far that women themselves would become victims of humiliation meted out by other women.

I stayed with Saira while she tried to get the paint off her clothes and washed her hair and face so that she would be presentable enough to go home. She was in a state of shock and was reluctant to leave the office and go home all alone.

Her distress made me frightened too. I did not have the courage to argue with the burka women if, God forbid, I ever encountered them on my way. It had never occurred to me that the burka campaign could one day become a part of the Azadi movement.

Wearing the hijab was the last thing I wanted to do. Not because I disliked it, but because the dupatta would never stay on my head, and I could not fasten it with clips, being allergic to all metal objects.

Baba had given me a detailed lecture on the importance of covering my head during my college days. He gave up when he realized my predicament.

I did try to cover my head in a scarf once in college, but my hair kept sticking out of the scarf like overgrown grass, and it made me uncomfortable to the extent that I even thought of cutting all my hair off—thank God for Sadia, whose timely slap knocked some sense into me and prevented me from carrying out my ridiculous plan.

Fortunately, I reached home without getting paint thrown at me. Neither did I encounter any burka activists on the road.

My horror subsided, but all the while I had kept thinking about Saira and how vulnerable she had looked in the office. I wondered if she had managed to reach home safely.

When the armed struggle started a few years ago, there was no mention of Islam or religion. It was purely an Azadi movement, with no consideration given to religion, caste or colour. Now, it had taken a new turn and most people considered it an Islamic movement. The Azadi movement and the revival of puritanical Islam (that too applying only to womenfolk) had become intertwined in such a way that it created confusion, not only in the valley, but in the international community, which had become suspicious of our objectives, as well.

Earlier, some outfits did engage in reformation in tandem with the Azadi movement by conducting raids on liquor shops and closing cinemas and video shops, but they were confined to some downtown areas and the target had been men or boys only. Now, it was women against women creating horrible headlines for the international press.

Women activists would, using the excuse of the Islamic movement, terrorize young girls to leave school or college. Many women in different offices had been forced to give up their jobs, and if anybody refused, they were subjected to harassment and violent acts.

All this was really frustrating and humiliating for girls who desired higher education, making something of themselves and doing something significant for themselves and for human society in general. But some women had crossed all moral barriers. The secular image of the valley was lost forever and the Azadi movement had turned into a nightmare for half the population.

There were attacks and raids on restaurants, internet cafes, Mughal Gardens and entertainment shops. There were even some cases of acid being thrown on women reported in the newspapers. Like others, Saira was so terrified that she did not come in to work the following day.

~

The pampered daughter of wealthy parents, Saira had lived a life I was not used to. She did not get a chance to face the reality of the life that half the population in the valley experienced every day. Kashmiri women were living a life of misery, poverty and humiliation. Saira was one of those lucky girls who did not have to travel on crowded buses or Matadors, wear cheap cotton dresses or face the soldiers at their doorsteps.

The paint-throwing by the burka women was only a one-off incident that had terrified her.

She did not walk under the heavy gaze of pockmarked soldiers, she did not have to make acquaintance with unwanted people in her house and neither did she receive marriage proposals from renegades. She would have learnt, then, to endure the pain and humiliation. What half of the population in the valley had been going through she hardly got a chance to see.

If she had seen Shiasta's mutilated body or known Fareeda's nightmares she would not have dared to leave her house, job or motherland behind. Rather, she would have become resilient like the rest of us women.

Saira had always believed in one rule in life: to 'cut off that part of the body which is beyond any cure'. I would convince her to listen to my mother, who used to say: 'No matter how bad the pain in your body is, don't get rid of it by cutting it off. Try to cure it.'

Saira had always been extremely ambitious and aimed for the big things in life. She achieved everything she set her eyes on. On the contrary, my battles seemed never-ending and brought no good results. I kept losing everything I was fighting for.

Saira's never-compromising attitude had developed a confidence in her that had become a distant dream for every woman in Kashmir. Most women compromised on everything: marriage, home, honour and life.

She did not marry a boy her parents chose. The boy she liked her parents rejected. In the end, she made a decision to not marry at all.

I did not count her among the 'tiger ladies' of Kashmir because she lacked the aura and grandeur they were known for. Such women never gave up their fight by using militancy as a crutch. The more atrocities they faced, the more resilient and strong they became. They endured what was beyond anybody's comprehension. They were an ocean of endurance and patience.

Our women had learnt over time that they could protect themselves in a more effective way if they all assembled outside their houses, in groups, while their men were held up in the crackdown.

Whenever security personnel stopped a bus or a Matador, the women would get off quickly and walk towards the bunker. They would quietly pray to God to save them from the wrath of surrendered militants while going through the frisking process and, at the sight of the signal, board the bus again at the other end of the road. They always kept their eyes open so as to fully see the gestures of soldiers, because they did not want them to think they were being rude by not obeying them. Once they reboarded the bus, they praised God for blessing them with a second life.

Saira did not have the chance or the inclination to share the life pressures that regular womenfolk in Kashmir were subjected to. She was never asked to sit in the scorching heat during a crackdown. She was the privileged daughter of a top civil servant known for his changing loyalties.

I had been close to Saira. But she was far away from me.

I envied her lifestyle and her free thoughts, but I despised her discreet decision of leaving the office, her home and her motherland without even saying goodbye to me.

PERIL

The 'Wear Burka' campaign had received huge publicity, and most of the local press seemed to promote it in a way that some non-entities or lesser-known women became the 'leaders' of the horde overnight. The pictures of public beatings or paint-throwing incidents on the front pages of newspapers kept most of the girls off the road and therefore away from educational institutions.

The scenes were reminiscent of the late 1970s, when the valley's girls were being threatened and humiliated by a special character referred to as 'Slacks Moulvi'. Many parents had objected to his indecent, harassing behaviour at the time, but to their astonishment, most people took pleasure out of his wickedness and allowed him to disgrace young girls in every possible way.

The Slacks Moulvi would stand outside the gates of women's colleges and beat, with a stick, those girls whose heads were not covered with a scarf. The boys from the adjacent college would stand around, watch the spectacle and laugh at his disgraceful behaviour. Only when most of the girls started staying home to avoid this menace, and parents expressed their anger against the government for not preventing him, did the police take notice of the severity of the situation.

However, the burka campaign had far more serious repercussions than the Slacks Moulvi, with most girls petrified to cross their doorsteps. The campaign essentially forced girls to wear the burka, cover their heads—or stay at home. Some preferred to leave the valley like Saira did.

When some moderately liberal women objected to it, I was asked by my station head to start a programme in which women would give vent to their emotions vis-à-vis the campaign. I had no choice but to produce it. However, I knew that nobody would dare to raise their voice openly against the burka campaign and the show would be a flop. To my surprise, however, the first programme was flooded with voices opposing the campaign and, despite the threats, women spoke openly against it.

'The "Wear Burka" campaign women are anti-Islam and are tarnishing our secular character,' one woman caller said.

'We want freedom based on secularism, not fundamentalism.'

'Kashmir is a Muslim-majority state and there is no restriction on religious practices. We do not need to display our connection to Islam by wearing a burka.'

'Some women are trying to divert the course of the freedom struggle by raising these petty matters like mandating the hijab.'

'Outwardly, they pretend to be real Muslims, but in their hearts they are the enemies of Islam.'

The unidentified women participants blasted the burka campaign, calling it 'an un-Islamic way' of treating young girls and harassing them. Many voices were being raised to stop this nonsense. The burka campaign was getting negative publicity in the media and so were the new battalion of women leaders. Most of them went into hiding.

The following day, some newspapers published the threats and warnings issued by newly constituted women organizations against those who were opposing the burka campaign. Pakistan-backed militant organizations issued statements in support of the burka campaign.

Despite their threats, the programme received a huge response and the majority of women wanted to participate in order to tell their own personal stories. Yet, some women continued to strongly support the campaign.

A young girl from the Shopian district agreed to come in to the studio on the condition that she would not reveal her name. And she wanted a live broadcast.

She showed me burn marks on her neck, arms and legs. She did not reveal anything before she went live on the radio to broadcast her terror.

'I was working as a teacher in a local primary school. On my way to school every day, there was a bunker I had to pass through. The security forces stationed there would follow me, take me to the bunker and interrogate me about the boys playing in the cricket field adjacent to our school. The soldiers wanted me to get close to the boys and gather information about their activities and contacts.

'They would beat me, drug me and sexually assault me. This ordeal went on for a few months. I left my job and remained confined in my home. The soldiers then came to my house and interrogated me about the boys in my neighbourhood. They tortured and raped me in my own home. One day, my mother found me in an awkward position. She was shocked and could not face the neighbours. She took me with her and made me jump with her into the Jhelum river. My mother died instantly. I survived because somebody saw me floating in the river near the village of Lasjan. Since then, I run at the sight of security forces. I have been living in the wilderness for the last three years. My only protection for the last three years has been the burka that you all loathe. I cannot sleep except in a burka, and I cannot even go to the toilet, because every time I take my burka off, I feel terrified that the soldiers will reappear and tear me into pieces. Can you guarantee me protection if I take off my burka, I ask you, my dear moderate women? And can you let me live a safe life if I take my burka off?'

Relating her ordeal, the young girl wept bitterly. Everybody present in the studio seemed to have felt her pain and wanted to cry along with her. She left the studio and did not turn back. I ran after her, but she had disappeared.

After the broadcast, there was a furore across the valley that resulted in the cancellation of the programme. People had come out on the streets to protest against the alleged atrocities caused by the security forces. Some separatist leaders along with students led the demonstrations and made it a big issue to further the Azadi movement.

Strangely, the Azadi slogans had completely transformed into Islamic ones.

My experiment in reality programmes had failed miserably.

My job was at risk because the authorities were angry with me. My life had already been at risk because the burka women had been offended by the moderate voices in the radio programme. Baba forbade me from leaving the house for a few weeks. I was under a lot of stress and braced myself for worse to come. Sometimes, I felt so terrified that I did not open the window to let fresh air into the room.

I made an official request for a transfer. The dust settled after a few weeks of chaos and I was neither sacked nor transferred.

I found that life had not stopped. It had just slowed down and become crippled.

Despite the death threats made by the burka women and the pressure tactics used by the officials, I kept moving forward, even though I had no idea where I was heading.

AUNTYJI

Before the uprising, we used to spend our evenings in the living room and talk about the Palestinian struggle. Leila Khaled and Yasser Arafat were our heroes. We would admire their daring attacks against Israel, cherish their dream and pray for their freedom. The story of the plane hijacking carried out by Leila Khaled was our favourite topic of discussion. Every time we spoke about her, there was a new revelation. Her zeal and courage would raise fresh hope among us and inspire our youths. I would wait for hours at the main gate for Baba so I could be the first to catch him, before he crossed the threshold of the house, and snatch *Huda* magazine out of his bag. The magazine had a full coverage on the hijacking saga and carried details about Leila's intriguing early-life stories. When I cut out Leila's front-page photo from the magazine, Baba was angry with me for many days. I put it up on my wall so that I could be reminded of her courage every day.

These days, we had not stopped sitting together in our big living rooms. We still gathered, but we hardly remembered Leila Khaled or Arafat, neither did we go to the attic to have a relook at their posters or stories of persecution. We did not wait to watch new releases, new videos or new shows. We all now sat in wait for All India Radio and Radio Pakistan's news bulletins and then proceed to compare these with BBC's current affairs programme *Sairbeen*.

We were concerned with looking for clues, gathering information and finding out the total number of causalities so that we would keep track of our relatives and our neighbourhood. We wanted to know where and how many crackdowns had been carried out during the day, and how many had been killed on the Line of Control. We got clues about the gunmen, how they had left security forces wondering with their daring guerrilla tactics. On the radio we would come across *Sadia-i-Radio*, which broadcast messages of freedom after a recitation of the Quran. We would feel happy at the mention of Azadi.

Switching on our transistor sets behind closed doors and shut windows had become our daily routine and our sole entertainment. We had a black-and-white television set that was dead because the power supply had remained off for almost twenty hours. When the supply was restored, all the light bulbs would trip due to fluctuation. Therefore, we had decided it was better to save our television set than risk ruining it.

Baba would become emotional while listening to news bulletins and relate to us the incidents of the early 1950s when, after the arrest of Sheikh Abdullah, people were tortured and intimidated if found listening to Radio Pakistan. He said, 'Some people were tortured with a hot iron placed on their bellies by the notorious police chief of that time. Listening to Radio Pakistan was like writing your own death warrant.'

I would ask Baba the question I had asked him at the time of the Bangladesh War, 'Baba, what made Abdullah sign the agreement and why was he arrested?' Baba would stare at the ceiling and shout at me, 'Why do you always ask questions I have no answers for? You'd better become a journalist!'

What Baba had gone through was nothing compared to what our boys had been put through. They were facing worse than that. Hot potatoes were replaced by hot-iron rods. No more irons on bellies—connecting genitals to electric wires had become the popular method of interrogation in our modern history of counter-insurgency. All the interrogation centres were supplied with special electricity connections, round the clock, for the purposes of torture and electrocution. Hundreds of boys were unaccounted for, many more either crippled or made useless. Not a single inquiry was made or allegations taken seriously by the government.

Listening to the radio at a low volume was still our only source of information. The radio had become our lifeline. We listened to patriotic songs during the day and would later find ourselves singing them without realizing it.

When we would realize what we had been singing, we would switch off the radio immediately. It made us peaceful within.

~

Since my return, Asad would not let me stay at Baba's house. He would discourage me by saying there had been frequent fake encounters in Baba's area than in any other place in the recent days and so it was dangerous to go there. 'Just go for a visit, but come back in the evening,' he would say.

One evening, we were huddled up in the living room to listen to the BBC news bulletin and find out what had happened in Rajpora, Pulwama, which had been under siege since the previous week. Only the BBC would give us a detailed account of the violence taking place in the different parts of the valley.

Moulvi Sahib was sitting close to Baba, waiting eagerly for the news broadcast. He was worried about his eldest son who lived in Rajpora. He had heard that the security forces had fatally shot a lot of people protesting against the constant state of siege. There were still a few minutes left for the news bulletin to start when the muezzin's call for prayers was stopped in the middle and the announcement for a search operation was made by the security forces, telling men to assemble in the mosque graveyard.

We all walked towards the front door, leaving everything untouched. But I did hide the radio set under the bed, so that the soldiers would not be able to get their hands on it. Many reports had been floating around recently that soldiers had stolen cameras, radio sets, watches and gold jewellery during the search operations. I had been told by Moulvi Sahib earlier that when soldiers saw a huge container of rice in his house, they asked him, 'Are you in the rice business?' Moulvi Sahib had laughed because the stored rice was for his personal use. It was merely a long-standing practice among Kashmiris to stock eatables, from rice to lentils to dried vegetables.

Another announcement was made by the Imam Sahib. Baba and Moulvi Sahib were struggling to reach the mosque quickly. Their eyes were fixed on the furious soldiers who were following the flock of men. Everybody from the neighbourhood was out on the streets, which were dark and cold.

The agony aunt of the neighbourhood, Auntyji, was, as usual, trying to ease the tension by poking fun at the situation. She sometimes made sarcastic comments about the soldiers, sometimes funny gestures, in such a way that the women around her laughed and wept at the same time. She would never let women stay alone in the house during search operations and advised them to stay together since there was strength in numbers. She was the one who would take the lead in talking to the soldiers and answering their queries.

Among all the women in the neighbourhood, Auntyji was different. She had a unique character—full of humour, always smiling and playing agony aunt to the many destitute women around. We called her 'Auntyji' out of love and respect.

Auntyji knew a lot of secrets concerning the men and their 'other' affairs in the neighbourhood. She never disclosed them though. Her free marriage consultations and counselling sessions could save marriages and resolve issues in minutes. The way she dealt with people was remarkable. She had a way with people, and within only a meeting or two, she would become everybody's favourite.

Whether it was a wedding or funeral in the neighbourhood, everything was supposed to go according to Auntyji's plan.

She was the one who had made all the arrangements on my wedding day. She was the cook, the decorator, the entertainer, all at the same time, and most of all, she was the mother who gave me away and wept like my Baba when I was leaving my girlhood home to start a new journey with Asad and his family. And the following morning, it was Auntyji again who had come by early to find out if I was coping well with the new pressures and obligations of married life.

Baba was Auntyji's mentor and had taught the Quran to her. He considered her a daughter even though she was only a few years younger than he was. Auntyji would never sit around casually or talk loudly in Baba's presence and would keep her head down instead. 'It is her solid family background that has made her a noble soul,' Baba would comment about her.

Sometimes, I used to tease Auntyji about her counselling techniques. I would tell her, 'You should have married Moulvi Sahib rather than a bald uncle, because you could have both opened a counselling centre and made so much money.' She would cover her face in her scarf to hide her giggles.

There was hardly a girl in our neighbourhood who had not found comfort in the warmth of Auntyji's embrace. Her own daughter often complained that she felt neglected because her mother had only time for others and not her.

In our close-knit neighbourhood, most of the women were used to sharing their secrets to delicacies among them. They would sit on the lawn, discuss issues, find solutions and comfort each other. Alongside, they would chop vegetables, clean the rice of dirt and small pebbles, deseed chillies and, towards the end of the day, enjoy tea from the samovar. This was the sort of counselling centre that functioned in the open and where secrets never remained confined. Watching the women enjoying in the sunshine, the men would also claim another corner of the lawn to discuss topics from politics to religion. There were no such comfort zones anywhere in Kashmir now.

Once again, the announcement of a search operation was made from the mosque, ordering everybody, including the women, to leave the house quickly. The security forces spread out in all the lanes and closed off the entry points to the area from all corners. They were close to the spot where Auntyji was standing with other women. One group of soldiers called Auntyji to accompany them into her house to search the premises. Auntyji's younger son was already out along with the other men and boys assembled in the graveyard for the identification of potential militants.

After nearly four hours of searching, her house was turned upside down. Not a single corner was left unchecked by the metal detector. The additional bedding stored in the big room was scattered on the floor, with the duvet covers ripped open. The pillows were torn open and the cotton filling was thoroughly examined. Auntyji did not object. She stayed calm and waited for the soldiers to leave. It was for the first time that Auntyji's house had been raided and searched this extensively.

The soldiers finally left Auntyji's house after being satisfied that there was nothing hidden there and marched towards the other houses in the vicinity.

All the men and boys waiting in the graveyard were told to walk in one line in front of a white Gypsy, in which sat a surrendered militant who was looking upon every terrified face to identify potential militants.

A boy identified as a militant was thrown into the Gypsy. He was shouting in anger, pleading his innocence. Another middle-aged man, the father of four girls, was ordered to come forward. The soldiers tied his hands behind his back and threw him into another Gypsy like a sack of rice. A 'young moulvi', hardly fifteen years old, was the third target of the Ikhwani.

Last of all, it was Auntyji's son who was pulled out of the row and told to jump into the Gypsy. The renegade had identified four men as militants. Everybody was shouting against the arrests, mostly objecting to Auntyji's son, whom nobody believed could be involved in the insurgency. He was quietly following the orders of soldiers.

The colour in Auntyji's face drained but she soon turned red with rage and anger. She fought and cried to get her son out, but failed. The soldiers waiting near the vehicles whistled, shouted and boarded the gypsies, ready to take the arrested men away.

Except Auntyji, everybody was shouting themselves hoarse. The crowd encircled her and shouted Azadi slogans. Without wasting a moment, Auntyji suggested that everybody accompany her to the local police station to lodge an FIR against the arrest of her son. The Imam Sahib of the mosque agreed and asked the procession to proceed to the local police station. Men, women and children—all marched towards the police station raising Azadi slogans.

The official of the security forces at the local police station assured Auntyji that he would find out about the arrests and update her in the morning. The local police officer, however, was reluctant to help. He rejected Auntyji's request and said, 'We have no reports of any arrests or crackdowns in the area. I am not authorized to register an FIR in such circumstances.' He did not allow the group to enter the gate. We all knew that the local police had no powers regarding the arrests. The local police was like a defanged snake.

Frustrated, broken and stressed out, Auntyji returned home with all her neighbours. She had no clue and there was nobody to help her. She stayed outside the house, at the gate, for hours, but nobody among the four arrested men was released. The neighbours had left, one by one, after a long wait.

Baba advised Auntyji to stay indoors and get some rest, so that she could regain some of her strength to fight the long battle to get her son back from the clutches of the security agencies. Everybody was praising her for being so strong and patient. Inside, however, she had turned to stone. The neighbours were comforting her, telling her to wait until morning, so that they could all again go down to the station and put pressure on the police to give information about the arrests.

My two younger sisters and I were all sitting beside her. Auntyji's daughter came by late in the night after somebody rushed to her in-laws and informed her about the arrest. She was quiet and stared at her mother.

Auntyji stayed awake all night, relating funny incidents and memories surrounding her children. She mentioned the marriage of her daughter, finding a match for the son who was arrested by security forces. 'He wants to marry an educated girl, but a housewife, so that she can look after me and my family properly.' There was a bruised smile on her face. At times, she would turn pale and take long, deep breaths.

Before the muezzin's call for prayer the next morning, Auntyji went to the washroom and was just about to begin her morning prayers, when Moulvi Sahib came running. He was wringing his hands and muttering to himself. We were all petrified to see him in such a terrible state. We knew he had come with some horrible news. His face went blank and he cried loudly. He was trying to find the words but kept trailing off.

We all ran towards the mosque. Auntyji could not run because her feet had become heavy like lead; every step she took was an effort. Her daughter was pulling her hair and screaming.

Baba could not breathe. Mehmooda held Auntyji's hand and dragged her towards the mosque. Our neighbours rushed out of their homes once they heard our screaming.

Yet another calamity had befallen us. One more Karbala—catastrophe—had happened. Everybody was wailing and running towards the entrance of the gate. It was still dark. The neighbours had encircled the mosque gate with lit candles in their hands. Four dead bodies had been left by the security forces near the mosque. Women and men, young and old, were beating their chests at the sight of the mutilated bodies.

Auntyji stood frozen. She became hard like rock. She sat beside the bodies. Her son's body was one among the four—tortured, lynched and thrown at the entrance of the mosque. Some distance away, stray dogs were barking loudly. People were shouting and raising slogans. There was mayhem and helplessness everywhere.

Auntyji looked at her son's body. She placed her son's head close to her chest and began wailing loudly. All of a sudden, she stood up and frenetically begged the people around her not to cry or wail, saying, 'My son has laid down his life for his motherland. If I had hundred sons, I would like them all to sacrifice themselves for our honour and Azadi. Please do not weep or scream today. Do not mourn my son's death. He is a martyr. Only pray to God to accept his martyrdom and protect us from the devil, accept our sacrifices and free us!'

People were in tears, looking at her brave face, which hid a mother's heart that was bleeding to death.

She took the scarf off her head and began to rub away the bloodstains on her son's face. Then she did the same to the other bodies. People were asking if they could help her. She gestured to Imam Sahib to come forward and take the shoes off the four bodies. Imam Sahib's hands were trembling with fear. Auntyji sprinkled cold water on their face and dusted their muddy, bloodstained clothes. The faces on the four bodies finally became visible and identifiable.

From a little distance away, we could see another mother was running towards us, wailing and screaming, on her way to see her son's dead body. Auntyji closed her eyes, unable to see her pain and agony.

In the midst of the shouting and wailing, Auntyji broke into a loud cry, calling her son home, piercing the heart of the sky. There appeared a light on the horizon. But in my neighbourhood the day had started with darkness.

After that day, Auntyji was not seen by anyone. She had confined herself to her house. Neither was she an entertainer nor an agony aunt any more. She hardly spoke to anybody in the neighbourhood. We all wanted to share her grief and console her. But she did not let us trespass into her world of despair. Pain and agony had become her domain and she let nobody share it.

~

I had known Auntyji since the day she married Bald Uncle about three decades earlier. Her marriage was a unique one and was remembered with fondness for a long time. She was very beautiful but had married the ugliest person in our neighbourhood—this was something nobody felt comfortable with. She was in a different league as compared to her husband, who was bald, had two front teeth missing with an unfortunate stout physique. The couple was a total mismatch, so their marriage was a topic of discussion in every household.

I recalled the childhood fun us friends had, hiding in the lane behind Auntyji's house, where we would watch the froth from Lifebuoy soap gushing out of her bathroom. We would burst the bubbles forming from the froth and smell the aroma of the soap Auntyji used those days. We would count the bubbles for hours and try and break each other's record of bursting the most number of bubbles. This was our big entertainment.

After her shower, Auntyji would come out of the bathroom and sit on the veranda to dry her curly black hair in the sunshine. We would talk about her sense of style, curly hair and her bad luck marrying Bald Uncle. The gossip session and giggling would continue for hours, often making us lose track of the time. Every time I would walk behind her lane, I would stare at the veranda that Auntyji used to sit in and smile. When she entertained us, I would ask her, in private, 'Why did you marry Bald Uncle?' In response, she would burst into loud laughter and spank my back, saying: 'You must never ask Bald Uncle this question. He is smarter than Dharmendra. You do not know how much he loves, cares for and comforts me. What more does one need in life? One must never believe in outward appearances.'

Since the death of her son, the fragrant soap bubbles had stopped floating out of Auntyji's bathroom. Life had altogether stopped in her house. Most of us tried to convince her to come out in the open and become the same witty, chatty Auntyji again. But she would never leave her room, where she had kept dozens of her son's photos hanging on the walls. She had immersed herself in his thoughts and perhaps even felt his presence in the room. Her confinement was a punishment for the whole neighbourhood.

It was after about a year that Moulvi Sahib went to see her and found her lying dead in the bedroom.

The neighbourhood came out in panicked droves as if an earthquake had hit us all. Imam Sahib decided to bury Auntyji beside her son in Shaheed Mazar in Eidgah, which was the resting spot for hundreds of people killed by the security forces.

My neighbourhood had changed forever. It was never the same again without Auntyji.

RETURN

It sounded very strange in the present circumstances that Sadia, born and bred in the city, had decided to live in a distant village. The continuing turbulence had forced thousands of families to migrate from rural areas to the city, which was being considered somewhat safer. Instead, Sadia decided to leave her urban life behind and settle down in the remote border town of Kupwara.

The alleged atrocities committed by the security forces were said to be much higher in remote villages than in the cities, but the reality remained hidden from the press and international media due to the affected areas being so physically inaccessible. Yet, the city dwellers continued claiming that they had been facing much more as compared to the rural dwellers.

The newspapers were flooded with reports that the security forces had unleashed a reign of terror in the border villages, with total control over everything, including running streams, orchards and paddy fields. The cases of gross human rights violations were highlighted by some organizations, but not a single complaint had been looked into by the government so far.

Human rights organizations were not allowed to visit the places in question, though they had received reports of rape, torture and extra-judicial killings through local sources. Nothing had been done to stop the atrocities committed in the name of counter-insurgency. Unnamed mass graves abounded in the remote locations.

We never expected Sadia to move to a village unknown to her, and she never expected us to stop her. In fact, she wanted to move closer to the border, so she could continue the search for her missing son more intensely.

Sadia had told Baba that she had decided to spend the rest of her life in Kupwara. She had come to bid farewell to Baba, Muna and me. She had made up her mind to leave behind her husband, her family and her past. She had developed this unique characteristic—stubbornness—during childhood. Once she decided on something, she would never give up, even if it was impossible to achieve.

We believed Sadia was fortunate to have Hassan for a husband—he never objected or interfered in her handling of domestic issues. Even if Sadia referred to the day as night, Hassan would never question her about it. Sadia enjoyed being the queen of her household and Hassan made sure to give her every comfort in life. Could Hassan leave everything in the city to live in Kupwara as Sadia had suggested?

Sadia wanted her husband to wind up everything in the city—his business, house, relationships and associations, and memories. She wanted him to live with her because there was still some hope in her heart that they would together find their son, even though her husband had given up on the search long ago, when his wandering from Kashmir to Bangalore did not bring any result.

But Sadia did not want to give up till her last breath. Everything else had lost meaning for her.

Earlier, she had received news from a distant relative in Bandipora that her son had been designated as an area commander by the pro-Pakistan militant outfit Hizb-ul-Mujahideen. He had been spotted fighting with the forces in the border village and was known to have been injured in an encounter. We were told that he had taken refuge in one of the houses built close to the Line of Control. After that, he had disappeared again.

Sadia and her husband had visited almost every house in the border villages adjacent to Bandipora. They had even gone deep into the dense forests to examine the secret tracks of the militants, shown to them by a local Gujjar shepherd. They were able to access some hideouts near the Line of Control and even met dozens of militants, except her son.

Again, she received another message from the same shopkeeper, who had given her information earlier, that he had seen her son twice in Kupwara along with his militant group. She made a quick decision to go and look for him in every house, no matter how much time it took. For this search, she was ready to give up her whole life. It made us believe again that Aziz might be hiding in Kupwara. We couldn't ignore a mother's instinct.

Sadia had packed her essentials so as to last a few days till she settled down there properly. She had already managed to transfer herself to a local primary school in Kupwara. Baba told us that she had already hired a small room with a kitchen as lodging and was ready to leave.

The Azadi movement had snatched everything from Sadia: Aziz, who was lost in the wilderness, her comfortable position in life, because her husband was now without a business, and she was on the brink of losing her home, family and relationships.

For the last three years she had hardly slept. She would wake up in the middle of the night crying and screaming. Almost every night she had terrifying nightmares. Hassan took her to a psychiatrist for treatment. The drugs had little impact on her mind. Her situation became worse and the psychiatrist left her on her own.

We were all wondering how she would manage to live in a place she hardly knew. We were unable to change her mind.

Just like Aziz disappeared from her life, she was disappearing from ours.

~

Baba was continuously sending messages for Sadia through travellers, traders and bus drivers. If anyone mentioned going to Kupwara, Baba would write a few lines asking Sadia to return home and send the messages along with them.

Each time, however, Sadia would write back saying the same thing: 'At last, I have found peace for myself. This is a real different experience living the village life and doing something for people who are needy and desperate. They have become like my family. Please do not feel sorry for me. I have discovered a new me. And I am quite confident that my Aziz is somewhere near me.'

In only few months, she had become popular among villagers. One of the traders told us that she would start her day cleaning and sweeping the graves that buried the unknown boys who had been killed by the army at the time of crossing over to this side of the border from Pakistan.

Somebody had told Sadia that her son was also buried in one of the graves after a fatal fight with the security forces on the Line of Control a few years ago. 'All the graves are without names. They only have numbers carved into them because nobody knows the identities of the deceased,' the villager revealed.

Sadia had made her new world her own. The local people had given her the new name of 'Saidamach', instead of Sadia, out of affection.

One early morning, while Sadia was teaching girls the Quran in the school compound of Kupwara, her son was watching her silently for many hours. The disappeared son had reappeared. He was listening to her *qirat*, watching her talk to girls, remembering her every gesture and looking for the changes she may have undergone in these past few years. Aziz was surprised to see his mother teaching in a remote village. Had he known earlier, he would have come to meet her. He wondered when she had come to teach in this school. He kept looking at her from his hiding spot behind the big tree.

After Sadia finished teaching the girls, she stood up and was returning to her room, when she heard a whisper: 'Mummy.'

Sadia stopped abruptly. She felt a chill run down her spine and looked around the graveyard, which was as silent as death. There was nothing visible except the graves. She wiped the sweat from her face with her chador, which she had covered herself in from head to toe. She started walking again, thinking maybe she was losing her mind. Upon taking another few steps towards the house, she heard it again: 'Mummy.'

She turned quickly back and looked around the big tree. There seemed to be nobody in sight. She came back towards the school, looking at the graves.

'Mummy.'

In a frenzy, Sadia was turning her head in every direction. Her heart was beating fast and her palms were clammy.

Aziz finally came out from behind the tree and stood at a distance, smiling at her.

Sadia, in turn, saw a boy resembling Aziz standing a few yards away from her. It was hard to believe the sight. She rubbed her eyes as if clearing her vision. She kept looking at him. She opened and closed her eyes repeatedly to confirm she was awake.

'Yes, there is my boy. He is smiling at me.'

Aziz was tall and bony like his father. But his dishevelled hair and slight beard on his long face had turned him into a different person today.

Sadia stopped for a moment and tried to pull herself together. 'Aziz!' She leapt towards him, but her legs were not moving. The few yards between them had become a mile. She ran with all her might.

Aziz came running towards her. Sadia touched his face repeatedly, as if making sure that he was indeed real. She touched his body, his hair. 'Yes, he is real. He has come back,' she muttered to herself.

She had no strength left to hug him. 'My son has come back.' She fell to the ground, eyes fixed on him so as not to lose sight of him even for a second, lest he disappear again into the thick forests. Aziz sat in front of her, took her in his long, bony arms, and kissed and hugged her like he was the parent and Sadia the child.

Her sobs were heard everywhere: in the village, the forests and even the four corners of the valley. Mother and son stayed like that for such a long time that villagers assembled around them, watching them in amazement, tears rolling down their eyes.

Some people were saying to each other proudly, 'Can you now believe her powers? She has got her son back from the grave. She is a real dervish.'

'My child has come back to me. I knew my God would never let me down. Nobody believed me. Baba lost faith in me. He had lost faith in motherhood. Nobody knows the power of a mother. Everybody wanted me to forget you. How stupid of them, telling me to die without seeing my son. Why didn't they recognize the power and strength of a mother? I could get you back from the grave.' She kept him close, his head on her chest, and Aziz was worried to listen to her irregular heartbeat.

Sadia was overwhelmed with joy. She was excited and requested every villager: 'Please tell my Baba that my son has come back. Tell him to learn to believe a mother, tell him Aziz has come back. Please inform my husband, who has lost his eyesight, that his son has returned. Tell him he will be able to see again once he sees his son.'

Her tears were like the torrential rain, about which there was a saying in Kashmir: 'This rain induces new life even in dead and decayed crops.'

Both mother and son remained sitting on the wet grass in the heavy rain, making up for the lost five long years.

That night, nobody slept much in the remote Kupwara out of sheer excitement. Everyone had come to visit Saidamach and talk about her miracle. They were all praising her and the powers she had demonstrated in broad daylight.

Sadia's husband left everything in the city and bought a new house in Kupwara. He ultimately closed down his business and went to live in the village for the rest of his life.

The reunion between mother and son had become a headline in every newspaper. This raised a new hope for the countless mothers whose sons had disappeared during the ongoing movement.

People came to our house to hear Sadia's story, which had reached every corner of the valley. Everybody believed in her divine power, but I believed in the divine power of a mother.

SUDDEN

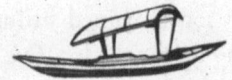

Normally, wedding preparations take three to four months in our community, but we had to start late because of the renovations going on in the upper storey of our ancestral house. Now it had been further delayed. We had been under security crackdown for the past two days. All the roads and streets were closed, and all our men were held up from dawn to dusk. Faiza's in-laws had no idea that we had been caught up in a security siege. And nobody was willing to put off the marriage either. There was only one day left for the reception of the *baraat* when the crackdown was lifted.

We jump-started the wedding preparations from the very next moment itself, so that we could finish all the required work and be ready to receive the bridegroom in time. All across the neighbourhood, however, the mood was, as usual, sombre and gloomy because of the exhaustion and humiliation people felt during this constant state of siege and searches conducted by the security forces. My in-laws wanted to complete the nikah ceremony as there was no time, nor any inclination, for bigger celebrations—and, mostly, no time left for major preparations.

Earlier, Asad and his brothers had thought of celebrating Faiza's marriage with lot of jubilation and pomp. Being the last marriage in the family, they wanted to make it a big and memorable event, but with the bleak atmosphere encompassing everyone all around, nobody dared to demand such revelry now. My in-laws were on their toes all day to do whatever possible to prepare for the baraat that had commenced from the groom's house a few hours ago.

After Faiza returned from Jammu following the Ikhwani's death, she was still petrified and would stay confined to her room. She had stopped living a carefree life and did not lecture us on philosophy any more. She showed no interest in her own wedding celebrations, behaving like a mindless zombie following orders.

I thought she would insist on seeing the groom before accepting the marriage proposal, but she raised no such concerns. Who he was or what his status was something she was least bothered with. She had accepted him as her life partner without raising any questions. Perhaps she knew he would be a hundred times better than the Ikhwani who had proposed to her without even considering his life and 'achievements'.

Faiza was the loved child in the family, and she had full faith in her brothers. She was confident that they would never let her down. Most of all, she was a strong believer in destiny.

The young girls of our neighbourhood came over to prepare the bride for the ceremony. They encircled Faiza, touched up her make-up and made small alterations to her wedding dress. It was like watching a film at double speed.

Faiza seemed composed and calm now. She had let the girls do whatever they wanted to do with her hair, face and wedding dress. She did not object to any demand made of her and gave the girls free rein to transform her into a fairy queen.

Her silence was tearing me apart. I wished I could read her mind, but I couldn't. Was she happy or cursing her fate?

Faiza looked wonderful and elegant in her bridal attire. She forcefully smiled at everybody, and was constantly being hugged and kissed by the guests, who were offering presents in cash and kind. The gifts were piling up on the shelves in the hall. Nobody seemed keen on opening the gift boxes because the time was really running out.

Muna was glued to her, not leaving her for a second. That made me a bit worried. I did not know how I would tackle him once Faiza left for her new home.

My son seemed lost, as if he was acutely feeling the pain of losing Faiza. He was only four years old, but seemed confused with all the hustle and bustle. He demanded that the bride take him to her room and play games with him. Faiza whispered something funny in his ear and soon they were both laughing.

The house, the neighbour's hall and the colourful makeshift tent in the lawn quickly became packed with guests, relatives and friends. It was a miracle that all the invitees had attended the ceremony even in this highly charged atmosphere.

The male relatives had started standing in rows on both sides of the long decorated street for the reception of the baraat. The bridegroom was only a few hundred metres away from our decorated lane. Women came running out of the house and held each other in a chain, singing traditional songs praising the bridegroom. Some children threw firecrackers in the air, a custom to welcome the groom. Asad had strictly advised them not to use firecrackers, but who would think of curbing merriment during merry occasions? The atmosphere was jubilant and the celebrations were at an all-time high.

In the midst of all the singing and the firecrackers, there came the sound of shots being fired. We all exchanged glances as if asking each other, 'Is that a shot being fired or a firecracker?'

There were a few more firing shots. All of us froze at that moment, silent and still, looking in the direction from which the firing shots were coming.

The firing suddenly stopped and started again. So did my breathing. There was a long silence now. We were all terrified and worried about the bridegroom. We heard a huge explosion followed by pin-drop silence. The guests ran in panic inside the house. Asad's Bhabhi was beating her chest. Imam Sahib was rushing towards the backyard, while children were clinging to their mothers, who were crying and screaming in terror.

Asad, Muna, Faiza, my brothers-in-law and me, we all started running to the point where the bridegroom was supposed to enter our lane. Some firing shots were again heard from a short distance away. Still, we ran wildly to see if we could spot the groom and his *baraatis*.

Asad was running barefoot. Muna ran after him. I ran after Muna. Faiza ran after me. And the rest of the relatives ran after the bride to stop her from going further. Faiza was dragging along her heavy studded wedding dupatta with great effort and pain. We were screaming and asking around if anyone knew about the bridegroom.

'Have you seen a bridegroom and his baraatis?'

There was whispering heard from another lane. The eerie silence was scaring us. After about fifteen minutes of wailing, from the opposite direction, a column of soldiers was coming towards us, warning us not to run in that particular direction.

'There are terrorists hiding in the house and it is under the army's siege. It is very dangerous, go back to your house,' shouted one of the soldiers.

Despite the soldiers' warning, Asad kept running to look for the groom. At the end of the lane he disappeared. We waited for him at the corner of our decorated street. It was a long, painful wait. It seemed as if he had been gone for ages. Nothing was in sight. Only firing shots were heard from a distance.

At last, we saw Asad coming back towards us. He had covered his head in his hands and we could not make any sense of that. We prayed to God: 'Save us, save our honour. Don't turn our happiness into tragedy. Have mercy on us. Have mercy on Faiza.'

All of us were eagerly waiting for Asad to deliver some news to put us out of our misery and tell us the bridegroom was safe. My mouth had gone dry and my heart was pounding. My throat became so sour that I had to put my fingers inside my mouth to relieve my irritation.

Asad took Faiza in his arms, kissed her and said, 'They are fine, the groom is okay, they will be here any minute now. Come, let us go inside and make preparations for their reception,' said Asad, too emotionally charged to talk further.

Faiza took my hand in hers and pressed it very hard. She was cold like ice.

Asad looked deep into my eyes and gave me a faint smile. *He has grown much older in these few moments,* I thought. He tapped my shoulder as if reassuring me that everything would be fine.

I placed my head on Faiza's shoulder. I wanted to cry out loud, because otherwise I felt my heart would burst open. Faiza hugged me and we both wept so loudly that all our relatives encircled us. The women started singing traditional songs in praise of the bride and bridegroom.

Asad revealed to his brother that the bridegroom had been saved by the same group of soldiers who had killed Moulvi Sahib's son-in-law. It was unbelievable. Could it be that the same people who had butchered Fareeda's husband some time ago had also saved Faiza's groom that day?

My teacher Madam Rashmiji used to say, 'Believe what you want to believe. The present is real and true. The past is gone and the future is unpredictable. So it is only fate that plays strange. It gives different shocks at different times. Better to not dwell on the tragic moments in life. Move forward with new experiences.'

1990: The station director of Doordarshan is killed by militants for his pro-government media policy in Kashmir.

ANOTHER MURDER

Madam Rashmiji was every student's favourite teacher at school. And I was her only favourite student among all my classmates. The day she saw me, she took me under her wing, making a huge, lasting impact on my impressionable mind.

My every action in school was praised by her. It was because of her that I took part in debates, symposiums, gymnastics and poetry writing. She would gloat with pride, saying, 'You are a gifted child, born with talent. You know you can do great things in life if you keep your priorities in order.'

Soon, my classmates realized her affection for me and how devoted she was to my personality development. I became the target of their jealousy. They would leave no chance to criticize me. But Madam Rashmiji took no notice of their attitude. When my classmates would leave me out of the hockey team, my beloved teacher would get me back on the team in the matter of a few minutes. When they were hesitant to include me in the picnic trip to Riyasi in Jammu, for no obvious reason, Madam Rashmiji got the whole trip cancelled by the school principal.

I did not know what had made her so fond of me. What I did know was that she had thought highly of my English handwriting: 'What lovely handwriting, running and symmetrical. Good evaluation techniques.' This was her first comment to me.

She would take my notebook, display it to the whole class and make the girls write in the way I did. She wanted me to stand out and be conspicuous. Instead, my peer group singled me out to my dismay. They made me feel like a pariah at times because of my closeness to the teacher. Sometimes, I wished that we were not as close.

Being in Madam Rashmiji's class raised my spirits and boosted my confidence. But at the same time it also made me suffer in isolation. My treatment at school would remind me of the situation I often faced at home, when Baba would pamper me by doing all my chores, which made my sisters extremely cross with me. They would start whispering the moment I would come out of my room. Only Baba would enjoy the look on their faces.

My teacher was the female version of Baba, playing out the same tactics in school. She became my role model without meaning to, even though I had no idea what the word meant. She was very simple, elegant and confident. And to acquire all her qualities became my sole aim in life.

She guided me and helped me achieve new heights in my educational career. If there was a cultural event, she made me organize it. If there was any dignitary or political personality visiting our school, I was the first one to be introduced to them. And if the school was required to send students to participate in inter-state debates or symposiums, my name would appear at the top of the list.

My personality development had gone from strength to strength, and my mind was opening up to new ideas and horizons. At the end of my school years, I was adjudged the best student of the year, and was the only student who received dozens of awards for excelling in debates and symposiums, and for organizing events in the school.

When I was about to complete my matriculation and leave for college, my teacher was about to be sent to another posting somewhere in Delhi.

'Madam Rashmiji will be leaving us soon. She had asked for a transfer to Delhi because she wants to stay close to her husband. I know many of you will not be happy to see her off, but we have to arrange for a memorable farewell for her,' our principal announced in the morning assembly.

Most of my classmates were watching me; I felt as if my face had been drained of its colour and charm instantly. I was looking at her, and she kept smiling at me, as though saying, 'Somebody will replace me very soon. And you should be prepared for surprises and shocks in real life, because you cannot stick to one person forever. Keep moving on or things will lose their charm soon.'

I believed our school was losing the best English teacher it ever had, while I was losing my role model, guide and mentor.

I went to see Madam Rashmiji off at the tourist reception centre along with her smart, ginger-haired husband, whose smile was like the first ray of sunshine after chilly weather. She was sitting close to him and seemed very happy. She caught sight of me and disembarked from the bus. She came to me and hugged me, repeating her parting words that I was to learn to fix a target in my life and work hard to achieve it.

'Never let others run your life. Be your own master and decide what you want to do. Work hard to achieve great heights in your life. Never give up your fight easily. You have a long way to go to cross the hurdles that are already there. I have faith that you will never let me down. When you reach the ultimate peak of success in your life, people will remember me and admire me for being the best teacher of the best student,' she said, having drafted a beautiful roadmap for my life.

We bid farewell to each other. My eyes were filled with tears, while hers were filled with the dreams and aspirations she had for me.

She wiped away my tears and again took me in her arms. Her smile cheered me up. Madam Rashmiji was the one person who prepared me to climb the tallest ladder in my life; she showed me the way to reach the success point, so that I would one day be able to tell her that I had not let her down.

We kept hugging until the bus driver blew his horn to warn the straggling passengers to board the bus quickly. Her husband was looking from the bus window at his wife—perhaps thinking about the bond of love student and teacher had developed for each other.

After Madam Rashmiji's departure, nobody was able to replace her, neither in the college nor in the university. Every time I passed my examination, I would yearn to find her and tell her that I had climbed one more step on my way to success, without losing even an ounce of my confidence. I did participate in amazing, memorable events in the university; once I was on stage, I would talk about her to the audience with moist eyes. She had such a huge impact on me that I could not imagine any aspect of my life that had not been shaped by her.

However, the reality was that she was nowhere around me, physically. When her memories were just about to gradually fade away, she reappeared in my life with a big surprise.

~

The morning transmission of the radio station had been recently restructured—it now broadcasted more devotional programmes, with an emphasis on Islam and its teachings. The intention was to create a sense of belonging among the listeners vis-à-vis the state, and make them believe that the station cared for the majority of the population and their sentiments. The programme content included Quranic verses and devotional music in praise of the Prophet and his caliphs. However, because of some factual mistakes in the Islamic dates, the programmes did not take off.

Instead of appreciation, it had raised an uproar among the listeners and the station had been flooded with dozens of complaints. It was general perception that the government had started the process of brainwashing the masses with the intention of curbing their sentiments towards Azadi.

The head of the state of Jammu and Kashmir took personal cognizance of the matter and informed the central information ministry to transfer the director of the organization for his ineffectiveness and insensitiveness.

All my colleagues were waiting to discuss the situation as well as the measures we could use to calm the listeners. I was quite sure that many heads would roll. In those days, the punishment was in the form of a transfer to the remote Andaman and Nicobar Islands. Both islands were cut off from the mainland, so life in general was very difficult there.

The meeting was convened by the station director; it went on for a few hours without any consensus on how to change the format of the programmes again.

While we were deliberating on the issue, a smart ginger-haired man suddenly entered the conference room. Accompanying the gentleman was his wife—Madam Rashmiji! The existing head of the station made a quick announcement that the ginger-haired man—Mr Shukla—had been sent by the information ministry to take charge with immediate effect. However, he did not say whether his job was safe or he had been made redundant.

Mr Shukla looked keenly at me, perhaps trying to recall if he had met me somewhere earlier. We all stood up to welcome him and his wife.

I was so overwhelmed that I rushed towards them to embrace my teacher and find out if she still carried the same warmth that had been the treasure of my life.

She walked towards me with the same affection, took me into her arms and asked me many questions about my life and career since she had exited the scene. She introduced me to her husband, thus raising my profile again, saying, 'She is the talented girl I used to talk about all these years. Can you believe she has become a household name in the valley! I knew there was a journalist living inside her, but I never knew she would achieve such success. A Kashmiri girl in the media—this is like a dream come true! I am indeed proud of being your teacher. You have made my day today.' Her husband, my new boss was smiling at both of us and looking on in amazement.

I did meet Madam Rashmiji on many occasions but I also maintained distance, because I did not want to be in the same situation I had faced in school.

The moment Mr Shukla took over as the new head of the station, he started to assess the broadcast programme content. He reshuffled the structure, programmes and introduced new talent to attract the listeners. Mr Shukla assigned me the toughest job—that of producing the news and current affairs programme, which was very difficult and tricky, given the volatile times we lived in. At times, he gave me an idea for a documentary feature or sent me to interview political leaders who had been hiding since the emergence of the armed struggle and were on the hit list of gunmen. To meet political personalities was to write one's own death warrant, but he did not let me show any reluctance.

It was significant in the sense that these leaders were the only lot that praised the government at a time when the whole population was demanding freedom from it. The majority of our listeners were criticising the radio for maligning the Azadi movement.

Mr Shukla would boast about my inputs in the morning meetings, in the presence of all the other officers, making them acknowledge my contribution. However, I would hate my involvement, because most of the programmes were either praising the government or bashing the Azadi wave. Impartial and independent journalism still remained a dream for me.

Yet, after a long time, I had found a thrill in doing challenging assignments again, including on-the-spot recordings of events across the valley. That gave me an insight into the situation in the remote area where the media did not even exist. I tried to highlight the basic issues of the population to play it safe. However, the basic issues were so many that the thirty-minute fixed slot in the evening transmission was hardly enough to accommodate them.

Sadly, Mr Shukla's efforts to produce programmes matching the people's needs and aspirations did not bring any result. People did not believe a single word we broadcasted, and claims and counterclaims were considered false. Militant bashing was deemed counterproductive, and radio employees were treated as anti-movement elements. Our listeners were more interested in Hindi film songs than news and current affairs programmes. Bollywood songs were as popular as ever. The people's only reason to listen to news bulletins on the radio was to keep track of casualties and of the changes that kept happening in the administration frequently.

Some of my colleagues claimed that they had even received death threats from militant organizations if they did not quit the job.

At the start of the insurgency, all central government offices were closed when most of the Pandit employees left the valley. Had there not been a few Muslim employees, the radio station would have been dead like the other departments. It was because of these few employees that things kept moving.

Mr Shukla did realize the dilemma the Muslim employees were in. He made it a rule that all his staff members would be escorted by security personnel from their homes to the office and vice versa. Every evening, he waited to hear from the security department that his staff had reached home safely and then only did he leave office himself, with full security, for his own residence. It was not a good idea to run through neighbourhoods with police escort—that made us more vulnerable and put us at a higher risk. Due to this, many employees preferred to stay at home forever. But because I preferred to come in to the office, I would disembark from the official vehicle before my lane, a little distance away, so that the neighbours would not sight me with armed escort.

Due to some technical fault in the transmitter, the studios were shut for the day. So we had to stay late to record the last segment of the programme, which had to go on-air early morning the following day. Our driver and security personnel were waiting for us in the duty room to drop us home. Mr Shukla had left earlier to attend some religious function at his residence, which was heavily guarded by the security forces.

I was about to finish when the duty officer rushed into the live studio. He was breathless, and was shaking and sweating. 'Mr Shukla has been shot dead outside his residence. We have to broadcast this breaking news!' No sooner had he announced the dreadful news that he banged his head on the heavy door of the studio and fell to the wooden floor. He became unconscious and could not give us any more details.

I rushed to the duty room and contacted the police control room immediately. The official at the desk confirmed that Mr Shukla had been killed, adding that he had been pronounced 'dead on arrival' at the hospital. 'He was shot four times in the head and neck. He would have died on the spot, I imagine. It has been confirmed that he was shot dead by some militant. The police are investigating the details.' The official stated the distressing details in a very casual tone, as if he was talking about a routine incident of violence. He hung up with a big thud.

First, I could not breathe for few seconds and then soon started choking on the lump in my throat. I did not sit on a chair, but on the floor in the duty room. The floor was cold and felt soothing to my inflamed body. I was dumbstruck with grief, like my other colleagues, and nobody knew what to do and where to go.

In a few minutes, however, the bizarre sight of my other colleagues running wild in the illuminated corridor of the building greeted us. They were frenzied, as if some beasts had been let loose to hound them.

Some were outraged, angry and were scolding the gunmen, the government and the radio station for their helplessness. Some soldiers entered the studio in amazement. The technical staff came rushing to get them out, but the soldiers ignored them and kept watching from the announcer to the machines all around. A few soldiers went close to him and searched underneath the various recording equipment. The announcer shrunk into his chair, looking around in fear. He was supposed to make an announcement for another programme as the on-air tape was running out. But he could not. The soldiers behind him were whispering something. He played another tape without an announcement. I could do nothing to comfort my announcer and was unable to get the soldiers out. The technical staff summoned the engineer-in-charge, who succeeded in convincing the soldiers to leave the studio.

I could not stop thinking about my beloved teacher and how she would be bearing this tragedy all alone.

~

The following day, early in the morning, I was at her doorstep. She was alone in her room, crying silently. Her two little kids were sleeping in the adjacent room, with no knowledge of how their lives had been irrevocably changed by someone they did not know. There were two security personnel at the main gate, stationed there to protect the person whose dead body was lying in the hospital mortuary. Another two guards stood at the entranceway watching how Madam Rashmiji was enduring the pain and agony all alone.

Her friends had not dared to come by and console her—they were afraid of those who had killed her husband—and were only looking through the corners of their curtain-drawn windows. They could feel her pain, but they had lost the courage to come out openly and share her grief. The movement had shown its ugly face—or maybe some had made it so ugly that even the initiators and pioneers of the movement were becoming ashamed of themselves. People had become less human and lost the plot.

When Madam Rashmiji saw me, she burst into tears, as if she had been waiting for somebody to listen to her screaming. I did not dare to look into her eyes. There was turmoil, there was terror and there was anger. I felt ashamed, sick and pathetic. Every time she looked at me, I avoided eye contact with her. Some guilt was eating into me.

I felt responsible for her husband's death. I did not know why.

She was the one who had instilled confidence in me all those years ago, and I was the one who took her confidence. She taught me the lessons of life, and I gave her the taste of death and destruction. She made me stand out, and I deprived her of her conspicuous happiness. I was responsible for her pain, agony and loss. Somewhere, in some part of my brain, I believed that whoever had killed her husband was somehow linked to me. There was some connection between the killing of people and the Azadi movement.

I sat beside her, not daring to console her. I did not want to sound like a hypocrite.

She placed her head on my shoulders and her sobs became louder. I was unable to breathe or scream. I just could not. My whole body had turned numb—cold and stone. I felt suffocated. I had let her down. I had shattered her dreams, her aspirations and her world. My Azadi destroyed her home, her future and her children. I never dreamt that my Azadi would be soaked in blood and destruction.

I wanted to run away from her, but I got lost in the unravelling deep, dark places of my memory.

I was roaming around the corridors of the radio station.

~

Joining the radio was not an easy decision, at least not for a Muslim girl who had always watched relatives raise their eyebrows every time she went to school or left her house.

Mine was a traditional family—women were meant to clean the house, please their husbands and bear children. I had never seen my mother look straight into Baba's eyes, let alone argue with him. The change happened when Sadia was born and Baba pledged to send his daughters to school against the wishes of his family. Only my mother supported him—she couldn't have gone against her husband. Mother used to tell us these stories in private.

It was a bumpy road because I had to fight so many battles. The situation was more difficult for Baba, who had to listen to the abuses of his relatives for the rest of his life. They found his actions disgraceful.

The radio was considered a despicable profession for Muslim girls. Baba's family disowned him when he sent my sisters and me to study further. And when he allowed me to work in radio, it was a stormy time for his traditional family; it left them shattered and agitated.

In the 1970s, only a few women singers and actors had dared to enter the premises of this huge organization called the radio station. For the rest of the female population in the valley, this was a forbidden city. The few girls who joined the station had no respect or value in our society. They were considered promiscuous like prostitutes, or people would treat them like clowns who could only make you laugh, no matter how much they were crying inside. Nobody gave two hoots about them, their emotions or their place in the society. The treatment meted out to female artists and singers by society was much more humiliating and insulting. Resultantly, they had no role to play in our social affairs and did not comprise the social fabric. Any girl joining the radio faced serious repercussions with respect to her marriage or status in the family.

I was neither a singer nor a clown. I was class-one officer, having successfully competed in the union public service examination board. However, to my relatives, there was no difference between me and the other artists. All my relatives, neighbours and friends started to belittle me because I had let them down by joining an organization with a bad reputation.

It was only Baba who stood like a rock behind me. My anxiety often made me think of quitting the media, but he would not let me do it and would instead encourage me to walk with my head held high in the presence of hostile relatives and neighbours.

'Those who despise you today will bow before you tomorrow, my daughter. Do not ever make hasty decisions. And do not let other people decide on your career. Decide yourself. You can quit at any point, if you think it is not right profession for you,' Baba would say, citing examples of the great people of the world.

It was very difficult for Sarla—the only female officer in the radio station at the time—to accept me. She took my joining the radio to mean that I was outsmarting her and trespassing into her domain.

I wished Baba would come to office to keep me standing on my own feet, like he used to do in presence of my relatives, because Sarla was so powerful and manipulative that I had once even almost gone to the extent of tendering my resignation.

Initially, Sarla would fight with me on petty matters in front of my colleagues. She would laugh, ridicule and make insulting comments to incite me. I kept silent. Then she wrote reports criticizing my programmes, made sarcastic comments during the programme meetings and mobilized groups to campaign against me. At times, it felt like the whole station was against me. I would see a strange expression in their eyes, as if they wanted to stay far away from me.

Sarla once stooped so low that she actually made an abusive comment about my religion too. I still did not react. I just kept going on without antagonizing her. My best strategy was to not give her any chance for a confrontation. However, she kept fighting me and did not stop her campaign to shunt me out of the radio station. I was always on my guard and kept strengthening my defence mechanism.

Sarla's ammunition of anger and her missile system of hatred lasted only two years. She soon tired of the effort and fell short of weaponry. In the end, she caved in and acknowledged my resilience and patience, which had remained unaffected till her defeat. She came around and offered me her friendship. It was a new chapter of my life.

In only few weeks' time, we became so close to each other that our friendship had become big news in the station, and then the gossip crossed the concrete walls of the radio station too. We laughed, shared secrets and enjoyed the best time of our lives together. We even exchanged the details of our hate campaign against each other in the days when we were still hostile to each other. From cooking to watching movies, we did everything together.

One day, she trusted me with a horrible secret, which left me speechless. I started keeping away from her, though she kept coming close to me. The secret was sacred for her, but a sin for me. I had never come across such a situation in the past.

Sarla's situation reminded me of the 'Parmeshwari case'—of a girl whose love affair with a Muslim boy had put the entire valley on edge on account of the underlying communal tensions. However, her affair was more dangerous than Parmeshwari's.

Kashmir was a secular society, but not to the extent that inter-caste or inter-religious marriages could happen easily and without uproar. Only a handful of prominent families could afford to take this risk. However, they were never deemed a part of the social fabric.

I knew that Sarla's affair could tear this society apart if anyone got wind of it. She was in love with a married Muslim man. Her disclosure made me restless and deprived me of sleep for days. This incendiary news would set the valley on fire at a time when there was already so much distrust between the two communities. More importantly, my family would not be able to bear the shame of my being a friend of a Hindu girl who was having an affair with a married Muslim man.

I wished I had not joined the radio and had never gotten close to Sarla. I did not want to lose Sarla or her friendship, but I could not carry on with her under the circumstances, as it would ruin everything I had worked for. This realization was a severe blow that made me crumble like a pack of cards. I knew I had to either lose Sarla or my own reputation. And if I did not intervene, the valley would face another bout of communal upheaval. So I had to make a difficult choice.

Sarla had an affair with a married man belonging to a reputed family. He worked in Delhi and, as it turned out, was a close friend of my teacher's husband, Mr Shukla. The affair had been going on for years. They had found a way to spend time and enjoy romantic evenings together.

Sarla's lover would come to Kashmir on a duty tour in the summer and spend quality time with her in a hotel. The wife of the Muslim officer knew nothing about the romance her husband was enjoying with a Hindu girl half his age. He would book them a cosy room in a five-star hotel on the banks of the Dal Lake.

I kept pondering over this relationship. Why did Sarla have to choose a married Muslim man? How dangerous it could be if people came to know about it. Sarla could lose her life and the Muslim lover everything.

'Doesn't your family object to this relationship?' I once asked Sarla.

'I have no family or relatives. My parents died in a bus accident on the national highway when I was only four years old. I live with my aunt, who paid for my education. She became a widow at the age of twenty-five. She's always lost in her own despair and so has no clue about my relationship. She does not care whether I live or die. She is half dead most of the time. I have been all alone since I was a child,' she confessed, her eyes reflecting pain and misery.

'Who cares what I do or who I talk to? He is the only person I have in my life. He loves me, cares for me and values me. Don't you think I too deserve a little bit of happiness in this cruel world? Why should I care for other people? Has anybody cared for me?' she said, anger and disgust writ large on her face.

'I am so sorry to hear about your parents. I asked you about them many times, but you never told me what had really happened to them. I didn't realize that you had been on your own since childhood. Indeed, it would have been hard for you in such circumstances when everything around you was in a shambles. I wish I could do something for you that could ease your pain. I still think you are involved with a man with the most baggage—a married man! You are young, beautiful and smart, but vulnerable too. He is a father figure to you, but he seems to have been exploiting your isolation, or your need to be with someone. That is unfair and unjustifiable. I might sound cruel to you, but if you put yourself in his wife's position, you would also feel ashamed. He has betrayed her trust also. Don't you think he is making a fool out of both of you?'

'You know nothing about how hard it is to be on your own. I have seen the cruelty of people. I have faced their emotionless faces. And I have stayed awake many nights because I was all alone in the house. My friend, I wanted protection from every perverse gazing eye, from the people who knocked at my door in the middle of the night. I wanted to share my fear and grief with someone who would listen to me. There was nobody except him, who spent dark nights with me to make me feel comfortable. He arranged for a police guard to stay outside my house. I feel protected in his arms. I feel safe when I walk on the road. I do not care whether he is a Muslim or a Hindu. What matters is that he loves and values me. Beggars cannot be choosers. I found peace and refuge in his arms. There was no Prince Charming waiting for me. It was only he who stood like a rock behind me. Otherwise, I would have fallen into an abyss.'

I had touched a nerve. Her wounds started oozing again. She kicked everything that came in her way. She became hysterical and kept sobbing.

I felt shallow inside. I had no right to shame her. However, I still wanted to tell her that she was treading on the wrong path. I was left with no courage to soothe her pain.

It was not easy for me to keep her secret. It was too heavy a burden to carry.

~

After having stayed away from her at least for a year, one early morning, I found Sarla at my house. She had come by to invite me to her wedding in Delhi. I was eagerly waiting to know whom she was marrying. My nervousness was written all over my face and I did not blink my eyes once. She gave me a broad smile and said, 'Don't worry, I am not marrying my Muslim lover. I am getting married to a Pandit boy.'

I quickly opened the invitation card to confirm what she had just said. I felt a wave of relief. Sarla was marrying a Hindu boy. Out of curiosity, I asked her about the relationship with the Muslim man and how she had ended it.

'Mr Shukla is the man behind this entire affair. He helped me end this relationship. I myself had felt that this relationship would never let me live in peace, even for a single moment. It would keep reminding me that something bad would happen in my life if I committed such a blunder. Mr Shukla made him understand what impact this relationship could have on the valley, even though my lover was ready to leave his family for me. It would have ripped the two communities apart. I could hardly bear the thought.'

She seemed calm and peaceful. 'All the wedding arrangements have been done by Mr Shukla and his wife. Mr Shukla is a messiah for me. He saved me, my honour and the valley.'

'And he saved my friendship with you,' I said, laughing, and we hugged each other.

The story of my friendship with Sarla ended soon after her marriage, when she left the valley permanently.

~

I heard a loud scream from the adjacent room. Madam Rashmiji ran towards her daughter, who was crying loudly due to fright. She had had a nightmare and hadn't found her mother beside the bed. 'Papa! Papa!' She was calling her father. Her mother took her into her lap and cuddled her saying, 'Papa is coming.' My heart skipped a beat.

I left them in their haunted house and rushed back to the office to help in arranging Mr Shukla's cremation. I felt deeply hurt, but I had nobody to share my grief with, because it was something that was best kept a secret. To mourn a Hindu's assassination was forbidden in the present circumstances. It was very hard to find even one Brahmin to perform the Hindu cremation rituals, except for a few Muslims, since nobody wanted to step forth.

The following day, all the morning papers had labelled Mr Shukla an agent of the government who was bent upon sabotaging the freedom movement. The print media had referred to a few programmes being broadcast on the radio as anti-Azadi, and had warned other employees to refrain from such practices or face the same consequences.

HOPE

I had failed to understand why Asad was so happy over the fact that I had to leave my job and stay at home after Mr Shukla's killing. Did he think I would concentrate more on the household now, or had he had enough of my journalism? Would he be able to bear all the expenditures on his own? Perhaps he had not thought about that yet. And I never raised the issue. Talking about money was always a very sensitive subject for Asad. For me the golden rule was to watch in silence.

Asad's brothers and their wives were pressuring me to give up my job because of the threats central government employees were receiving after Mr Shukla's assassination, but I had received no direct warning from anybody so far. Baba was not in favour of my quitting the job.

Asad was wavering, and would sometimes take his family's side when he was discussing me with them. Then he would backtrack and say that I should continue at the radio station when he was alone with Baba. I was confused and frustrated like him, torn between his family and my Baba's disagreements.

I was indecisive as usual. Nobody bothered to ask me my opinion, which hardly counted in this patriarchal society. It was against the custom to let women decide any matter, even if she was the sole breadwinner of the family. I left them to discuss, argue and fight over the issue.

I decided to talk to Tahira, who was younger than me, but was very clever, self-centred and thought beyond what was expected of someone her age. Her advice was all that I wanted before I implemented my plan. Tahira had bothered to come to office only once or twice after Shiasta's murder, but she was the first employee to get her salary on time and nobody had ever noticed her absence.

It was very painful for me: the moment I left home, my neighbours would stare at me. And when I stayed indoors, they thought it was because the gunmen had threatened me. Upon catching sight of me, they would start whispering and give me scornful looks, as if I had committed a sin in being an employee of the central government. Either way, it was torturous and humiliating.

I felt nervous initially. Soon, I realized that I had become paranoid, or perhaps it was the case that my personality had grown too melancholic due to the prevailing situation. I was suspicious of everyone.

~

Tahira was not at home. I was told by her mother that she had moved to Jammu along with her children. Because of the closure of the schools in the valley for a long time now, she made her children join schools in Jammu. Her old mother was looking after the house and property comprising a few rented shops. The irony was that Tahira had not bothered to inform me or the office of her departure. I felt disappointed and dejected. Was there something the matter with me that it was always I who was left behind repeatedly by friends, foes and colleagues?

I became desperate to talk to somebody and seek their advice on quitting my job. But there was nobody—not even my sisters, whom I had not seen for the last seven months. As Asad used to say, 'Everybody is moving forward. There is nothing wrong if your sisters do not come to see you. Relationships change with the time.' Regardless of whether it was 'moving forward' or detachment, the situation was hard for me to accept. Something strange was happening.

~

It was in the beginning of 1993 that I decided to visit the radio station, without caring about the neighbours' glances and whispers. I walked with my head held high. I laughed at my courage and confidence. It was something new in me that had made me walk the streets without fear or shame.

There was heavy traffic on the road. Lal Chowk had regained some of its hustle and bustle and people were everywhere, shopping for Eid. Everyone was already in a festive mood. Droves had come out like processions queuing up outside the bakery, the butcher's and the textile shops. It looked as if normalcy had returned. Long lines of mobile shops were flooded with customers on the Hari Singh High Street. Besides the locals, the security personnel too were shopping for embroidery and dry fruits. Had it not been for the enormous number of security personnel on the road or their bunkers, Lal Chowk would look like it had regained its pre-movement glory. Money was being spent like water, and there was a race to buy and sell and trade amid the heavy traffic. Civilians and paramilitary forces were shopping like two harmonious communities of the valley. Perhaps they had come to terms with living amongst each other.

It took me more than two hours to reach office, a route that normally took me forty minutes.

I found that the radio station employees, only a few in the office, were still under shock. They were only talking about Mr Shukla's killing and the impact it had had on the radio programmes. A few Hindu employees—who had not bothered to leave earlier during the emergence of the armed movement— had now left for good. Muslim employees preferred to stay at home and wait for the dust to settle. A few officers had been brought in from Delhi to run the show. There was minimal attendance on the part of the local employees, who did nothing except take their salary at the end of the month.

My office room was calm and empty.

I found not a soul inside the studios. The radio building seemed totally rundown and dilapidated. All the rooms were full of dust. The toilets had become filthy and were stinking. Overgrown lawns were surrounded by bunkers and military vehicles. Whisky bottles were piled up next to the security bunkers.

The canteen, library and auditorium were closed with heavy padlocks. Outside, on the exhibit walls, the historical photos of cultural functions and events held in the auditorium were layered with dust.

It was quiet and cold inside. The silence was eerie.

Outside, on the road, everybody was running as though chasing one another. During the turmoil, people had developed the bizarre habit of running instead of walking. Shopkeepers, vendors, employees and students were seen running as a matter of routine now. On the contrary, the security personnel seemed calm and at ease, and seemed to be enjoying the pleasant weather of the valley.

I walked towards the administrative block in the backyard of the building, where dogs were sniffing through garbage containing recording tapes, cartons and scripts. Somewhere from the Jhelum river, a foul smell had emanated, polluting the surroundings. In the corner, outside the building, was a Sikh employee Kulwant Singh, who was sorting out the huge post scattered on his desk.

It was very unusual to find Kulwant Singh all alone because he was always surrounded by the other Sikh colleagues, all of whom he got employed in the radio station since the eruption of the armed struggle. Muslims often envied the Sikh community for their closeness to each other.

During the political turmoil, the Sikhs had remained neutral and avoided any violent incidents. Internally, they were not in favour of independence, but they did not leave the valley like the Kashmiri Pandits did.

However, the Sikh community in Kashmir was not much different from Kashmiri Pandits. When it came to Kashmir demanding Azadi, the Sikhs belonged to the nation, but when it was the Sikhs demanding the separate country of Khalistan, they readily supported the Punjab movement.

Kulwant Singhji was about to retire after twenty years of service in radio, and for the last eight years he had been sorting out my post or making tea for me, and he walked miles to the market to buy the milk. He was sober, gentle and talkative.

The moment Kulwant saw me, he stood up and greeted me with the same warmth: 'Madamji, I have not seen you in ages. How good to have you back. I hope your family is coping well in the circumstances.'

'I am fine, so is my family. It is good to see you as well.'

'Madamji, would you like to have tea or kahwa? It will only take me five minutes.'

'No, no, please do not bother. Next time, certainly. I am in a bit of a hurry this time.'

The moment I stepped up the staircase to enter the administrative block, he remembered something and gestured to me to wait a bit.

'Madam, there is a letter for you, good thing I remembered. It has been pending here for almost six weeks. I have kept it safe in my drawer.'

'Oh, a letter for me? Who is my admirer?'

'It looks like the letter has come from some foreign country.' He opened the upper drawer of his desk and took an envelope out. He came towards me and handed me the letter.

I hardly glanced at the letter and put it in my handbag.

'Thanks so much, sardarji,' I said, and stepped into the administrative block to sort out my annual leave. There was nobody present. The empty block gave me the creeps.

Instead of walking further down the administrative block, I took a few steps back to leave the building. I kept looking towards the door, expecting someone to come bursting forth and kill me. There was so much fear that I had to trust my instincts. My heart was beating faster than normal and the palms of my hand became sweaty and itchy with fear.

I ran towards the door and left the building in a hurry. Kulwant Singh was still sorting out his mailbag. Before he could start talking again I rushed further down the path. Outside, the soldiers at the gate looked suspicious of my unusual behaviour, but did not say anything. Without looking around, I ran on the road like the others towards the bus stop. I had to keep reassuring myself that nobody was chasing me.

~

I lost myself in the crowd while waiting for the bus. It was at this point that I vowed not go to the office any more until the situation got better and a little bit of normalcy returned to the valley.

When the bus conductor demanded the ticket fare from me, I was gazing at something outside the window. What he was saying I could not understand, but my unflinching gaze made him so nervous that he looked at the driver for direction. One of the passengers on the left seat jolted me out of my reverie, saying: 'Sister, give him the fare.' I was awoken from my slumber and regained my composure.

'Just a second, please.'

I opened my purse to pay for the bus ticket. There, I found the envelope Kulwant had given me. I had not opened it yet. I looked around to make sure nobody was watching me.

I curiously opened the letter to calm my frayed nerves.

My goodness, this was unbelievable.

I burst out laughing. The passenger beside me got startled by my behaviour and said, 'Is everything okay, sister?'

'Yes, everything is perfect,' I replied. My eyes became moist and my lips went dry. My strange reaction was not due to terror, it was due to joy and exhilaration. Baba's dervish had performed one more miracle. I closed the letter, placed it in my purse and made sure it was properly zipped. I tried to act normal but my heart was beating so fast.

The bus halted at the next stop, where dozens of passengers were waiting to board. I hurried past them and started running towards Baba's house instead of going to mine. Approaching his place, I found myself shouting loudly in merriment—the same way I used to whoop and cheer in my childhood, when I passed my examinations.

'Baba, I have some breaking news. I have got a job in Britain!'

I was euphoric and wanted Baba to come out and hug me, like he used to do earlier, when I would wave my progress report at him.

But Baba did not come out like he would have done earlier. Instead, he gestured to me to come inside quietly, because it was not the right time to share one's joy with the world. The area was again reeling from last night's crackdown, which had left one youth dead in broad daylight.

I became sombre and stepped inside without expressing any further excitement. Baba was sentimental; he kissed my forehead and said, 'My God is great, and so is my murshid.'

A few years ago, I had applied for a producer's job in a media organizations in the United Kingdom. After the long interview process, I had not received any responses and had forgotten about the matter—not because I did not perform well, but because the surrounding situation did not leave me with an idle moment to think about other occupations, when the only occupation was to remain safe. Sometimes, Baba would remind me about the application and try and make me find out what happened of the potential opportunity, but hardly paid him any heed.

After a long time, the organization had offered me a job, asking me to fulfil a list of formalities quickly. My rejuvenation did not let me wait and I applied for a visa the very next day.

ÉMIGRÉ

Most of my relatives, friends and neighbours had come to see me off. Why wouldn't they come? I was the first person in Asad's family to have got a prestigious job in one of the most reputed organizations in England. Until now, we had only seen Europe in our dreams or in English films.

Those relatives who had loathed me my whole life were also present to bid me farewell. They had resented me, initially, for being a girl and then for working in the notorious media sector.

Those close relatives who had abused my Baba for letting me to join the radio had also come. Also present were those who had come to maintain a strategic connection with me, in case they needed my help in the future.

They were all showing me gratitude and respect. I was surprised over how, all of a sudden, I had become a celebrity to them.

There were only a spare few who felt genuinely happy for me.

But almost everybody was pretending in their own way.

My sisters were pretending not to show their sadness that I was moving far way, so that I would not feel weak and fragile.

They were recounting the days when I would not budge from the place I used to study in, wait for the library books that were allotted to other students and hound Baba to buy me magazines and newspapers out of his meagre income.

Those who wanted to see my backside gone were pretending to be very upset at losing me to an unknown future. It was difficult to figure out whether they were pretending to be happy for me, or whether they were cursing my lucky stars in their hearts?

The hall of the top floor of my house was full with guests. Some were coming and some were leaving. My in-laws, my sisters and my Baba, all were sitting together, eating, talking and smiling. Who should boast about my success—my Baba or my in-laws? I locked eyes with them. Baba seemed serene and calm today. Asad's eldest sister was condescending to the guests sitting beside her: 'Her luck changed the day she married Asad.' My sisters found this hard to stomach and soon Mehmooda took the lead in reacting to her, saying, 'She brought fame and fortune to this family. It was Baba's hard work and sacrifice that was rewarded today.' My neighbour wearing a green dupatta nodded her head in acknowledgement. Asad's sisters ignored her, in a way, as they did not listen anything anyone said.

The samovar was bubbling away and brewing cinnamon and cardamom, the aroma wafting pleasantly over the room. A few of my relatives had brought me gifts, which I had no time to open from their wrappings. I handed them over to Faiza for her to keep safely.

This was the first occasion after my homecoming that I was the centre of attention in my family. Everybody was looking at me, thinking about me and trying to get noticed by me. I really enjoyed the moment and wanted it to last longer.

Asad would come into the hall with relatives and leave after making them sit next to me. He made sure the guests were taken good care of.

It took me weeks to decide how I would settle in another country after I got my visa. I decided—rather, Asad decided—that initially I would go to England all alone, leaving Muna with him till I settled down.

Asad insisted that I should first find out the nature of the job, find a place to live and figure out whether I would be able to adjust to an alien environment. 'What if you are unable to do the job and they send you back?' Asad made a good point, but it made me lose my confidence and faith in my capabilities. Yet, I agreed with him.

I understood what Asad said and it made sense: 'Sort out your job, find some accommodation and then send us a ticket—we will be there with you in only a matter of eight hours.'

Asad had called Faiza and her husband to stay with him so that Muna would not miss me as much in her presence. I felt bad about my son, who appeared to be upset and sad. I did not dare to take him in my arms because I knew he would burst into tears and so would I. He was sitting in Faiza's lap and talking to her while glancing at me. My selfishness had overpowered me. In the core of my heart I was cursing myself and asking again and again: *Why do I have to go?*

Some of my relatives were praising me and my capabilities: 'You are Baba's gifted girl, you have shown your mettle.'

A few distant relatives sitting beside Baba started teasing me, in jest, when Asad came with guests inside the hall.

'Should we call you memsahib now?' There was laughter. I was embarrassed in front of my old, frail Baba.

'Oh, you will hardly recognize Asad if he does not run to join you.' There was loud laughter again.

'Lucky you, Asad! Start counting the foreign currency, my friend.'

'Could you find a job for my son also? He is more qualified than you.'

'Don't drink alcohol or go to nightclubs.' I was blushing and sweating.

'Asad, you have no idea what you are getting into. It is a vicious circle, my brother, just remain alert, I am warning you.'

There was a queer mix of noise, sarcasm and ludicrous gesturing all over the hall. Our society was very unique in a way that we would always share the grief of others but we would hardly share others' happiness and joy. It was not our style.

I left the guests in the hall and took Baba to another room to say goodbye. He wanted to come to the airport, but I did not let him. Because, inside me, a little girl was crying, thinking how would she ever live without her Baba around her?

~

Two dozen relatives, all packed in cars, were following my taxi to the airport. It was as if I was leaving for a pilgrimage to Mecca and my relatives had come to seek my blessings. They wanted to give me the same send-off that Hajji had been given. What a sweet surprise.

The cars were halted by the security forces at certain checkpoints on the way to the airport. The well-suited gentlemen and the well-dressed women in the cars prevented the soldiers from checking further, whereas the cars in the right lane were searched and frisked minutely. My relatives were not asked to get down from the cars when I was asked to show my air ticket and open the suitcase I was carrying with me. The moment I crossed the checkpoint, Asad burst out into loud laughter. He was perhaps hiding his embarrassment.

In the airport lounge, everyone waited in a row to give me one last hug before I went for a final security check-up. All the displays of affection seemed so bizarre and artificial that I felt an intense urge to run away. Everything seemed unnatural and unreal. People's eyes were moist and faces gloomy. I was thinking that if I had been so dear to my in-laws, why hadn't they showed it earlier?

Asad and Muna were the last to say goodbye to me. How ironical—Asad had become emotional and attempted to hide it under his fake smile. *Is he sad because I am leaving, or is he also just pretending like my relatives?* Throughout the turmoil, I yearned to stay close to him, but he had gone far away from me. Am I running far away from him this time? Does he really want to remain close to me? Sometimes we laugh at your own fate.

Asad did not say a word and kept Muna close to him. My heart was breaking.

I was the last passenger to board the plane, leaving everyone behind the large glasshouse, from where I could only see their silhouettes. I became emotional and overwhelmed as I moved further away from them. My inner voice was torturing me, *Why am I going and where?* I had this sinking feeling in my stomach. The air hostess made a gesture, asking me to enter the plane quickly.

So what if I am going now? I will be back very soon. I will do wonders in journalism here in Kashmir. The situation will become better and I will live my life as I lived earlier, without fear and terror. I will never ever give up my dream. My heart ached with pain and the ache became too sharp. Had I lost too much without achieving anything?

Had I become the occasional pigeon that breaks free from the rest of the flock and ends up lost and confused? *Shouldn't I stay with my flock?*

At the top of the staircase, I took a deep breath. The cool breeze coming from the lush-green forests surrounding the airport was fresh and soothing. The forests topped with snow-capped peaks were in deep slumber. Everywhere I turned my head, my motherland looked sad and gloomy like me. We were both crying and bleeding silently. We both had lost so much and in return had received nothing.

The dark-grey cloud near the horizon had covered the whole sky. The earth and sky were one.

Under the cluster of the clouds laid the unknown grave of Shiasta, who might be in deep sleep herself, somewhere in the thick forest.

Behind those huge pine trees lived Sadia, who had found peace and solitude among the unmarked graves of fighters.

On my right, at the foothills of the Takht-e-Suleiman hill, Fareeda's husband was buried under many tons of rock soil.

And at the other end of the runway laid Auntyji, whose laughter could still be heard in the neighbourhood.

I had treasured them all in my heart, protected and preserved their precious memories. They became bright, little indelible blood clots in my chest the moment I stepped on to the plane.

Each one of them and many more had become engraved in my soul. Whatever I saw and endured during the ongoing turmoil, I did not know how soon it would fade out from my memory. But what I did never ever forget were the tiger ladies of my motherland—their love, endurance, pain and pride was the treasure of my life and, therefore, invaluable beyond measure. My gratitude for them grew deeper, thicker and stronger every moment the plane was taking me farther away from them and from my motherland.

Inside the plane, I lost the soil under my feet and my heart missed a beat. I was lost in my thoughts, at the height of 30,000 feet. I looked deep into the soul of my valley, my gloomy and tormented motherland, which had lost so much.

Over the Pir Panchal Mountains, the thick clusters of black clouds were hitting our plane; most of the passengers were frightened by the turbulence. I wanted to treasure the fresh and pure air of the misty, majestic mountains. Through the small window I could see my bruised land silently enduring the pain. The whole world praises and enjoys its beauty, but has remained tight-lipped over its long and painful years of suffering. If I had been able to do nothing to ease the pain of my motherland, would I at least be able to show it to the world through my eyes, heart and soul? There arose a strange feeling in my heart—a glimmer of hope that I would open my heart to the cruel, tight-lipped world.